THE REST WILL COME

Christina Bergling

THE REST WILL COME

Limitless Publishing, LLC
Kailua, HI 96734
www.limitlesspublishing.com

Formatting: Limitless Publishing

ISBN-13: 978-1-64034-167-8
ISBN-10: 1-64034-167-6

Dedication

For Handy

CHAPTER 1

Emma did not realize the keys were in her hand until she smashed them into his face. The sickening squash of the impact surprised her, and she found the warmth of his blood on her hand unexpected.

She could only hear what he said echoing in her head.

You know, my heart is just not in this.

At some point, she had unwittingly laced the ragged points of metal between her knuckles. In the sad and dark parking lot, as he said it had nothing to do with her and she should not take it personally, she had unconsciously clenched the spikes between her fingers. Her body curled around her rage while her mind gagged on his unenthusiastic lies.

They stood there frozen, tangled in his injury. The breeze was swirling into Emma's gaping mouth, drying out her widened eyes. She permitted her gaze to travel down the length of her own arm as time itself seemed to slow and ensnare them in the moment.

The keys protruded from her fist like barbed

brass knuckles before disappearing into his leaking flesh. The skin contorted around the intruding metal. Blood actually spurted, leaping up onto her hand and forearm. The blood fountain operated in the rhythm of his heartbeat, which was rapid and desperate.

With her fist still firmly implanted in his face, Emma finally looked at his eyes. Or rather, eye. One eye floundered under the gushing blood. The remaining eye bulged from its socket. The twitching iris found Emma, and time completely stopped as their expressions of shock mirrored each other.

The two stopped breathing. His body slowly started to tremble, beginning at its connection with Emma and reverberating out into that stunned eye. In the low light of the worst dive bar she had been in since college, Emma had not noticed how strikingly flat and mundane his eyes were. A tired, muted brown.

When he had walked in, she had registered that he was attractive. The judgment was a knee-jerk reaction, an echo of the endless string of wasted nights with an exhaustive parade of douchebags. She felt the tug of her lingering priority. First, he had to be attractive, then he could be a decent guy. She knew how far that had gotten her.

With her keys jabbed into this latest jerk's face, Emma considered maybe this approach had been part of her problem. He had been merely another indistinguishable online dating profile. Matched.com, eCompatible, Fish of the Sea, they were all a homogenous blur.

He was looking for a partner in crime. Or a

soulmate to start a family with. Or a good girl he could talk to. Or whatever.

They all sounded the same, and they were all equally hollow and inaccurate. Month after month, they became impossible to separate or recall. On her phone, she took screenshots of their profile pictures. She linked the pictures to their names and numbers to have any hope of identifying the right prospect. Was this the guy with a thing for tigers? The one who posted tons of pictures with his nieces? The one with a profile composed entirely of shirtless selfies? The one who was serious about working on his fitness? The one who grew pineapples in his backyard?

Their interaction began with a virtual wink. Emma hated the whole winking concept, cringed every time the notification appeared. If a suitor winked at her from across the bar in real life, she would not have been able to roll her eyes fast enough. Then he began asking her stupid, patronizing, infuriating questions. *What kind of kitchen appliance would you be and why?* She actually laughed at her computer screen while she tried to concoct the right answer. Though his emails that followed were hardly more inspired, every email and eventual text read down the same canned and useless dating script, the same words and details she only began to confuse with other guys. Ultimately, hours of investment culminated in hearing his actual voice over a month later.

As with every other ill-fated first date she had endured over the past few years, Emma had thought, *why not?* He was not especially striking on the computer screen or over text messaging, but why not? She had to keep trying, had to meet someone new. What had resulted was a procession of first dates that did not yield someone new. Rather, each date was with the same subpar candidate over and over and over again.

This date, however, had deviated into this dank parking lot with her keys in the candidate's eye.

He had selected this deplorable location, a bar in a small town between their two cities. This entire date that his heart was no longer in had been his idea. He was the reason Emma was standing in the flickering streetlight, listening to the cars on the interstate, second knuckle deep in his bloodied face.

Emma had arrived at the bar first. As her tires rolled into the nearly vacant parking lot, she cringed, her body drawing in on itself. The building hugged the sound barrier wall for the highway, crouching low and sad in the shadows. The fluorescent beer and liquor signs glowed out from the small windows like possessed eyes in the darkness. One lonely streetlight illuminated the parking lot.

She parked her car directly under the feeble light and thought, *What the hell was he thinking? What am I doing?*

With the engine still purring in the car, she held her phone hesitantly in her hand, pressing the power button to light the screen. She involuntarily and habitually rolled her eyes as she moved her fingertip over the touch screen to call up their text conversation. She had to remember which one he was, which mundane life details they had already discussed.

Mark: Hey beautiful, I'm really looking forward to finally meeting you tonight!

There he was, perched atop a hill in Garden of the Gods with Pikes Peak in the background, like a poster child for Colorado tourism, in the profile picture she had captured from the dating site. She scrolled farther up into the past.

Mark: I used to be in the Air Force but just stayed in Colorado Springs when I got out. I loved the mountains too much. All my family still lives back in Nebraska. I see them occasionally.

Right, the former Air Force guy who now loved hiking and worked from home for a software company.

She backed out of the conversation to her home screen. Only a picture of a vacant beach at sunset. No messages, no escape. The light timed out, and the phone went black again. Emma flipped it on and let it die two more times, flirting with the hope that some distraction from anywhere would appear to save her. When it did not, she opened the door and stood in her heels on the uneven asphalt.

Her phone still hung in her doubtful palm as she walked into the bar. Her fingers flexed against the case like a security blanket, clinging to a lifeline out of this place. She found herself already drafting the texts in her head to tell Ronnie how horribly this one went. Ronnie's last message was still in Emma's inbox.

Ronnie: Good luck! Text me when it's over.

Emma wanted to text her a million things already. Like how she was still nervous as with every other first date; how the drive down was a pain with traffic; how this bar was awful and she was terrified to walk inside; how she needed this guy to be less than a douchebag; how she was so painfully sick of being single and just wanted things to happen, like they had for Ronnie years ago.

Instead, she waited. She would have plenty of time to give Ronnie the latest update in her dating soap opera afterward.

As she scraped her heels along a bar floor so dirty it felt sandy, Emma's heart clenched firmly against her throat. Two withered regulars looked up mechanically from the bar and stared at her, letting their glazed-over eyes linger long enough that she wrapped her jacket tighter around her body.

Dim lights cast strange shadows over an eclectic menagerie of random trinkets hanging from the walls. While touted as a bar and grill, the scene reminded Emma of a bar she frequented in her misspent and underage youth. The reflex memory of the environment forced the phantom taste of kamikaze shots and acidic vomit up the back of her throat. Nostalgically.

She pressed her hand to her mouth and moved slowly, nearly creeping to the first open table of many. She perched at an angle from which she could see people enter through the door, trying not to attract any further attention. From the dilapidated state of the two regulars, she was relatively confident her date had not yet arrived.

Tucking herself into the lacquered wooden booth, Emma snatched her phone up to her face again. No notifications, no texts, not even a spam email. She settled for absentmindedly scrolling through MyBook, looking at statuses and pictures without actually seeing them. She did not want his initial impression to be her glued to her phone. She did not want to be trapped in the reality around her either.

She set the phone on the table in front of her, screen down, then heard the door squeak over the low, mumbling music. People all looked the same walking into a first date. Anxious, somewhat awkwardly shifting, eyes wide in a blending of hope and fear. Senses pricked to seek out the date as quickly as possible so as not to be exposed waiting alone, or worse—stood up.

He walked in with those dumb brown eyes engaged and scanning. Aside from the fact that he was the only other patron in her demographic, Emma recognized the desperation in his gaze and knew he was her date.

She sized him up automatically, allowing her eyes to rapidly drink in what he had to offer. Even seated in the booth, she determined he was tall enough, taller than her. He would never tower over her; her head would never nestle beneath his chin as she always wanted; still, he would be the slightest bit taller. She snagged the familiar train of thought and shook it loose, recalling that she had learned he needed to be more than simply tall and hot.

As he walked closer, he noticed Emma. His eyes identified the only female in the establishment, and relief spread across his face, stretched in a decent smile. When he sat down in the booth across from her, Emma mused that his grin could possibly get her into trouble. If she reached a little, she could imagine sleeping with him.

Good enough was a start.

"Hi, I'm Mark," he said, extending his hand.

Of course he was. Mark, John, Chris. Emma had read a thousand of their profiles, went on first dates with what seemed like hundreds of the same generically named men. She was so exhausted from the entire experience that she could vomit in his outstretched palm. She repeated that one of them had to be The One. She smiled sweetly and reached across. When she shook his hand slowly and deliberately, she gauged the warmth and smoothness of his palm against hers. The hand of a software developer.

"So, this place is not what I expected," he said, sweeping his eyes around and lowering his head in embarrassment between his shoulders. "I have never been here before. I didn't expect such a…"

"Dive," she said it for him.

"Right, exactly." That smile again. "I'm really sorry."

Emma grinned back, turning her face to lift her cheek toward him flirtatiously. The motions all felt so familiar. She played her part well. "That's okay," she replied.

"What do you want to do? Do you want to stick it out? Should we find somewhere else?"

"It doesn't matter to me. Whichever you prefer."

"How about one drink while we look for another place to eat?"

"Sure. I mean, how bad could they mess up beer?"

In the absence of any kind of wait staff, he politely walked up to the bar and retrieved warm, flat beer in questionably clean mugs. Emma thanked him while pretending not to examine her drink. She took a sip and held back the grimace as the sour edge of the flavor flattened over her tongue. Looking at him warmly, she swallowed it thinly.

He had his phone on the table between them, swirling over some app about local restaurants. There were not many options.

"How about this one?" He gestured to an entry in the list. "Mexican place about two miles from here. It has a whopping three stars."

"How many stars do you suppose this fine establishment has?"

He scoffed. "You want me to look?"

"Mexican is fine by me."

"Cool. We'll finish these beers and head over. So tell me about your job again? Data entry, right?"

Emma awarded him points for actually reading the emails and being able to recall her correct occupation. He probably had mined their text conversation in the parking lot, just as she had. Her mind reeled before it was her turn to speak. *Shit, what have I already told him? What have we talked about over email? He was in the Air Force and*

9

works for a software company now. He is not the one with the five-year-old son or the two ten-year-old daughters because all his family is in Nebraska. Did he say he had an ex-wife and a kid? Or just an ex-wife? Have we talked about my family at all or only his? Was it merely work we rambled about? He was the one who loves hiking. His picture is in Garden of the Gods, so he has to be.

Emma knew that all they would ultimately do was rehash the emails they spent weeks sending each other, simply because neither of them vividly remembered which candidate they were auditioning. They would both politely pretend this was not the case, that they were so interested in this person who stood out from the herd, but that was exactly what always happened.

At her core, Emma hated the first date interrogation.

"You're from Nebraska, right?" Emma said, leaning on the texts she had skimmed.

"Yeah. I was born and raised out there. My family is still out there. I joined the Air Force right out of high school to get out of there. I was stationed all around, then ended up in Colorado Springs and just decided to stay there. I love the mountains. I really like hiking."

I was right! Emma gave herself an internal high five.

"What about you? Denver girl?"

"Yeah, I'm actually from Colorado, a rare native. I grew up partially in Colorado Springs. My dad still lives down there with his wife. I moved to Denver with my mom and brother after they got divorced."

Emma's eyes shifted about subtly while she talked, flitting from Mark's eye contact to a pass of the bar to the drink menu on the table. When she returned to his eyes, she noticed the decline in their trajectory. His gaze drifted down, sliding along her neck and to her chest without registering she was looking at him. Smoothly, he met her eye contact and flashed his teeth.

"So what is data entry exactly?" he said, leaping back to the safe, reliable job topic.

"Nothing exciting. It's actually pretty boring, but it's better than working multiple waitressing jobs. I plug into music and zone out for a few hours while I work."

"Sounds like software development."

"Probably," Emma laughed.

As their beers disappeared, Emma tried to gauge how she felt about Mark. Although she found him attractive enough, she was not sure she responded to him on any other level. Nothing he said produced any reaction in her beyond the tedium of the first date, but perhaps that was only her physical disgust at being forced through the ritual yet again. While his childish examination of her cleavage did make her want to wrinkle her nose, he was a guy. She had to accept he was going to examine her body as much as she had gauged his height and degree of attractiveness when he walked in.

She found no aversion to him mingled in her lackluster and muddled feelings, so she decided that would be enough to build on. It would have to be, or she would have to endure another first date with another guy.

Finally, they set down empty mugs.

"Should we migrate?" Mark asked.

"Sure," Emma replied. "Let me use the bathroom first."

Mark looked different when Emma emerged from the restroom. His hands were shoved down deep into his pockets, his shoulders up closer to his ears. He stood rigid, almost on edge as he looked around. That sly smirk of his had dissolved.

He did not say anything as he escorted Emma to her car. He swung his hand beside his body now, cradling his phone in his palm, dragging his feet across the ragged asphalt. Emma rounded behind her car and stopped beside her trunk. She could feel the change in his demeanor bristling along her spine.

"Do you want to ride together, or should I follow you to this place?" she asked, cocking her head to examine him.

Mark did not look up at her. He stood there, clinging to his phone.

"You know, Emma, I don't think this is going to work," he said, low and quiet.

"What do you mean, the restaurant?"

"No, this. You know, my heart is just not in this."

***

Gradually, by degrees, Emma's senses returned to her. First she actually heard the cars on the distant interstate and recognized how close other people could be to her assault. Then she saw the wash of the florescent bar signs on the parking lot and remembered the few staggering would-be witnesses inside the bar. She jerked her paralyzed hand only to realize her escape was hindered, her fingers trapped in the keys that were embedded in his flesh.

As the shock absorbed into her brain, the panic blazed up around the edges.

My keys are in his face. Holy shit, my keys are in his face! What did I do? What was I thinking? What am I going to do now? His eye is fucking gone. There is no way I won't go to jail for this.

Her torso collapsed on itself as her head dropped and her shoulders rounded in sympathy. Yet she remained tethered to him by those bloody keys.

The jarring realization momentarily derailed Emma, even with Mark starting to wilt beside her. A sputter erupted from his lips, and the blood droplets spattering her face snatched her back to the present moment, to the real time of her crime.

His one surviving eye was no longer crazed and engaged. The eyelid flirted on the surface as the eye adopted a distant reach. He wobbled on his feet, knees going weak and gummy. His instability dragged her along, tangling them in an awkward dance. Blood started to drip from his parted lips. The flowing red wave consumed her hand, and she began to panic as she lost sight of that part of her body.

Oh God, he's going down.

She whipped her head around frantically, searching for an inspiration in the empty parking lot. There was only her car directly beside them. Her spacious trunk bumped up against her hip. She jolted at the idea and dragged him closer to her car.

She hesitated at the thought but only for a split second. Before she had accepted her decision, she slapped clumsily at her pocket, hunting for her keys. Then she hung her head at the obvious realization that those keys were laced into her fingers and punched into his face. Another level of distress pressed her heart into her throat as she looked around wildly.

She had no other choice. She allowed her free fingers to trace her other arm up toward his face, cringing and hesitating as she moved into his blood. She squeezed her eyes shut and fumbled around the mess interlacing them. Thankfully, her thumb found the trunk release button on her key fob from memory. The rubber button was slick with his blood, but when she depressed it, the latch released behind him.

He did not even notice; he was too lost in his own decline.

The trunk lid lifted slowly, as if inviting him in. Emma took a deep breath and squeezed her eyes shut. She pressed a breath out through her tense lips.

Do it. You have to do it. Just do it.

She forced herself to plant her free hand into his shoulder and shove him back toward the trunk. He did not resist. She did not know if he even noticed. He was delirious from his blood loss, awash with his injury. His nerves were far too occupied to worry about Emma clumsily trying to stuff him into her trunk with one hand. With little force, he toppled against the frame of her car, limbs splaying out like an overturned turtle. His head rocked from side to side, confused, and he ejaculated a sound somewhere between a moan and a scream.

"Shitshitshitshitshitshitshit!" Emma hissed.

She braced his collapsing body with her hip, jutting her pelvis toward him as she imagined she might have done to him under completely different circumstances. If he fell to the ground, she would never be able to heave him up.

The keys made an awful squishing sound as they jostled the wound in his face; more of his blood poured over her knuckles. She pressed her hip harder into his drooping body and felt the tremor rippling through him. A strange, gasping wheeze pushed through his lips, escalating into an awkward moan. Frantically, Emma gripped his shoulder and swung her head around to survey the parking lot again. Her hair slapped against her face and into her still-wide mouth as she scanned the darkness.

Nothing. They were still alone.

She turned back to Mark, whose boring face was becoming more unrecognizable by the blood-drenched second. His body weight crushed down on her wobbling pelvis, heavier and heavier. He would soon be crumpled on the ground, perhaps on top of her, and then there would be no avoiding detection, no denying what she had done. What else could she tell a police officer with her hand still embedded in his face?

Emma sucked the air back into her lungs, tasted the metallic smell of his blood, and shoved against his shoulder. Pushing him downward, she bucked her hips up to guide him over the bumper of her car. Mark's limbs thrashed, maybe deliberately, maybe haphazardly. She could not tell if he was clawing against her, if he was cognizant at all.

At last, he crested the hump of the bumper, and his body weight worked in collaboration with her, guiding him into the flat, empty bed of her trunk. His back hit first, and his head bounced after it, dragging her along with it. His one eye shut, his breathing became slow and weak against the side of her hand, and his body fell still.

Emma had to disentangle herself. Her fingers snared in her key ring against his face felt like manacles around her wrists. They were weighing her down, trapping and confining her, exactly like the handcuffs the police would snap on her. They kept her locked in her attack and all the consequences that could follow.

Mark was not moving. She jerked on her arm. His head followed with the wet sound of the wound, yet they remained connected. Even the blood flow had slowed. She pulled again, harder. His head came up from the trunk, still clinging to her keys, but she found more space between her knuckles and his eye socket.

She paused again, spinning to suspiciously sweep the scene. She waited for one of the sad barflies to walk out and witness her trying to wrench her hand out of Mark's pulverized face. Still nothing.

Emma lifted her foot and placed a high heel on the bumper of the car. She planted her palm on

Mark's chest and shoved against him, tugging on her arm again. The traumatized flesh and cartilage groaned while she grunted. She simply could not get enough leverage.

Wobbling on one heel, she moved her other foot inside the trunk and positioned it beside her palm on Mark's chest, pressing the heel down into the fabric of his shirt. She breathed in and pulled as hard as she could, pushing and kicking against his chest. Her arm shook, then with a loud pop she was released.

Emma toppled over backward and met the unforgiving asphalt below. Her liberated hand dropped to the dirt, keys still in her grip. She wiggled her fingers and peeled them from sticking together in his thick blood. She sat up quickly and pulled her heels beneath her, attempting to stand unassumingly, slammed the trunk lid shut, and darted toward the driver's side of her car.

With the door closed behind her, Emma felt more concealed. She hesitated briefly, allowing the shock to swell back over her. Without her realizing it, her eyes had welled up and tears spilled down her cheeks. Hot and frantic tears.

She lifted her hand to extract the keys from her fingers. When her eyes met her own gnarled paw, she did not recognize it. She did not want to touch it. Cringing, she stripped the keys from between her fingers. Chunks of flesh or eye or who knew what part of Mark encrusted each key, filled in each groove of the teeth. She could not bring herself to examine them closely.

The thought crept up into her disoriented brain,

softly, almost naturally: *Clean off the keys. You can't get his DNA in your ignition. Use something you can burn.* The rationale comforted her, made her feel more genuine. She let her breathing deflate as she reached into the pocket of her door and brought out a napkin.

She wiped each key meticulously, using her nail behind the paper to dig into each crevice. She had watched enough crime scene investigation shows and documentaries to know it was not enough to eradicate the evidence. Still, it was better than nothing. And having her keys look familiar brought some measure of calm over her chest.

She needed to get out of there. Flee the scene. Then perhaps she could figure out what she would do next.

Emma's eyes were fixed and distant as she drove. She saw the road in front her, only she was not present behind that sight. Her consciousness was locked in that moment, infinitely looping the instant in the parking lot. Over and over, she relished the vindicating and disgusting feeling of his face collapsing against her blow; the uncomfortable warmth of his leaking blood; heard the weak rasp of his breathing as he tumbled into her trunk.

You know, my heart is just not in this.

Hearing the words in her brain reignited her rage.

My heart is just not in this.

Every time she replayed that sentence, each time his voice said it again, her regret and panic receded, disappearing under the swell of her righteous anger.

He had dragged her out on another first date she did not even want to attend. He had invited her to this horrible bar so inconveniently far from her house, where she could have sat resigned to her single fate in yoga pants with an inappropriately large glass of wine. He had baited her with the chance that, though he may not be enticing online, he might be *The One.*

All of that, to leave her after one horrendous beer.

What had happened while she was in the bathroom? What had he seen in her that was so revolting that she was not even worth dinner? What possibly could he have had better to do?

The more she thought, the faster her heart pounded hot and heavy against her ribs. The more she wallowed in his offense, the more she relished the memory of her keys jabbed straight into his stupid eye. She wound her hands around the steering wheel tighter, gripping until the blood was forced from her knuckles.

He deserved this. Just another asshole. Another dick! How can they all be like this? Is there not one decent, marginally attractive guy out there? How can this be so hard? I'm done. I'm so done.

A familiar pain opened up in her chest, that same gaping hole that grew deeper and heavier with each failure in this dating endeavor. It felt like a weight on her ribs, crushing the life out of her. The pressure replaced her breath with thin, acidic-tasting anxiety. It felt like a cavern below her heart, expanding in emptiness and isolation, growing gradually until it would be large enough to swallow her. That uncomfortable, anxious sensation rippled out. Desperation reached its tentacles into her limbs, making them unsettled, and wafted up into her eyes until they were filled with its reflection. She felt sadness at the growing reality of her hopelessness.

The same familiar thought danced through her darkness. *I just want a family.*

With that poignant and too-familiar concept, her anger withered into despair. Her body retreated and she dropped her grip from the steering wheel, lowered her shoulders away from her ears, and folded in around the safety of her pain.

They keep getting worse. How can they all be like this? What is wrong with me that I can't find anyone? I'm hot enough. I have a job. I'm not bat shit crazy. I'm a good person. Why is it so hard? It shouldn't be this hard. It isn't this hard for anyone else. It's me; it has to be me.

You know, my heart is just not in this.

Emma closed her eyes and let a scream shake the windshield.

Then she heard something shift against the sound of her tires on the road, something moving in her trunk. He was still alive. She pulled herself from wallowing in her very familiar lament and returned to the situation at hand.

What in the hell do I do with this douchebag?

It was easier to refer to him as a douchebag. She could scarcely remember his name before or during the date, though now the name Mark might be permanently branded into the soft tissue of her brain. She did not want to think about him as Mark, the Nebraska boy who loved hiking; she needed to focus on him as the loser whose heart was not in it.

That justified what she had done.

Either way, she still needed to get rid of him, preferably without ending up in prison in the process. What she knew of criminal justice she had gleaned from a healthy enjoyment of crime shows, documentaries, and criminalistic dramas. She did not know if that would be enough to save her now.

Emma abandoned her depression of her single status and released the rage over Mark's emotional assault, fixating on the logistics of getting out of this mess. A plan would be comforting. A task would focus her mind away from the turmoil rising up around her on all sides.

Most importantly, she needed to get rid of the evidence which, in this case, was mostly the body. The body that now seemed still somewhat alive in her trunk. She was not sure what, if any, evidence she had left splattered in the parking lot. It would be far too risky to return to find out. After disposing of the body, she would need to remove all traces of it from her car and her person.

The body was the more pressing matter.

There would be no escape if she brought him in for medical attention. If he survived, which was increasingly unlikely, it would be prison for her. There would be no family, definitely not one she wanted, behind cold steel bars.

She could not allow Mark to completely deny her of that.

Where would one dispose of a body? Did people even manage to get away with murder anymore? Perhaps the right defense attorney could weave a brilliant insanity plea for her. Online dating undoubtedly could make anyone certifiably insane.

Just one juror would need a bad online dating experience to be amiable to reasonable doubt.

The resolution to her problem ended up dancing elegantly over her mind, poetic in its perfection. As she flipped on her blinker and moved to exit the interstate, Emma realized that her path to this unfortunate moment had started with her first ill-fated step down the aisle on her wedding day.

CHAPTER 2

Rain fell from the sky on Emma's beautiful outdoor wedding venue. It should have been a sign. The weather itself warned her against her vows, yet so infatuated was Emma that she experienced only blind elation. She saw only Justin, and when she looked at him, an entire life laid out behind him, complete with the house in the suburbs and the two or three children he would give her.

He was the answer. She felt that in her core, so she could only feel blissful about sealing it officially, rain or not, recalling that her mother said rain on a wedding was good luck.

Emma sat in front of the large mirror in her hotel room, adjusting and readjusting the neckline of her wedding dress. She wanted her breasts revealed tastefully; no one wanted stripper cleavage on their wedding day. The dress kept shifting down slightly whenever she moved. She had succeeded a little too well at her fast and detox leading up to her wedding day.

Ronnie stood behind her, her arms folded across

her body and a mimosa dangling from her hand. Emma was relieved that Ronnie had cleaned up so well for the occasion. Ronnie did not have the same constant and stringent considerations about her appearance that Emma did, and did not, as she so often put it, give a shit what others thought. She was on her third mimosa of the morning in front of both Emma's mother and grandmother.

Still, Ronnie was there, not belligerently intoxicated, or fighting with Emma's more refined bridesmaids yet, and that was all Emma could ask for.

Emma straightened the top of her dress once more and turned to Ronnie expectantly. "How do I look?"

"Beautiful, of course," Ronnie responded. "Your tits going to stay in that thing?"

"Yes!" Emma pouted and tugged at the dress again. "They have to."

"I told you to get off that diet shit."

"It worked, didn't it?"

"Yeah, until you're showing your nipples to the priest before you even say I do."

"Shut up!" Emma could not help but snicker. How her mother would die right there in the chair. "I'm getting married," she said, almost to herself.

Ronnie smiled back at Emma. The expression spread over her lips, but her eyes did not participate, instead remaining flat and distant. It was no secret that Ronnie and Justin did not get along in any sense. Ronnie's disdain for Justin had been forever sealed by a pizza. When she and Emma were college roommates, Justin decided to eat the entire pizza Ronnie could not afford and had left in the fridge overnight. He could never recover from that in her eyes. To Ronnie, that encapsulated the kind of man he was.

Beyond that, Emma simply could not see why Ronnie did not think Justin was as wonderful as she did. She knew Ronnie did not understand him, did not know him the way she did. Or perhaps she was jealous that Emma was committing to a real relationship while Ronnie rotated through noncommittal casual encounters.

One day Ronnie would figure it out and catch up to Emma. Then perhaps she would appreciate Justin.

"I'm going to smoke," Ronnie said, moving to the balcony.

Emma wrinkled her nose and moved back to the mirror again. "Where is your date?" she called out the open door.

"He's not my date," Ronnie replied with smoke curling out from her mouth.

"You brought him to a wedding, he's your date."

"No, he is the guy I am going to sleep with after your wedding. So much easier than hooking up with one of Justin's sleazy groomsmen."

"Okay, where is the guy you're sleeping with after my wedding?"

"His job is to ensure I have plenty of alcohol to keep me well lubricated the whole reception and then to well lubricate me after the party." Ronnie laughed plumes of smoke.

"Very classy, Ronnie. Because you finding alcohol on your own has ever been a problem?"

"Ha! God no. But it is so much easier to have a minion to do it for me. He should have at least one purpose besides sex."

"How gracious of you."

"I'm a cunt. You know this."

"Ronnie! My mother is right outside."

"Yeah and she knows this too."

"I love you anyway."

"You'd better. I'm wearing this hideous dress for you!"

"That dress is absolutely not hideous! It's tasteful, and you'll be able to wear it again."

"Yeah. Right."

Ronnie sneered, again without her eyes. Emma told herself again that it had to be jealousy. More importantly, it did not matter. This day was about her and Justin. Even if Ronnie got sloppy drunk, even if she had some sort of dramatic meltdown, that would be her "date's" problem. Tonight, it would be only Emma and Justin, starting the life she always wanted.

Emma's father held a white umbrella over them as they walked down the soggy aisle. Her heels sank into the wet ground, plunging into the fabric laid down as a path in the grass. It took the exertion of every one of her leg muscles to steady each step and make her parade look graceful. All eyes were on her, as she wanted, as she had been dreaming about since her dress fitting. She would *not* wobble and fall at her own wedding. She clung to her father's forearm and listened to the splat of the droplets on the umbrella above drowning out the Wedding March.

Justin stood at the summit of the aisle under his own umbrella beside Emma's army of bridesmaids. Ronnie was making a concerted effort not to look irritated and bored. When she and Emma made eye contact, Ronnie put on her biggest alcohol-fueled grin for her. Ronnie loathed weddings, which made her participation all the more meaningful.

When Emma looked back at Justin, her heart swelled, and that life completing excitement flared again. She clutched her hand tighter around her father's arm. He responded by folding his fingers over her hand as he did when she was a child and too scared to walk into a new classroom, back when she lived with him and he was still there for every first day.

Justin looked over at his best man, Tom, and they bantered in some nonverbal joke. Dimples pierced Justin's cheeks as he chuckled at his buddy. Then he outstretched his fist to bump knuckles with Tom. By the time Emma was halfway up the aisle, slow, soggy, and unstable, Justin's eyes finally met hers. He smiled for her, but his dimples did not dig in as deeply as they did at Tom's joke.

She told herself his eyes lit up for her, that he was reflecting her devotion and excitement. This day was the beginning of all he would want for himself because he was getting her.

The reception was a blur. Emma had invited everyone she had ever known. She wanted the grand wedding she had fantasized about while she sat alone at lunch between her classes after her mother had abruptly moved them to Denver. She wanted a full support system to launch them into their new life; she wanted to see all the relationships they had built around them. And she wanted her wedding to be seen.

From the hallway, she could hear the music bumping and conversation humming on the other side of the door. She wound her fingers tightly into Justin's and pulled him close. He smiled at her with his recklessly dangerous smirk and kissed her like he meant it, hand at the base of her head, eyes closed. She grinned back against his lips when the DJ announced them.

"Please help me welcome Mr. and Mrs. Justin Atwater!"

The voice boomed, and the doors swung open to the sea of faces and flashing lights. Emma put on her widest grin and allowed Justin to lead her across the floor. The crowd was a tapestry of upturned lips and clapping hands. The music and the cheers engulfed them.

Justin led Emma onto the dance floor and expertly twirled her around, allowing her wedding dress to balloon around her waist. As the song ascended over the crowd, he wound her up in his arms, and they began to dance. She followed his steps around the floor, pressing her face against the warmth of his skin and deeply inhaling his copious application of cologne.

Bliss. This was her bliss.

The music faded around them, and the clapping swelled to replace it. A ripple of clinking glassware rose from the crowd, and Emma pressed her lips into Justin's on command. Beaming widely and deliberately, they made their way to the bridal party table.

As they walked, Emma caught sight of Ronnie taking shots with her date at the bar. Even from a distance, Emma took note that Ronnie's companion was not the wide-shouldered, buzzed-headed, tattoo-clad stereotype she had come to expect. Ronnie's date looked somewhat normal, unimposing, a shorter man with dark and uninked skin. When Ronnie looked up, Emma jerked her head to signal Ronnie to follow them. She was pretty sure Ronnie rolled her eyes, but she took her companion's hand and did as requested.

When the two couples converged behind the beautiful table settings Emma had painstakingly selected, Ronnie and Justin did not even bother to look at each other. Each expertly pretended the other did not exist with the fluency of years of practice.

"Hi, I'm Emma," Emma said, leaning in and outstretching her hand to Ronnie's date.

Ronnie sat back and allowed Emma to introduce herself.

"Terrence." He shook her hand genuinely, maintaining gentle eye contact. "It's very nice to meet you, and congratulations."

Emma was temporarily stunned by Terrence's simple sincerity. Of the numerous deplorable men she had met on Ronnie's arm, Terrence did not belong.

"Why thank you, Terrence," she replied, giving Ronnie the wide-eyed I-really-like-this-guy look.

Ronnie rolled her eyes and took another deep drink of her cocktail.

"Justin, this is Terrence," Emma said, tapping Justin on the shoulder.

"Hey, what's up, man?"

Justin offered his hand without bothering to grant Terrence any true engagement. He was too busy staring off onto the gyrating dance floor at an awkward mix of Emma's busty high school cousins and relatives too drunk or too old to hold a rhythm. She could not necessarily blame him for brushing Terrence off. Aside from his distaste for Ronnie, the men she dated never lasted more than an appearance or two maximum. What was the point of meeting them?

Emma secretly tucked a genuine hope for Terrence down inside her chest.

With a plate of lean, dry chicken and some soggy vegetables mingling with the wine in her stomach, Emma made the rounds with Justin as his wife.

By the time she reached Ronnie, Ronnie had crossed that very crucial line into drunk. Emma always knew by her eyes. Ronnie could drink with the best—or worst—of them and had cultivated an impressive tolerance over her alcoholic years, but her tell was always in the coverage of her eyelids. At that certain intoxication level where she tipped over into excess, her eyelids drooped to halfway shade her eyeball. The opening of her eyes would then steadily decrease until she would close them and be passed out for the foreseeable future.

Ronnie's eyes peeked up at Emma in the dim swirling light of the reception with half of the pupil showing. She was no doubt on her way out. Terrence was not beside her, so Emma assumed he was minioning her another drink or puking after trying to keep up with her.

Ronnie smiled, a pure drunken look that captured her face and dragged it down off her skull, and lifted her limp arms to Emma. Emma shook her head and let Ronnie wrap her up in a paralytic hug.

"I love you so mush," Ronnie slurred into her ear.

"I love you too." Emma laughed and patted Ronnie's head as she would her toddler cousins.

"Good wedding?"

"Good wedding."

Ronnie smirked again for a moment, then something else crept across her features. Her lips twitched and moved toward words multiple times, leaving them unspoken. She would not be able to help it; eventually, she would let whatever questionable thought was batting around her inebriated brain fall out on the floor in front of them.

"Emma, I have to ask you something."

Emma braced. If Ronnie ever hesitated to say something, especially annihilated as she was now, it was never anything good.

"Sure," Emma replied reluctantly.

"Why Justin?"

"Oh come on, Ronnie, not this again. Not at my wedding."

"No, no, listen. You married down to my level. Like, what are you doing? A fucking tatted up bartender with a criminal record? Shit, he belongs in my bed more than he belongs in yours."

Emma face froze, and she shot Ronnie a steely

look.

"I don't *want* him in my bed. Jesus. You *know* I don't want him in my bed. You know what I'm saying."

"I love him. Isn't that enough?"

"If that's enough for you, then yes. I just had to ask."

"You don't have to like him."

"Oh, I don't. But what I think of him doesn't matter. He's your husband now."

"Yes, he is."

Emma tried to fight the icy feeling creeping through her veins. Ronnie was always so venomous when she was drunk, always pushing to get a toehold inside someone's head. She made sober Ronnie look like the portrait of self-control.

"I'm going to go find Justin," Emma said.

"Look, I'm sorry, Emma. You know I didn't mean anything by it. I am happy for you."

Sure she was. Emma once again told herself it was Ronnie's immature jealousy and focused on what she had, what she had cemented tonight. She pitied Ronnie for planning to bed and discard what seemed like a decent guy like Terrence. She could insult Justin all she wanted if it made her feel better about her life.

Ronnie's eyelids had drooped even lower when Emma turned to walk away. She shook the conversation from her brain and plunged back into the party that was all about her. She chatted with the remaining guests, circling the room in search of Justin. She spotted him in the corner with Tom and his groomsmen again, fist bumping away. The scantily clad groomsmen's dates stood looking bored in their dresses more appropriate for the club than a wedding.

"Hey! There's my beautiful wife." Justin raised his arms and snaked one around Emma's shoulders, drawing her in. "Hello, beautiful wife."

"Hello, husband. Where have you been?"

"I've just been here, you know, with the bros. Are you about ready to wrap this thing up so we can get headed to our honeymoon?"

Justin kissed her to punctuate the word honeymoon, and she smiled, forgetting her flush of anger at Ronnie's questions and Justin's typical vanishing act.

"Yes, I am. We just have to toss the bouquet and garter, and we are off!"

"You think anyone is sober enough to catch those?"

"Not at all. We should have done it right after the cake, but it's tradition."

"Well then let's go throw some stuff!"

***

On the plane to Hawaii, Justin laced his fingers into Emma's, allowing his palm to trace the lines on hers. She cuddled into his arm and pressed her head into his shoulder. He kissed her hair and breathed against her scalp.

Emma felt a deep, unadulterated happiness, thinking how perfectly life had lined up for her, now for them.

CHAPTER 3

There was a wet bikini on the floorboard of Justin's car. It was not Emma's bikini. It was some other woman's used, soggy bikini. Right there out in the open. For anyone, for *her,* to see.

Emma stood in her driveway under the blazing Colorado sun with the car door open. Her hand still gripped the top of the doorframe. Her eyes went wide and immobile, her head cocked awkwardly to the side, and the soft breeze swirled through her hanging lips.

She did not know what to do. She did not know how to think.

There was another woman's wet bikini crumpled up on the floor of her husband's car.

Without thinking, Emma took the cell phone from her pocket and dialed the number automatically.

"Ronnie. Get over here now…No. Now."

She hung up and stood petrified and unmoving until Ronnie walked up beside her and craned her neck to peer into the car at what had Emma so captivated.

"What is that?" Ronnie asked, squinting from behind her sunglasses. "Is that a swimsuit?"

"Yep," Emma answered robotically.

"I'm guessing that is not your swimsuit."

"Nope."

"There is another bitch's bikini in Justin's car?"

"Yep."

"Well whose fucking bikini is it?"

"I have no idea."

"Just some bitch."

"Just some bitch."

"Where is that rat bastard?"

"Work. He took my car today. He was getting the oil changed on his way in. I came out here to grab some sunglasses to walk down to the store."

"And some bitch's bikini is on the floor."

"Yep."

"What the fuck!"

"Exactly."

"I'm going to murder him."

For once, Emma and Ronnie were on the same page about Justin.

Emma hesitated in her shock until Ronnie peeled her hand from the car door and pushed it shut. She allowed Ronnie to take her shoulders and lead her back into the house and out of the sun. Ronnie maneuvered her to the couch and sat her down, blank and near catatonic.

She kept seeing the tiny, crumpled pile of patterned material. Tiny red cherries on black fabric. A heap of red strings tangled everywhere. She kept imagining the woman who filled out that bikini, who peeled off that wet, clingy bikini in her husband's car. Which one of the cocktail waitresses or shot girls from his work was it? Which desperate regular or college-aged groupie was it? Was she hotter than her? Did she have bigger tits? Did she let him have sex with her right there on the passenger seat, the passenger seat Emma rode in when Justin held her hand on the shift stick?

Emma's mind was whirling behind her vacant, immobile eyes.

"Emma. Emma!" Ronnie called her back. "What are you going to do?"

"I-I don't know. I've never been cheated on before. What am I supposed to do?"

"Um, you have to date them to be cheated on. How would I know?"

"You never suspected Terrence."

"Hey, Terrence and I are most certainly not dating, so there can be no cheating. What he does on his own time is his business, so long as he doesn't infect me with it."

"What should I do? Do I confront him about it? Do I pretend I never saw it? There could be plenty of explanations."

"Explanations for some soggy bitch's bikini stripped off in his car?"

"He's cheating on me. The bastard is cheating on me." Emma flew to her feet and started pacing frantically in front of the couch, picking at her fingertips. "First he suddenly doesn't want kids anymore, and now he's sleeping with some girl in a bikini in his car!"

"Wait, what? Emma, he doesn't want kids?"

Emma stopped, frozen in the shock of her accidental confession. She had not wanted to reveal it. Saying it made it real, cemented it into the world and made it something she had to deal with. A choice she had to make. She did not want to prove Ronnie right about him so few years into their marriage.

Emma's eyes quivered when she stopped wringing her hands and looked up at Ronnie. "He told me a couple of months ago. He doesn't want kids anymore. He said he doesn't want to change his lifestyle. He doesn't want to be all tied down like our friends who have kids. He doesn't want to change."

"A couple of months ago? Emma! Why didn't you tell me?"

"I don't know." Emma dropped back onto the couch cushion, tears spilling down her cheeks in waves. "I really didn't want it to be true. We were talking about going to counseling, and I thought maybe we could work it all out without having to tell anyone."

"Oh, Emma. All you've ever wanted is babies."

"I know," Emma squeaked, succumbing to her sobs.

Ronnie wrapped her arms around Emma's shuddering back and rested her chin on her shoulder. She let Emma cry as she held her calmly.

"Emma," Ronnie said when Emma's tears had subsided a little. "Do you even want to be with him?"

The question launched a new wave of sobs. "I don't know. I hadn't decided. I do love him. I was trying to figure out if I loved him enough to stay without kids. If he's cheating on me, maybe he doesn't even want to be with *me*."

"What are you going to do? Are you going to confront him?"

"I don't know. Is a bikini even enough evidence?"

"Does it need to be? When does he get home?"

"I won't see him until tomorrow. He won't get home from the bar tonight until after 4 am."

"If he's even at the bar."

"Ronnie…"

"I'm sorry, Emma, but come on."

"I have to know. I have to know if it's just a bikini or if it's a bikini because he's cheating on me."

"Fair. So you confront him."

"I confront him."

They let the words die between them, both retreating into the quiet that followed. Emma tried to force the image of Justin crawling on top of some bar trash in the car out of her mind, but it played over and over relentlessly, more graphic with each rotation. She tried not to hear his voice in her head telling her he did not want to have children. Ever. She tried not to feel her heart fracture with each echo and hallucination.

Ronnie kept her company in her misery and her internal madness until Emma could not endure it any longer and retired to her bed. She was surprised how easily sleep found her in her turmoil, how it cradled her and swept her away under a heavy blanket. It felt right to give up, to flee, to hide. It would be better if she could disappear in her bed and no one found out what happened.

***

When Emma woke up the next morning, her eyelids were so heavy that she was well conscious prior to unveiling the world, the world she wanted no part of now that she had to confront Justin to confirm he was having sex with another woman. With other women. Cheating on her instead of giving her babies.

Every synapse in her brain begged her to curl back into the mattress, bury herself under the sheets. Self-preservation pleaded to avoid, deny, ignore. Nothing good would come of knowing he betrayed her and chose someone else over her.

She had to know. The doubt would eat her alive. She could not lie beside him, share a house with him, without knowing. They certainly were not having sex lately. She had thought it was because his reversal on children had made her cold, uninterested. Was it instead because he was being satisfied elsewhere?

It would all drive her mad. She had to know.

Emma wrenched out of bed onto doubtful legs. Justin had graced his side of the bed the previous night. She could tell from the way he left the blankets kicked to the foot of the bed with no regard to how that uncovered her. She was so deeply wrapped in her depressive coma she had not felt him enter or depart the bed. She did even bother to look at the time.

Justin was downstairs in "his" room, the spare bedroom he had claimed for his assortment of short-lived hobbies, strumming on the guitar he had picked up at a flea market the previous week. He had downloaded a slew of how to play videos the next day and was feverishly committed to them in the rare moments he was actually within the walls of their house.

The guitar case was propped up against the wall beside the plastic crate of spray paint cans from when he was going to perfect the technique of graffiti art, next to the thirty boxes of shoes from when he was going to start selling Jordans on eBay, and across from the tattoo gun and tote full of inks from when he was going to learn how to ink people. None of these interests ever endured. In less than two weeks they were left abandoned along the wall and a new hobby was introduced. They were simply more ways he did not spend time with her.

Justin stopped strumming when Emma pushed the door open.

"Good morning, beautiful wife." He flashed those damned dimples at her. "You were wrecked. What happened to you last night?"

Emma could not even force a curl in her lips. Could not find her voice to respond. Her heart knocked hard on her ribcage.

"Hey, what's the matter?" He stood and moved toward her. She instinctively took a step back. "Did something happen, Emma?"

Emma walked out down the hall until she reached the couch. She sat down tentatively and looked back at him. He followed her, confused and perplexed, perching beside her. She swallowed hard on the knot in her throat.

"I found a bikini in your car yesterday," she finally said. There was no point in saying it any other way.

"A bikini?"

"Yes, a wet bikini on the floor on the passenger side."

Justin's eyes moved around while he held still and calm beside her. "Huh. Okay. So there's a bikini in my car."

"Justin, why is there a bikini in your car? It's not mine. Whose is it?"

Emma started to quiver. The trembling started in her hands then reverberated up her limbs until it shook her face and the tears brimming in her eyes. Justin looked up at her, shocked at all the emotion she was displaying, and half-chuckled.

"Oh no. No, babe. You think I'm cheating on you? No, no, no. It's not like that."

"Then what is it like? Why is there some girl's wet bikini in your car?"

"Oh, babe. No. You remember Jason? We used to work with him at Pedro's?"

Emma nodded mechanically, narrowing her eyes.

"Jason is at the Terrace Hotel now. He came into the bar one night and hooked me up with the key to their pool and hot tub. We all go there when we get off work some nights."

"Why did you never tell me about this? You're going to this hotel hot tub after work and you never even tell me? Whose bikini is it? And why is it in your damn car?"

41

"Emma, Emma, calm down. It was just a shot girl from the bar. She was way too drunk, and I gave her a ride home. That's it."

"She stripped off her bikini in your car?"

Justin laughed, and Emma's anger flared.

"No, no. She changed before we got in the car. She must have just tossed it on the floor and forgot it. She was pretty wasted. I was worried she might puke in my car."

"Again, why didn't you tell me any of this?"

"You want to know when I give a drunk coworker a ride home?"

"Are you cheating on me?"

"Emma." He leaned heavily on her name. "Of course not. I gave her a ride home. Come on, you know better. Come here."

Justin snaked his fingertips into her hair and pulled her face to him. He kissed her like he had not in months. He kissed her like he meant it, like he wanted her, like he needed her. He kissed her like she mattered, the way he kissed her before she had any doubt she was the only one.

Another tear rolling down her cheek, Emma closed her eyes and kissed him back, trying to make herself believe him.

CHAPTER 4

Emma wanted to believe him. Every minute, she tried to believe him; she told herself to believe him. Why would he lie to her? He loved her. Why would he cheat on her? He could not find some bar skank who was better than her. He only gave her a ride home.

And he would snap out of it and want children again. His doubt was only a phase.

He loves me. He loves me. He loves me.

She poured the words over her mind, hoping they would permeate her thoughts, hoping that thinking it hard enough would make it real. He had married her; that had to mean something.

A terrible weight continued to build on Emma's chest. There was a crushing pressure each time she tried to inhale and her breath fell short. The apprehension wound its way around her heart, squeezing it tight in her compacted chest, then reached up to seize her neck. A permanent knot resided in her throat, like a fist holding her esophagus.

She could not breathe.

No amount of positive thinking or rationalizations or hopes lightened the pressure she felt sinking down heavier by the hour; nothing loosened her airway. If anything, the more she tried, the worse her anxiety became. Like picking at an angry scab.

"Jesus Christ," Ronnie said as she walked in.

"What?" Emma said in a weak and distracted voice, looking up from the couch.

Justin had left shortly after waking up. He had some excuse about helping a friend move that Emma scarcely heard over the deafening sounds of her own thoughts and doubts. She was partially relieved that he had left her alone in their house as usual so she could embrace her unadulterated despair. She called Ronnie over to help her through it.

"What happened last night? You look like absolute hell," Ronnie said.

"Thanks," Emma replied sadly.

"Have you slept? Eaten?"

"I've slept. Sleep is easy. But eating, not really."

"Okay. I'm going to make you something to eat. You are going to tell me what the fuck happened after I left yesterday. How did Justin explain bikini girl?"

Ronnie haphazardly tossed her purse onto the couch beside Emma and marched into the kitchen. She always moved through Emma's house as if she lived there, without inhibition or hesitation. In this particular case, Emma was glad to let Ronnie run her home and her life. She did not want to think about food or sleep. She could not think about anything besides a crumpled, wet bikini and how much Justin's mouth tasted like lies when he kissed her.

Ronnie buried her face in Emma's refrigerator while Emma shuffled into the kitchen and draped on a stool at the counter. She felt so weak, drained. Everything about her was heavy. She wanted to relent to that crushing sensation on her ribs and curl into a sad little ball.

"Spill," Ronnie said, lining up sandwich ingredients in front of Emma.

"I asked him about the bikini."

"And? What did he say?"

Emma thought perhaps Ronnie was enjoying this, maybe she wanted to be right about Justin all these years later. Possibly Ronnie was happy to be having the conversation she always knew they would. When Emma looked at her with watery eyes, she met the concern for which she knew Ronnie. She may have hated Justin, but she did not want to see Emma suffer for it.

Emma took a deep breath and sat up to spit out his sloppily spun story.

"He said a group of them from the bar went to the hot tub at the Terrace Hotel downtown, and this girl was wasted so he drove her home. He said she forgot her bikini in the car, but she was wearing clothes, and they didn't have sex or anything."

Ronnie rolled her lips under and pressed down on them with her teeth. She kept her eyes on the food in front of her, assembling the sandwich.

"Say it," Emma said.

"Well, do you believe him?" Ronnie dropped the sandwich in front of Emma and looked into her eyes.

Emma looked down at the sandwich, stared at the striations of colors and ingredients through the tears welling up over her sight. "I don't know. I mean, what he says makes sense, and I should believe him. But…"

"Bite."

"What?"

"Take a bite."

"How am I supposed to take a bite and answer you?"

"Bite."

Emma reluctantly gathered up the sandwich. It had no taste when she pushed it into her mouth. Ronnie waited patiently, folding her arms across her stomach while she watched her chew.

"You didn't actually answer my question," Ronnie said when Emma had finished swallowing.

"What do you mean?"

"You said what he said made sense and you should believe him. You didn't tell me if you do believe him."

"Do *you* believe him?"

"Emma, you already know the answer to that."

"Yeah, I know how you feel about him."

"That still doesn't answer the question. Do you believe him?"

"I don't know."

Emma could not say she did not believe him. Even if she didn't, saying it would make it real. Saying it would make Ronnie right. Saying it would mean everyone would know what he was and how he had fooled her. Every single person at her wedding, every single person in her life would know that he had sex with someone else, that she was not good enough to keep him.

"Okay. That's okay. What are you going to do?"

"I don't know."

Emma dropped her head to the counter again and took handfuls of her hair.

"Calm down. It's okay. Calm down. Bite."

Emma snapped her head up and glared at Ronnie. Ronnie simply placed her hand on her hip and stared back at her until Emma took another begrudging nibble of the sandwich.

Back on the couch, Ronnie shoved a glass of water into Emma's hand.

"Drink."

The food and water took the edge off Emma's anxiety. Only the edge.

"The way I see it," Ronnie said, "you have a couple of choices. You can believe him and move on with your life. You can not believe him, deal with it, and move on with your life. You can not believe him and try to work it out. Or you can not believe him and be out."

Ronnie made it sound so simple.

"I don't really like any of those choices."

"Yet those are your choices. I know it's awful and you never wanted to be here, but here, we are."

Emma hated it when Ronnie was right.

She rolled her choices around in her brain for a long time, allowing Ronnie's voice to echo off the walls of her skull so she could hear what they sounded like the second time. She pictured herself letting it go, forcing his story down her throat and pretending the whole bikini never existed. She imagined gagging on her suspicion, choking on her doubts. Then she slipped into the scenario of leaving, of dividing the Christmas ornaments, of being alone in a big empty house. Of being single again.

Nausea flared up along the back of her throat.

"Ronnie, what the hell am I going to do?" She dropped her face into her palms and let her tears wet her hands. "I can't pretend it never happened. I can't believe him. But I don't want to leave him. I do love him."

"Do you love him enough to give up having kids?"

There was the real question. Like a sucker punch to Emma's gut, there was the ultimate question from before the sodden bikini on the car floorboard.

"I don't know!" Emma sobbed. "All I ever wanted was children. Ever since I was a kid I wanted a baby."

"I know," Ronnie said, wrapping her arms around Emma and pulling her into her shoulder. "You don't have to know now."

Ronnie held onto Emma until the cries stopped shaking her body.

When the door closed behind Ronnie, it echoed in the seemingly cavernous house. In the silence, Emma's anxiety welled up, and the walls began to close in on her. She could not stop the thoughts, the flashes, the pictures of a naked girl in her passenger seat, Justin biting on her earlobe like he did to

Emma.

The image made her physically sick. Being alone in the house as she now feared she might always be made her physically sick, like her chest was collapsing, like she was coming out of her skin.

It was all too much.

She realized she was still huddled against the front door, palm pressed against it after shutting it behind Ronnie. She would have given anything to have Ronnie here forcing food down her throat, still cussing Justin—anything not to be trapped alone with herself.

The woman who was not enough for Justin. The woman he had to supplement. The woman he did not want.

Did he even love her anymore? Did he even ever love her at all?

She did not want to think about it, but the thoughts in her head throbbed like the sick pulse in her veins.

She did not believe him. In the quiet of their house, in the frothing pit of her stomach, she knew. Her mind insisted on throwing flares of doubt, misdirections of denial. Yet in her gut, she knew. Even in the way he had sex with her the night before, she could feel it on him. His betrayal, his detachment.

He had cheated on her with the bikini cocktail waitress. Her body would believe nothing else.

Was the bikini waitress the only one?

Emma's skull threatened to split in half. She wanted to dig her fingers into the fissure and pull until she heard the satisfying crack of splitting bone.

She wanted to rip her head apart, and then it would just be quiet.

She finally peeled her fingertips from the door and curled her hands into her chest. She staggered unsteadily and reluctantly deeper into the house, tears distorting the light around her. She coiled on the couch, pulled a blanket over her face, and shut out the world.

The light was fading from the windows when Emma was stirred by the chime of her phone.

Ronnie: What are you going to do?

Ronnie was relentless. She would not permit Emma to wallow aimlessly for a second. Emma rubbed her raw and sensitive eyes hard then drew the phone into her blanket nest.

Emma: I have to know.

Ronnie: How?

Emma: I have to find proof.

Ronnie: How??

Emma: I don't know yet.

Emma knew Ronnie wanted to tell her to leave him, the way she had wanted to tell her to leave him ever since they started dating.

Why did she have to be right about him? Emma had been telling herself for years that Ronnie and

Justin simply did not get along, that Ronnie was secretly or subconsciously jealous that Emma had life all figured out. She never wanted it to be that Ronnie knew what she was talking about.

The surface layer of her mind said she could still prove her wrong; she could prove that he was telling the truth. Doubt and denial were as comforting as the blanket in which Emma buried as sleep swept over her agitated mind again.

"Emma. Emma."

The voice came out of the distance in the dark.

"Emma. Babe."

Slowly, the voice started to take shape, become familiar. That familiarity made her cringe, made her pull her limbs tighter into her body under her blanket.

"Emma, wake up, babe."

It was Justin, from whom she was shrinking away. She opened her eyes and made out his shape sitting beside her. She could tell from the shade of the darkness that it was late, that the night was folding over itself and beginning to ease toward morning. She could smell the bar on him. The thin, sharp edge of stale alcohol, the frayed trail of the cigarettes he smoked in the back alley.

The skin of a girl in a bikini. But maybe she was imagining that last one.

Heischeatingonyouheischeatingonyouheischeatin gonyouheischeatingonyou.

The thought pulsated on her brain, and she jerked her head to shake it loose. She forced her mind above her body, shoved down her instincts and her panic. She would wait for proof.

"How was work?" Emma mumbled, her voice still groggy with sleep.

"The usual. It was a good night. A lot of twenty-first birthdays."

"No late night swimming?"

"Not tonight."

He unearthed her from the heap of blankets, taking her hand. Her fingers twitched and winced against his touch. She forced herself to breathe. She would have proof, and until she had that measure of verification, she would still be his wife. Just in case there was no proof to be had.

The warmth of his skin against her palm sickened to her, making her anxious. Buried in the sensation, the stark and vivid desire to pick up the poker from beside the fireplace and jab it into his chest radiated. The cool metal would feel at home in her hand, the weight shifting in the arc of her attack comforting. Her heart would exhilarate when her weapon met the resistance of his body. Over and over, she visualized the blunt tip puncturing his chest and the happy spray of blood. She would cherish the dumb look of shock on his smug, lying face.

Emma shook her head hard, trying to dislodge the impulse, trying to break away from what was clearly the fragments of a nightmare. She was not a violent person; she did not think like this.

But she also did not get cheated on.

She's just a fat dumb slut, and nobody will ever want her again.

The voice reverberated in her head and she jerked her neck, twitching to shake it free. She realized she must have looked insane.

"Emma, are you okay?" Justin leaned in closer and moved to encircle her shoulders with his other arm.

Emma faced away from him. "Yeah, I'm fine. I was deep asleep. I'll just meet you in bed."

Justin flipped on the TV and dropped to the couch as she moved into the bathroom. Again, that flash of stabbing him hard with the fireplace poker blazed over her sight. Her entire body seized and fluttered at the vision of the blow. She squeezed her eyes shut tight until she saw patterns of light bursting behind her eyelids. Then she squinted into the mirror.

She scarcely recognized her reflection. Looking at her gaunt and puffed face, she realized that she was not carrying on any deception. Even Justin could not be so dense as to not be able to tell she had been crying all day, to see the utter weight dragging down her features, to notice the absence of any light in her eyes. Even if he did not love her anymore, he could not be that oblivious.

Emma placed her hand on the glass to obscure her reflection and closed her eyes. Those hot tears burned at her eyes again, brimming up against her lids. She did not know how she could have so many tears to cry, how they could continue and never relent.

She wanted to know. She needed to know one way or another. Justin's betrayal would be a relief compared to the awkward limbo where she was presently tormented.

He never came to bed that night. Emma woke

alone on their cold mattress with the sun ripping across the room. She nearly felt hungover from how all the crying had drained her, from all the fluids she had wasted. She caught herself comforted by his absence, liberated in not having to feign being okay, even if it also took a stab toward proof. Why would he not come to bed with her? So he would not have to sleep with her after having been with someone else?

She found him on the couch where she left him the night before. He had shed his shoes and pulled a blanket over himself to pass out on the cushions. The TV still droned in the background. He opened his eyes as she shambled into the room.

"Why didn't you come to bed?" she asked.

"I passed out down here, watching some stupid show."

He sat up and discarded the blanket, picking up his phone from the table, typed away at the keyboard, then placed the phone back on the table. Face down.

Justin had always been potentially more married to his phone than to Emma, constantly clicking or swiping, perpetually chatting with this superficial friend or making plans with that one guy he knew. Still, in their torrid relationship, he had never been secretive. He openly took calls and returned messages and read emails when he was in the middle of a meal or conversation with Emma.

In all that, he never put the phone face down.

In the suspended silence, the phone vibrated, muffled against the wood. Justin snatched it up to his face, unlocked it, and typed in a response. Then he again placed it face down on the table. Very deliberately, not in the normal fashion he would toss it on the closest surface.

Emma felt her eyebrow rising then snatched it back down.

Justin tapped his fingers on the back of his phone, smiling lazily at Emma. "I'm going to hop in the shower. I'm meeting the boys to shoot some hoops before heading in to work today." He stood from the couch.

And I am going to check your phone to find out what you are hiding, Emma thought.

Justin took a step then froze, reaching back to gather up his phone. He moved forward and kissed her on the forehead like a father to a toddler. Emma's heart sank a little as he walked away with his phone in his hand.

Why would he need his phone while he was in the shower now? It was on there. The proof she needed was on that phone, she was sure.

With the sound of the shower running and Justin's music blaring over it, she searched out her own phone. She already had four texts waiting for her from Ronnie.

Ronnie: Well that was a worthless day of work.

Ronnie: How are you feeling?

Ronnie: Are you alive over there?

Ronnie: WTF? Hello, Emma?

Emma was somewhat surprised Ronnie had not shown up to check on her considering she was throwing cuss words in acronyms at her. Perhaps she knew her well enough to know she had retreated into sleep to escape.

Emma: I'm alive.

Ronnie: Took you long enough! Sleeping it away?

Emma: Yeah.

Ronnie: So how is it today?

Emma: Still bad. I'm finding it hard to fake it around him.

Ronnie: So don't.

Emma: I need the proof. I need to know.

Ronnie: I think you already do. Where is this proof going to come from?

Emma: His phone. He's being super shady about it.

Ronnie: You think he's dumb enough to keep cheating texts? Don't go snooping on his shit like one of THOSE girls. Just confront him. Leave.

Emma: I'm looking on the phone. Whenever he leaves it.

Ronnie: I don't think it's a good idea, but do what you gotta do. Call me after.

Emma: K.

It must have been easy for Ronnie to always confront everything, to not give a care to what she might lose and always dive into her problem headfirst. What did she know about a relationship? Terrence hovered in the peripheral of all her stories ever since the wedding, but what did she know about being married? Or about possibly ending a marriage? It could not all be so simple.

Emma's fingers felt anxious again, shifting nervously against her leg. She imagined Justin's phone in her hands, the screen against her fingertips. The answer she needed was right there, if he was not guarding it so closely. It was surely why he was guarding it so closely.

Her fingers froze as the thought broke across her mind. What would she do with the answer? If she had proof, what then? Would she leave? Would she forgive him and work it out?

The realization shattered over her mind that she had no idea what she wanted anymore.

CHAPTER 5

It would be weeks before Justin abandoned his phone. Long strings of nights passed where he never showed up in their bed and Emma would find him sleeping on the couch, still in his clothes from his shift at the bar. Clumps of hours of watching him type away on his phone and keeping it face down in front of them or secured in his pocket.

So much time passed that complacency made a home in the back of Emma's skull. The distastefully awkward marriage gradually wore on her senses, grinding its way into becoming the new normal.

If nothing changed, Emma did not have to make a decision. If she did not know, she could continue on in this suspended animation, this limbo where it all might not be real.

If Ronnie would stop asking her what she was going to do, perhaps she could even convince herself to ignore that malignant little bikini.

It was like she had a roommate. She surely did not have a partner. Justin made brief cameos into her life between playing basketball with the boys, working closing shifts at the bar, attending any concert that would come through town, driving up to go hiking in the mountains on his days off. When she actually thought about it, the scarcity of their overlap was not much of a change, barely a deviation from how they existed before the bikini.

When had they stopped being husband and wife? When had he stopped being in her life at all? She felt like she was support staff to his life, always complacent in whatever plans he wanted to make, in whatever he wanted to go do without her, always accommodating for whatever he wanted for her. Never rocking the boat.

The devolution of their relationship must have happened so slowly, incrementally, as if Emma was sitting in a pot as the temperature gradually climbed. She had not noticed anything until the water around her started to writhe and bubble, until she found some woman's wet bikini on the floor of his car.

The marriage she saw when she opened her eyes disgusted her. She remembered loving him when they got married, but when she actually considered Justin now, she scarcely knew him, much less felt any connection with him. Was this going to be the father of her children he no longer wanted? Were they going to march into old age as roommates wearing rings?

When she thought about it, Emma's heart sank and her head throbbed. Every time Ronnie asked her how she felt, what she was going to do, or when she was going to leave, Emma wanted to punch her in the face.

If she did not think about it, she did not have to decide. She did not have to change absolutely everything about her life. She did not have to reveal the failure and now sham of her marriage to the world and everyone.

Then Justin forgot his phone.

Emma walked into the kitchen after he had departed for work, savoring the quiet in the house and the lack of pretense she found in being alone. The coveted device sat lonely on the counter. After so much fixation, so much fantasy of holding it, Emma was left stunned immobile. She blinked to ensure the phone truly sat unprotected on the kitchen counter.

She brought her hands anxiously into her chest and wound them around each other. She stepped out of the kitchen and looked out the front window to verify Justin's car was gone. Then she crept back into the kitchen and slunk over to the phone as if she was being watched, as if she could be discovered at any moment.

Not knowing how to be sly, she bumbled over the blending of doubt and excitement in her chest. She looked around guiltily again then snatched up the phone, curled her fingers around it, and brought it close to her face.

No passcode.

Moron.

With a flush of exhilaration she unlocked his phone and opened his messages.

Justin had saved every text message he had ever received on the device.

Moron again.

There was a conversation with her, left neglected for weeks, one with his mother, a barrage from his many friends. One stood out at the top. The most recent.

Jessica.

It was just a shot girl from the bar, Justin's voice echoed in her head. *She was way too drunk, and I gave her a ride home. That's it.* And when she had asked again later who the bikini belonged to, *I don't know. She's just a shot girl from work. I don't know her name.*

Who the hell was Jessica? Emma already knew the answer as she opened the conversation.

Her tongue swelled in the back of her throat; her heart pounded in her ears. The world around her contracted and closed to the breadth of the phone screen. Every nerve and synapse in her body pointed toward her eyes, waiting reluctantly and impatiently to read the proof. Tears brimmed in her eyes as she lifted a shaking finger to scroll the conversation.

Jessica: What time do you get off tonight?

Justin: I'm first cut so maybe around midnight.

Jessica: I'm off. You coming over?

Justin: Hell yeah.

Justin had told Emma he was closing. Again. A wave of nausea undulated from the pit of her stomach and came slamming into the back of her throat. Her cheeks contracted; her lips pursed. She scrolled farther back.

Justin: You left your bikini in my car.

Jessica: Oops.

Justin: My wife found it.

Jessica: Oh shit!

Justin: I told her you were drunk and I just gave you a ride home.

Emma's vision flickered out. Her fingers seized and she dropped the phone to the floor, sprinting to the bathroom to puke until dry heaves shook her body.

Proof. The proof Emma had wanted and did not want at the same time. He had preserved their entire incriminating conversation history, like he wanted to get caught. Like he wanted out.

She knew about me. She knew he was married. She knew he was lying to me.

When Justin burst back through the door, Emma sat stoically on the couch, tapping his phone against her knee. He must not have even made it to the bar before realizing his error. The tears and the nausea had faded, and Emma posed like a statue, numb and overwhelmed, done waiting for him.

Justin slowed when he saw Emma waiting with his phone, eyes still wide when she stood up and extended it out to him. Gingerly, he squinted and reached out to take it.

Emma felt the fireplace poker in her hand again, saw another flash of the blood coming out of his chest, felt the impact in her fingertips. Every fiber in her body wanted to take that step backward to retrieve the weapon, wanted to heave it up and through him. Holding his phone out to him felt wrong. Everything that was not killing him right now in their living room felt wrong.

Justin tucked the phone in his pocket and stood looking at her.

"Emma, I—"

"Tell Jessica to keep better track of her swim wear," Emma said robotically.

"You went through my phone?" Justin threw up anger first. She could see him mentally indexing the contents of his phone. "Emma, look, I can explain."

"Can you, Justin?" Emma glared at him. "Go to work. We have to pay Credit Financial this week. I am working eight goddamn shifts this week. We will talk about this when you get off. Midnight, right?"

Justin's eyes and mouth hung open. "Right," he said softly and confused.

He kept staring at Emma with wide eyes as he walked slowly toward the door. Emma kept thinking about how the fireplace poker would feel so right against her palm. And in his chest cavity.

When the door closed behind him, she collapsed to her knees and sobs wracked her body again.

Justin did not come home that night. He was not sprawled out on the couch when Emma rolled over and stumbled out of their bedroom to check at 2 am.

***

Emma knew the bed beside her was still vacant before she opened her eyes. Her hip felt like it was levitating at the all-too-familiar absence of his weight on the mattress. She did not want to open her eyes. The light was bright, and seeing it would make the day real. Once her eyes dilated, this collapsed mess would once again be her marriage and her life.

She brought her fists to her eye sockets and rolled them gently over her swollen and crusted eyelids. So many layers of tears were dried on the tender skin. She did not want to touch the raw flesh any more than she wanted to deal with the problems causing it. She took a deep breath, letting the air fill her chest and push her lungs against her ribs. Even her sides felt sore from sobbing.

Emma was slowly becoming unable to distinguish the pain in her heart from the pain on her nerves.

She peeled begrudgingly from the sheets, even as every cell in her body cried for the denial she could find in sleep, the escape. She stood on unstable legs, her toes sinking into the carpet, and felt the thin dehydration stretching along the inside of her skull. All those tears down her cheeks, bleeding her eyes. She floated drunk or hungover or somewhere in between, lost in a detached haze.

When she opened the bedroom door, Justin was sprawled out on the couch. He had snuck back in the wee hours. His leg dangled off the edge of the couch, tangled in a blanket. His mouth hung open, drooling and stupid. All the physically enticing features she always saw in him, that she prioritized in him, dimmed as something hot and acidic bubbled at the back of her mind. He began to look more unrecognizable to her by the day.

Looking at him felt like a blow to the chest, the emotion creating an impact on her flesh. Emma steadied herself against the banister then sank down to sit on the first step where she could still see him snoring below her.

When she closed her eyes, all she could feel was the cold handle of the fire poker in her hands, her grip choking the unyielding metal. All she could see was his dumbstruck face when she plunged the sharp end into his chest. All she could hear was the wet gasp in his throat and the sucking of his chest wound.

She only sat at the top of the stairs in their house, cradling her head, the sound of his breathing grating against her brain like a serrated blade.

Fire poker in his chest.

It was all she could think about. It was the only thought that kept the burning pain in her chest from violently rising up to swallow her mind whole. She kept seeing it flashing over and over. Each of his inhalations was Emma pulling the poker back, winding up the blow; each exhalation the sickening puncture into his chest and his wide-eyed shock.

She wanted the pain in his eyes, she wanted the shock in his face, instead of feeling both laid hot, heavy, and suffocating on top of her.

Emma did not know how long she crouched paralyzed at the top of the steps. Her eyes were locked open, her chest rising and falling dreadfully. She wandered far removed in her murderous fantasy.

If only her flesh had the courage.

Emma remained catatonic until Justin's waking breath rippled through the stagnant air. She gazed down to watch him stir out of the trailing end of sleep, the way he did countless mornings beside her. Mornings when she thought she could not be happier, mornings when she thought she loved him.

Emma heaved up against the crushing weight on her chest before he could see her. She felt so full she could barely move, as if she was inflated by her pain. The torrent of emotions sloshed and writhed beneath her surface, made her feel disoriented in her own skin. Her consciousness felt like a bobbing lifeboat in a dark, violent, and unfamiliar sea.

When she padded unsteadily into the room, Justin made eye contact with her. The connection triggered a flare in her. All the tumultuous wayward emotions solidified, focused, drawing a point in her wounded mind.

She wanted to kill him.

"Morning," he said cautiously.

Emma had so much to say she might vomit actual words at his feet. Unfortunately, her mind no longer communicated with her voice; her tongue lay thick and useless behind her teeth, as if her pain forced her to forget how to speak.

"Look, Em," he started, looking down at his hands.

He poured that familiar tone, that gentle ease into feigned remorse that had seduced her before all too easily. That had beguiled her the night after the bikini. Emma shook the depressive slack from her face and hardened into a look that forbid him to finish the lie.

She knew now that they were all lies. Lies were his native tongue.

He fell silent, not knowing what to do. The air heaved in the quiet, felt thick in Emma's slow breaths.

"You didn't come home last night." Her voice sounded foreign and unpracticed to her.

"Em, I—"

She glared at him again. "You knew I knew. You knew I knew about her. About *Jessica*. You knew I knew when you got off work. You knew I knew you would be with her." She looked Justin dead in the eyes. "You really don't give a fuck about me."

When she said it, it was the truest thing Emma had heard in a long time. He did not care about her. At all. He did not consider her as he recklessly lived his life. She was like furniture in their home, something to sit on or look at. Emma found clarity in that truth, soul-crushing, suicide-inducing poignancy.

"You don't give a fuck about me," she said again, whispering desperately to herself.

"Emma, I—p…"

Emma lifted her hand to block his empty words. "Did you ever? Did you love me? Why did you even marry me? How many other women have there been? How many did you sleep with then come home and lay next to me?"

The idea of even more adultery brought vomit

into the back of her throat. She pursed her lips and doubled over, moaning chaotically.

"No!" she said before he could even reply. "I don't want to know. I don't want to know."

She wrapped one arm around her heaving stomach and cradled her head in her other palm, wilting into a ball on the carpet. She did not care how she looked to him. She did not care how pathetic her sobs may have sounded echoing in his face and against the white walls. He did not want her anyway; she was never enough.

Justin stood over her as she wept into the floor for too long. By the time he moved, Emma had forgotten he was there. He crouched down and placed a hand on her shaking back. His touch felt vile to her, and she writhed violently away, curling up against the entertainment center with her tear-stained cheeks bright red.

"Don't touch me. You had sex with her hours ago when you knew I would know. Don't touch me with that hand."

Justin tossed up his arm and let out a sigh, dropping himself onto the coffee table behind him. "Emma, what do you want me to do?"

Die.

"I want you to be the man I married. I want you to be my husband. I want you to not lie to me about everything and go around cheating on me like I'm an idiot. I want to have the life we were going to have, the children we were going to have."

"That was the life *you* always wanted. That was always *your* plan."

"So this is my fault?"

68

Justin rolled his lips in and turned away. "So what do you want to do? Counseling? Just end it?"

Emma looked at him dumbfounded. He was trying to wrap this up, trying to expedite her pain because it made him uncomfortable. He was trying to get out there back to whatever life he had created without her.

"Are you going to change?" Emma asked.

"No, I don't think so."

"Are you going to want kids again?"

"No, definitely not."

Emma let her mouth hang open a moment in surreal disbelief. "Then we're done."

"Okay." Justin popped up and almost clapped his hands to break the moment. "I'm just going to get out of here for a while. I imagine you don't want to see me."

"Don't you think we should maybe decide what we're going to do?"

"You said we're ending things."

"Justin, we're married. You don't just *end* things. We have to get a divorce. We have to divide things. We have to figure all that out."

"Yeah, well, you know, whatever you want. We can do that later."

Justin hopped into his shoes, already moving toward the door. It must have been such a relief to him. He was free.

He left Emma in a silent house, a prisoner of her grief.

CHAPTER 6

Emma could hear Ronnie giggling through her front door, and something about the sound increased the weight on her chest. Everything around her was so bright and so loud; the world itself was assaulting her. The streetlights shone down, slicing the dark and causing her to squint. The whoosh of passing cars and the edge of Ronnie's muffled laugh abraded her ears. She wrapped her fingertips into the cloth of her hoodie and tied to curl into it, to disappear among the thin folds.

Her eyes throbbed from so many unrelenting hours of crying. The lids were so raw that it hurt to blink. Her head felt heavy and depleted, her dehydrated brain weighting her skull. When she reached her hand to the door, her arm quivered in front of her.

Sound and light poured over Emma like a wave when Ronnie opened the door. She recoiled and shrank away from it, attempting to step back into the shadows.

"Emma?" Ronnie squinted then reached for her,

pulling her into the abrasive light.

Emma looked like a zombie. All the color had drained from her face, making her features appear gaunt and lifeless, drawing all the attention to her red and abused eyes. She had lost herself in one of Justin's hoodies, though she did not know why she was wearing it. She had reached blindly into the closet and fled the empty house. From the mingling of shock and concern on Ronnie's face, she must look as horrid as she felt.

Ronnie dragged Emma through the door by her shoulders.

"Emma," Ronnie said, "what the hell happened?"

Emma tried to find the words to articulate what had happened, the phrases to encapsulate the recent implosion of her entire life. Terrence sat on the couch behind Ronnie, a silent stun upon his features. Beer bottles and opened containers of Chinese delivery littered the coffee table.

Emma had interrupted a date.

"It's over," Emma mumbled before the wretched sobs began anew.

Ronnie wrapped around Emma and did not say a word; she simply held her. From beneath Ronnie's arms, Emma heard Terrence get up and gather a few things.

"I'll give you guys some time. Be home later," he said to Ronnie, kissing her on the cheek on his way out.

After the door closed behind him, Ronnie dragged Emma to the couch and flipped off the TV. She took Emma's face in her hands, wiping the overflowing tears with her thumbs. Emma did not want to look her in the face. She did not want this to be happening; she did not want any of this to be real. She had spent the past hours since Justin vanished trying to convince herself it was not. Saying it again only made it feel all the more authentic.

Ronnie repeated, "What happened?"

Emma struggled to breathe through her tears, forcing the air out between thin, taut lips while she choked on the sob. She strained to swim above the pain, to grasp at a lifeboat of lucidity against the swirling tide in her mind.

"H-he finally l-left his ph-phone," Emma stuttered. "Forgot it completely when he left for work."

"Moron."

"Oh! He's so much more stupid than that!" Anger exhumed her words from the fog, tugged her voice out from under the depression. "He saved the entire conversation with this bitch. From the bikini and before. Everything. Right there on his phone. Ronnie, she knew about me. They talked about me. They LOLed about me."

Ronnie sat up more rigidly, grew taller. "That *bitch*."

"Which one?"

"Both of them."

"It gets worse."

"Fucking of course it does!"

"So I confront him. You would have been proud. I didn't cry, I didn't beg him for answers. I told him I knew and to get home after work so we could deal with it."

"Yes! Good for you."

"He didn't come home. He knew I knew about this girl. He knew I knew when he would get off work. He knew I would know he was with her, and he didn't come home. He went and fucked her then came home and slept on the couch."

Ronnie tensed beside her even tighter, her face blooming in shades of blood. Emma knew this look well. This look usually ended in them getting kicked out of wherever they were at the time.

"Then I fell apart," Emma said.

"Well, yeah! Jesus!"

"I started blubbering and raving like a crazy person. All 'you don't give a fuck about me, you don't love me, you never loved me.' Falling down crying. Screaming at him. It was embarrassing."

"Who cares? What, do you need to save face in front of him? He deserved every minute of it."

"And more, but I don't like him seeing how much he's hurting me."

"Fair enough. Then what happened?"

"Nothing," Emma said. The sadness crept back into the edges of her sentences. "He didn't care. Ronnie, he was relieved. He couldn't get out of there fast enough."

"Well of course, Em. He has been outside of your relationship for who knows how long? He's already over it. He's probably glad to not be hiding it anymore."

"It's more than that. I don't even recognize him anymore. In these few weeks, he is a completely different person, and I don't know who is real—the guy I married or the guy now. I think the guy I married never really existed."

The tears started to squeeze out again at the thought of her huge lie of a life. Emma felt so impossibly stupid and oblivious. Ronnie said nothing, only rubbed her back.

"I know, I know," Emma said, burying her face in her hands. "You were right about him."

"I didn't say anything."

"But you were thinking it."

"That is the last thing I was thinking right now."

"Either way, you were. He's a complete piece of shit."

"That doesn't make me happy. I never wanted to see him hurt you like this. Even to be right. And you know how much I love being right."

"Yes, it's like a sickness."

"A sickness because I'm so good at it."

"Too soon," Emma laughed through her sobs.

Laughing felt strange yet distantly familiar. It hurt Emma's cheeks to turn up, but the sliver of levity eased the weight for an instant.

"When is the last time you ate?" Ronnie asked.

"Um, maybe yesterday sometime."

"Oh no. No, no. You are eating now."

"Ronnie, no. I really don't want to."

"Shut up."

Ronnie got up and marched into her small, understocked kitchen.

The thought of food repulsed Emma. She could imagine the dry, ashy sludge in her mouth, rocking around between her lazy teeth, gagging her. She wanted no part of it. She did not want taste on her

74

tongue, did not want the sensation of digestion in her gut. She wanted to starve away her feelings, waste away her body until she disappeared completely.

However, Ronnie would not be contested. It would be pointless to argue.

Emma's phone sang from her purse on the floor. Ronnie reached down and snagged it.

"It's Noah," Ronnie said, holding out the glowing phone.

"No, I can't talk to him while I'm like this."

"Emma, he's your brother."

"I know he is, which is why I can't. He'll remember when our mother was like this after our parents' divorce. I don't want him to see that I became her."

"Talk to your brother."

"Later."

Ronnie dropped the phone back in the purse and headed to the kitchen.

"You are not your mother just because Justin cheated on you."

"Aren't I? Doesn't that make me *exactly* my mother?"

"I know it brings it all up, but plenty of women get cheated on. Guys are assholes."

"It wasn't just that she got cheated on. He cheated on her with Mrs. Davies from down the street when her dumbass son Jeremy was constantly at our house. Everyone in the neighborhood knew. It was quite the scandal. My mother was humiliated. She cried all the time. You know, like me right now. She was so pissed and embarrassed she could not even deal. Like me right now."

"Oh ouch. And you had to watch all that."

"I remember her embarrassment. And Jeremy Davies was such a little asshole. I never realized why he was always over. He just was. Driving me crazy. Then when we all found out, he was at our house again taunting me."

You might as well just kiss me now, Emma, because we're going to be family. Your dad is my daddy now. He doesn't want your stupid mom anymore. He doesn't want your ugly mom! She's just a fat, dumb slut, and nobody will ever want her again.

Emma heard Jeremy's voice clearly in her head, the way his fatty cheeks muddled his words. The abrasive sound climbed out of her depression and deafened her. She shook her head until the room around her resurfaced.

"We got in a fight," Emma said.

"You got into a fight? Emma? Emma got into a fight ever in her life?"

"Well," Emma hesitated on the memory as the focus in her eyes wavered, "I guess it wasn't a fight. I hit him."

"Jeremy? Like, you punched him?"

"We were playing in the basement and I hit him with a metal pipe that was down there."

"Emma! What?"

"In the head. More than once."

"How is it that you've never told me about any of this? Not your mom's humiliation, you assaulting a kid with a weapon."

"It's embarrassing. And my mom put me in a lot

of therapy after."

"I knew about the therapy. I just thought it was for the divorce. What happened to this kid?"

"Noah came down before I could really hurt him. He went to the hospital, and that was even more drama, but he was fine."

"I'm at a loss here. I don't even know what to say."

"Well, that is a miracle!"

"Shut up."

"My little attack made things even worse for my mom. More drama and embarrassment. I think that's why she immediately moved us to Denver and got all obsessed about finding a new husband and getting back to where she said she was supposed to be."

"Okay, let's work on not letting that happen to you. You already live in Denver at least, and you definitely aren't still assaulting people because Justin would have had that shit coming!"

Emma snickered in spite of herself, and thought again of the fireplace poker.

Wallowing on the couch, her head felt the slightest bit lighter not being in that vacant house, at having vomited all her pain, even her past, into Ronnie's lap. The fading conversation had been the first time she had said anything coherent about how she was feeling since she had picked up Justin's phone. Hearing external thoughts made it seem almost possible that she might still be sane.

Almost.

Her head still felt dreadfully heavy, so Emma leaned onto her elbows and juggled her skull between her palms, rocking, letting her fingertips sink into her cheek. She glanced over at the dormant flat screen TV. Had the television doubled in size? She furrowed her brow, then noticed a gaming system below, wires snaking out and pooling on the floor around it.

Ronnie hated video games.

Bewildered, Emma sat up a little straighter, lifted her weary head to survey the usually monotonously familiar space.

Work boots and male sandals were stacked among Ronnie's black sneakers.

"Ronnie?"

"Yeah, yeah, here I come."

Ronnie appeared carrying a plate, which she heaped with selections from the Chinese containers. Emma found the gag in her throat. Ronnie forced the plate into Emma's lap.

"Did you get a new TV?" Emma asked.

"Um, not exactly." Ronnie started gathering up the Chinese containers and moved away from Emma.

"Ronnie, why do you have a gaming system? And boy shoes? Is Terrence living here?"

"Maybe," Ronnie said, her back still to Emma.

"Ronnie! When did that happen?"

Ronnie dropped the boxes in the refrigerator and turned back around.

"Maybe a couple weeks ago."

"How could you not tell me that? This is huge, Ronnie! At one time you barely let them sleep over. How did this happen?"

"Em, you had too much going on. I couldn't tell

you I was moving in with Terrence while you were dealing with Justin cheating on you and your marriage ending. It wasn't going anywhere."

"I don't want you keeping things from me because my life is a mess."

"I wasn't. I was just focusing on you first."

"Oh my God, Ronnie. You live with a boy."

"Eeew, I know."

"Do you love him?"

"No!" Ronnie paused. "Maybe."

"Ronnie!"

Emma had officially crossed into an alternative reality. A horrible and disorienting world where her marriage was a hollow lie and a failure and where Ronnie was having sex with one person and allowing him to stay in her house longer than twenty-four hours.

"I say again, how did this happen?"

"I don't know really. We just sort of decided to not fuck anyone else."

"Which you also didn't tell me about."

"His lease was up at his place, and somehow, it became him moving in here."

"Holy shit."

"Holy shit."

"Awww, Ronnie. You're growing up! I'm so happy for you."

"Are you?"

"Yes. I can be happy for you and still be unhappy for myself at the same time."

"Fair enough. Now eat, woman."

Emma looked down at the piles of rice and noodles quivering in her unstable lap. She poked at a grain of rice. The texture felt vile against her skin. Ronnie leaned forward with a stare that said "*EAT*." Emma sighed and brought the forkful to her lips. Merely the scent of the comingling ingredients made her stomach seize up. She took a deep breath and shoved the food between her teeth.

Immediately, her body rejected the idea. She slammed her hand down, nearly tipping the plate all over the floor. Dry heaves rattled her ribs, and she pressed the back of her hand to her mouth.

"I can't, Ronnie. I just can't."

"Fine," Ronnie said, removing the plate. "You leave me no other choice."

"What?"

"Ice cream for dinner."

***

Emma woke up the next morning dissolved into a blanket on Ronnie's couch. She had slept paralytically once more—one slow, pathetic respiration above being dead—and her joints ached from being crumpled in one position so long. She moved clumsily with both mind and body protesting every shift. Every part of her wanted to sleep into oblivion.

More evidence of Terrence and cohabitation greeted her in the bathroom. A towel branded with the image of some superhero Emma did not recognize was slung over the towel rod, a canister of shaving cream and a manly razor crammed into the corner on the edge of the bathtub. Ronnie's toothbrush now had a companion in the white crusted plastic cup. Ronnie had finally permitted someone into her home, into her life. For the first time. A tight stab pierced her chest. Even Ronnie's toothbrush had more companionship than she did.

Emma placed her palms on the cold counter and hung her head. She blew the breath out thick between her lips when the tears welled up again. At this point, she did not remember what it felt like to not be crying, to have any sense of clarity in her head.

"Em?" Ronnie said through the door.

Emma squeezed her eyes shut to cinch off the tears, wiped her cheeks, and opened the door.

"How are you feeling?" Ronnie asked when Emma stepped out into the hall.

"Fat," Emma said, cradling her stomach. "I can't believe you made me eat an entire thing of ice cream."

"You wouldn't eat food. Desperate times."

"Food sounds so unappetizing right now. Eating is the last thing I want to do."

"Then you get force-fed ice cream until that changes. I didn't expect you up so early."

The bedroom door was closed behind Ronnie. Terrence must have come home while Emma lay half dead on the couch. Their couch now.

"Yeah, I have to work."

"Oh come on, Em. You can skip it."

"No I can't. I already missed two days. There's no way Randy will let me duck out on another. I have three jobs; I can't miss work. For any reason."

"Have you told him what's going on?"

"No. I told him I was sick. With how I sounded,

I don't think it was hard to believe."

"Tell him what happened; take another day."

"No," Emma snapped. Then softer, "I don't want anyone to know."

Ronnie tilted her head and raised an eyebrow.

"At least not yet," Emma whined. "I need to get my head around it first."

"How are you going to hide this?"

"Hide what?"

"This!" Ronnie gestured up and down over Emma. "The fact that you look like you've been shit out of a dinosaur then run over by a truck."

"Jesus. Thanks, Ronnie."

"Honey, awful shit has happened. You look awful, nothing wrong with that. But you can't hide it and you won't be able to keep it a secret. Like I have always told you, you're too transparent."

"Well, for now, I'm going to try. I need the money. We owe Credit Financial this week or they are going to send us to collections. Plus the mortgages, plus the motorcycle payment."

"For all of Justin's debts."

"I know. I know!" Emma mashed her hands over her face. "I married an idiot. He dug us in over our heads in debt, convinced me to buy a second house and a car and a motorcycle. I've been working three jobs to keep us afloat while the debt collectors keep calling, and he's out working at a bar some nights and fucking cocktail waitresses in bikinis. I know!"

Ronnie remained silent, letting Emma scream and lean against the hall wall.

"How did I get here, Ronnie? How? How is this my goddamn life?"

"I really don't know, Emma. You were always the one who had it all figured out, who knew what she wanted in her life."

"Look where that got me. I'm alone. Justin's been cheating on me for longer than I want to know. I'm working three bullshit jobs to not file bankruptcy. You have a job that throws the money at you and have finally moved in with someone."

"You're right. I don't know how any of this happened. Do you think we switched lives at some point, like some *Freaky Friday* shit? Because your life sounds like it should belong to me."

"We must have. You didn't do some voodoo on me in the college, did you?"

"Well, you know I have always been secretly fluent in the dark arts. And you did always nap on my fucking couch when I had insomnia."

"Clearly, I deserved this then!" Emma laughed, and the darkness lifted for a brief moment. "What the hell am I going to do, Ronnie?"

"Honestly, I have no idea. But today, apparently, you are going to pull your shit together and go to work."

***

When Emma shambled back into her house after two shifts, she was as exhausted physically as she was emotionally. Her flesh felt like it complimented her fractured mental state. It felt like she had an excuse. It was a relief to feel so tired and sore that she could not think. She had happily plunged into the distraction of tasks all day long, except her face hurt from forcing the grin and saying, "No, I'm fine. Just don't feel very well," on repeat.

Under the cover of night, she limped from her car to the dark and hollow house. In no way did she want Justin to be inside waiting for her, she only did not want to be alone with her thoughts. She should have gone back to Ronnie's welcoming couch. Only she could not face seeing her uncharacteristically happy cohabitation with Terrence.

There was no place for her, no position that made the pain more bearable, no perspective that made it all feel less real and catastrophic.

Emma had not eaten all day. Being busy was an easy enough excuse. Ronnie was not there to shove ice cream down her throat. With the more detached apathy and tunnel vision focus of coworkers, her starvation could go on unnoticed and unimpeded. The burning emptiness where her stomach usually sloshed felt appropriate, played in harmony with the symphony of pain on her nerves.

Emma did not even bother to turn on any lights. She was familiar with the layout of their house. She left her shoes and coat by the door, dropped her keys, purse, and tips on the counter, and heaved her weary bones up the stairs. She might have been asleep before her head actually contacted the pillow.

***

Shifting and rustling in the morning house below her roused her from her coma. She would have been frightened if she cared what happened to her anymore, if she did not know from the bumbling disregard in the movements that it was Justin. She rolled her eyes hard, causing her wounded eyeballs to whimper.

She did not want to see him. She never wanted to see him again. She could not stand having to confront the reality behind the man she thought she loved. What remained was only some unfamiliar, dumb, cheating asshole. Someone she would have never permitted herself to see herself with once upon a time.

She had chosen him. She had given everything to him. In front of everyone. And that was the worst part, the pain that twined tightly around every wrinkle in her brain.

Whining as she thrashed out of her pillowed nest, she dug deep through the endless layers of depression, scratching down to rediscover her anger. She drew the rage up and pushed it out over her flesh in a protective layer.

Anything to be able to deal with him.

When she walked down the stairs still in her rumpled uniform from last night, she found Justin dragging bags up from his office in the basement, his playroom. Emma walked around him to gather up the purse, keys, and tip envelope she had abandoned in the dark hours ago.

"What are you doing?" she asked without bothering to look at him.

"Just getting some stuff. I think I'm going to blow town for a couple days. You know, clear my head."

"What about work?"

"I'll take off."

"On the weekend? Justin, you make all your money on the weekend. We have to pay the motorcycle and both mortgages by the end of the week."

"We'll figure it out."

"Will we? Will we? Like we're figuring out this separation? Are you just going to leave me high and dry on all this stuff?"

"Em, I wouldn't do that to you."

"Yeah, and I didn't think you would cheat on me and leave me either."

Justin looked down and gathered up the bags to move toward the door.

"That's right," Emma said. "Don't own up to it. Don't deal with it. Just continue doing whatever the hell it is you want. Never mind me, your wife, or anyone."

The door shut behind him, and the sound echoed through the house.

Emma stood there alone, still holding the envelope with her tips in it. Tips from the third job she worked to pay *his* credit card debt, to pay for this house *he* insisted they buy. She wondered when she had become his bitch.

She was his bitch.

He was having sex with some cocktail waitress in a bikini, and he was leaving her. Alone in this stupid house *he* had to have while they rented their first house to unruly college kids who did nothing but damage it.

The screen door slammed shut behind her as she fled the house. She paid no attention to Justin loading his car with all his pointless, unconsummated hobbies. She completely lost concept of her body, her mind so enveloped in shock. He could not stop stunning her with his new levels of idiocy and detachment.

She did not realize she was running until her feet pounded the asphalt, bare skin slapping at the textured road. She did not feel the pain, did not feel her feet. She did not feel anything. A horn blazed loud in her ears as a truck slammed on its brakes in front of her. She did not react. She could only stare at the driver with wide, maniacal eyes.

She kept running. She pumped her legs and slammed her unprotected feet into the pavement mindlessly until her pulse throbbed through her temples, her breath burned in her lungs, her muscles cried out in their own acid. She ran until she could not think and could not feel anything beyond the exhaustion.

It was that day Emma became a runner.

CHAPTER 7

Her heaving breaths swirled past her open lips, the reverberation of each stride rippling up her body. Her foot struck the pavement mid-sole on her overpriced, personally fitted running shoes before she coiled the leg behind her and thrust out the next. Even with the chaotic gangster rap threatening to deafen her through the quivering earbuds, the sound of her own breathing encapsulated her.

Her heart throbbed to support the rapid, gasping inhalations, sending the blood pounding under her skin. The edge of her sight wobbled in rhythm. The sweat beading across her forehead and upper lip and trickling down the curve of her spine was not beckoned by the sun or the temperature around her; heat brewed in and radiated from her core. Her furnace burned hotter with each stride and puffed breath, wafting up waves of heat to lick over her face.

Emma's eyes surveyed the curve of the greenway sprawling in front of her. Her sight registered the tall line of security fences hugging a neighborhood of backyards, the low water level of the creek trickling sluggishly alongside her, the twist in the branches of the sprouting trees, the bobbing figures of other runners on the trail. She did not actually see any of the scene.

Emma was lost in the run.

The concrete below her crawled up against her toes, easing up in an incline, dragging her up a hill. She drew out her strides, heaving her legs up slower with her quads, leaning forward to employ gravity for aid. As the grade increased, her breathing struggled. She clenched her teeth and spat her exhalations out, swinging her arms toward the crest.

The hill climaxed and spilled her out into a downhill stretch. Emma let out a gasp in relief with acid writhing over the muscles in her legs, teeming and tingling from her hips to her ankles as she pumped them forward. She leaned back upright and dropped her exertion to coast through the heavy steps down the reward hill. Her heart climbed back out of her skull and the heat flared down, dropping below consuming inferno.

Her breath remained desperate while gaining pace with each inhale. Her body moved mechanically, methodically, mindlessly. Right, left. Leg, arm. Breathe in, breathe out. Just keep going. She disappeared into the monotonous melody, below the pain on her nerves where her thoughts could not find her.

Where she was free.

The hill meandered and waned in front of her jog, and her finish line crept into view. The culmination of her miles edged into sight, the same point at which she started. Almost there. The weight lifted out of her exhausted muscles and heaving chest as an awkward depleted rejuvenation rushed over her.

Faster. She pushed her tired legs faster. She stopped listening to her body completely. She stretched out her run to her physical limit, reaching with each movement, pushing harder each time her foot struck the ground. She launched off of her steps, sending her breathing into a panicked yet strict rhythm through thin lips.

When she slammed past the imaginary line on the pavement, Emma put the brakes on. Her heavy footsteps dwindled until she fell into a gentle walk. Her entire body vibrated, her skin was on fire, and her head felt like it was floating. A smile was playing on her lips. Her chest heaved, the sweat pouring. She only felt euphoric, elevated, elated.

Emma loosed her phone from the sleeve on her arm and stopped her GPS tracking app. Her pace had been better; she was getting faster. Every time, she pushed to her physical edge, and every time, that got her a little further.

Her body flushed and tingled beneath the shifting layer of sweat secreting over the length of her skin. The stupid, unadulterated smile stretched absentmindedly across her cheeks, contorting her face upwards in a pattern too often forgotten. The brief relent of the weight on her chest permitted her to actually breathe. Its absence made her feel like she was floating. She felt happy. Simple and unrefined, free from thought.

The heat still radiated out from somewhere

buried at her center. Though her inhalations became thicker and more fluid, she was perspiring more than in her dead sprint, if that was possible. She could smell her own exertion on her upper lip and feel it sliding down her back, pooling above her eyebrows, lining the hinges of her knees.

In this disgusting, saturated throbbing, she was free and content, momentarily divorced from her life and lost in the synapses of her physical body.

With each cooldown step, her lungs and her heart slowed back toward their resting rates. The heat billowing from her core vanished abruptly and instantly, leaving a chill icing the edge of her sweaty film.

Each step was also one closer to her car, one in the direction of reality, where there was more than the sound of her breathing and the collision of her shoes with the pavement. She would run into oblivion if she never had to come back, if she never had to deal with or think about the mundane realities anymore.

Emma lifted her phone and wiped the sweat from the screen onto her race tech shirt. She did not hear any notifications through her blaring music and deafening breathing, but a barrage of text messages, emails, and social networking indicators greeted her on the screen.

Welcome back to your dreaded reality, they seemed to say.

There was a message from Ronnie.

Ronnie: Screw that d-bag. Dinner at my house tonight. T will be out. I'll order food and get

wine. No excuses. Get your ass here!

This was the reality Emma ran from that day: talking to Ronnie about her latest dating disaster, making it real and binding by confession. Before the run had even cooled on her soles, there it was.

There was no escape, even on the trail, so she drove home, showered, and got her ass to Ronnie's in yoga pants and a sloppy bun.

When Ronnie's door opened, Emma saw the full wine glass suspended in front of her face. Ronnie extended the drink to Emma at the threshold, smirking some combination of a welcoming grin and an I-told-you-so air. The deep red liquid quivered at the surface and refracted pink light against Emma's face.

Blood red, like the color that flashed when it became clear Dylan would not be answering her texts.

Blood red, like the color she fantasized about loosing from his neck.

She welcomed the blood red of the wine and how familiar it felt. She wrapped her fingertips around the glass and brought it to her lips. She took a long pull of the liquid before she even entered the apartment.

Ronnie nodded approvingly and walked back inside. Emma followed her mechanically and pushed the door closed behind her, crumpling on the couch.

"All right. Spill," Ronnie said, bringing a pizza box out to the table.

The smell of the melty cheese and savory sauce

made Emma want to vomit in her mouth. She dove back into her wine glass, where the aroma was thin and abrasive.

"I don't want to." Her voice echoed sadly on the inside of the glass.

She kept the curve pressed against her face and watched her exhalations steam patterns above the liquid. Ronnie dropped her head to the side and raised an eyebrow harshly. A glare flirted on the edge of her lashes. Emma knew that look. She whined and threw her arm over her eyes like a child.

"Stop being ridiculous," Ronnie said.

Emma sighed and pulled her head back up, casting Ronnie a defeated gaze. "I don't want to talk about it anymore. I don't want to deal with it anymore. This whole dating thing is stupid. Another guy who turned out to be an asshole. Another guy who didn't want me. I'm still divorced. I'm still single. I just want to be done. I just want the family I was supposed to have already."

"That escalated quickly. I only asked you what happened," Ronnie laughed, pushing Emma's drink up by the base.

Emma half smirked and gulped at the liquid again. The sedative arms of the alcohol reached up to cradle around her brain, and the slightest edge of her tension began to dissipate. Only the hole in her chest plunged deeper.

"What happened with...what was this one's name again?"

"Dylan."

"Right. Dylan."

"You make me sound like a hoochie," Emma whined, "like there are too many names to keep straight."

"Look, I'm not naming any of these puppies unless they decide to stop acting like strays."

Emma choked on a chuckle. "What does that even mean?"

"Details. Spill!"

"He poofed."

"Disappeared?"

"Disappeared. It has been a week. No calls, no texts, no returned messages. Just poof!"

"Ugh. And you're sure he doesn't have some shit going on?"

"How would I know if I have no idea where he is?"

"Were you guys dating yet? Officially, I mean."

"No. I mean we hadn't had that talk, but I thought that's where we were going. It seemed to be what he wanted."

"So what are the rules here? At what interval do you have to check in with someone you haven't committed to?"

"Ronnie."

"No, seriously, I have no idea here. I never 'dated.'" Ronnie lifted her fingers in air quotes.

"I don't even know anymore. No, there is no real rule when you're not official. But if you are trying to date someone, it's simple good form to reply to a message, to not up and freaking vanish."

"Fair enough. If you say so. You know I always wanted the bastards to poof!" Ronnie giggled into her wine glass.

"Speaking of your not dating, how is Terrence?"

"Not so subtle subject change!"

"Give me a break. We'll circle back, I'm sure."

"Always. T is good. You know, the usual."

"Adequately vague, the usual. You know, it's okay to be in a relationship. You have lived together for multiple years now. It's okay to act like you love him."

"That sounds gross," Ronnie laughed. "No, no. Once it becomes like every other relationship, it will go to shit like every other relationship. As far as I'm concerned, we are fuck buddies who cohabitate."

"And love each other."

"Fine. And love each other."

"Where is he tonight?"

"Gaming night with some guys from work. They order pizza and drink beer and play some stupid shooting games I can't stand while I get the apartment to myself to drink wine with you. Everybody wins."

They clinked glasses and both drank deeply.

"I remember when you brought him to my wedding. You said he was your guy of the night. Look at you now. Practically married. In such denial the whole time. 'No, we're not dating. No, we're just sleeping together.' Uh huh," Emma mocked.

"Whoa, whoa, whoa! I am not married."

"Practically married."

"I am not practically married."

"Sure, sure. Exactly like you're 'not dating.'"

"Shut up."

Emma smirked gently against her glass, grasping at the enjoyment of agitating Ronnie, reminding her of all her own denial and hypocrisy. Even if her eventual happiness was also a stab at that hole inside her chest, the wound edged in an envy that alarmed Emma.

"We are not here to talk about my partner," Ronnie said.

"Husband."

"Partner! We are here to talk about this situation with…?"

"Dylan."

"Right. Dylan."

"Do you think I'm being a psycho?" Emma grumbled. "Can I really get mad when we're not together?"

"Sweetie, you've always been a psycho." Ronnie winked. "No, you can be mad whenever you want. But *why* are you mad?"

Ronnie lowered her chin and adopted her calm and analytical tone, gently stepping inside Emma's head. Emma was familiar with Ronnie tucking right beside her in her brain, some strange blend of a comfort and a violation.

"I'm mad because he poofed."

"Right. I guess I'm wondering if you care about him specifically or if you're upset that things didn't work out again."

"You mean, was I really that into him or just having someone?"

"Yeah."

"Very possibly the someone. He let me hope. He let me actually think he could be the one. I was

96

stupid enough to see the happy ending and think I was finally there. I think I almost started to trust him." Emma paused. "Shit, I'm mad at myself."

"Em, I know you're mad that you're single when you don't think you should be, and I know you're mad that you're divorced. Justin took the life you thought you were having away from you. I know this whole time you're thinking you're wasting more time not having the kids you want."

"Exactly." Emma nodded with her head hung low while the familiar tears burned back into her eyes.

The way Ronnie was able to see through Emma's face and words and extract the buried truths made Emma uncomfortable in her own skin, made her writhe against her own body. Ronnie said the things Emma did not want to say aloud or even silently to herself. She did not want to deal with the way all roads led back to the babes yet unconceived and unborn.

This violent and painful dissection of her mind made Emma want to avoid Ronnie or omit telling her anything vulnerable, but after Justin had so effectively blindsided her, she found herself addicted to these brutal truths. She never wanted to be caught so unaware again, never wanted everything ripped away while she covered her eyes. She came to Ronnie for comfort while also to have her head cracked open and be told what lay hiding inside.

She wanted to be mad at Dylan. She wanted to expend her energy hating him. She did not want to deal with what was wrong with her or how she was unhappy with her life. Emma wanted to curl up and cry or crawl into a hole and die. The way Ronnie said it made it sound like it was her fault. Instead of Dylan simply being wrong, Emma now again bore the responsibility of choosing him. She blinked past her tears and dove into the therapy.

She sighed and leaned back into the couch, watering the pain twisting in her belly with more wine, allowing it to blossom and change shape.

"So do I even give a shit about him? Or am I unhappy overall?" Emma asked, looking off at the blank TV, her pathetic reflection staring sadly back at her. She could not endure eye contact with Ronnie when she was this emotionally exposed.

"Let's not let him off so easy just yet. He poofed; that still makes him a douche. But did you like him, Emma? I mean him for him. Were you falling for him?"

Emma rolled the questions over and over in her mind until they felt blunted and smooth. She conjured Dylan's image in her brain, the way he leaned back when he smiled, the way his cheeks lifted his designer glasses when he laughed. She had liked him, hadn't she? He had been so attractive that her face flushed when she met him. She had felt that spark seize her nerves when he revealed his vivid grin on their first date. All of that had to be him in the moment, not merely what she promptly imagined for their future.

But what did she know about him? Where he worked, that he had a younger brother and sister. Aside from his well composed appearance, dazzling face, and the fact that he preferred sex with her on top, she could not think of anything remarkable about him. Nothing else about him made her flutter.

"Goddamn it, Ronnie," Emma breathed.

"I'm sorry. I know you don't like to hear these things. I know you just want it to work out, but I cannot watch you entangle yourself with another douchebag."

Ronnie fetched the bottle, filled their glasses, and set it close. The alcohol lay heavier upon her with each sip. Ronnie appeared to remain unaltered.

"We don't know for sure that Dylan was a douchebag," Emma protested.

"Aside from the fact that he poofed?"

"Well, yeah."

"He was pretty."

"So?"

"So he was a douche."

"Ronnie, you can't say that."

"Yes, I can. Ninety-nine percent of the time, hot equals douche. It is social Darwinism. Hot doesn't have to work at it, so hot does not develop non-superficial qualities. Hot equals douche."

"That's bullshit, Ronnie. Terrence is pretty."

"No, Terrence is attractive. An accidental attractive he does not strive for or seem to be aware of. He doesn't look like he walked off the Jersey Shore like these asshats you can't resist."

"Ronnie!"

"Tell me I'm wrong. Go ahead, tell me. You have horrible fucking taste, Emma. Case in point: Justin."

Somewhere beneath her alcoholic blanket Emma bristled at hearing his name. Sometimes she hated how much of a bitch Ronnie was. Deep down Ronnie enjoyed this on some level, rubbing Emma's nose in her epic mistake.

Emma stewed and pouted for quiet and saturated moments while Ronnie patiently waited, sipping her wine. Ronnie knew exactly what she was doing. She had made a home inside Emma's head since she was force feeding her ice cream post-divorce now years ago.

"So what am I supposed to do?" Emma snapped. "Be with someone I don't find attractive, who I have no spark with?"

Ronnie rolled her eyes. "No. But dude, the spark is bullshit girl code for wanting to have sex with someone, not some mandatory magical connection. I think picking them because they're hot, because you have a physical reaction to them, is really hurting you. Maybe you should try picking them for other reasons."

"Jesus, Ronnie. You make me sound so shallow."

Venom had infiltrated the therapy session. Ronnie did not need to be able to read Emma to hear the edge and defense in her voice. She took a deep breath and adopted a gentler tone.

"Emma, you *have* been shallow in this whole dating thing since Justin. I'm not sure why. That was fine with the casual partners you started with to distract you, but that can't be how you select a partner. Hot doesn't raise the kids you want. A six-pack doesn't take care of you when you're sick. A perfect tan doesn't make him faithful."

Emma let out a single yell from the pit of her

belly, from below that aching hole in her chest. What did Ronnie know? She had casual-sexed *her* way to a relationship. She had only actually been in a relationship with one person, never had her heart ripped out when one ended. How could she possibly know what Emma should be doing? How could she spout all this knowledge from a life she never lived?

"I hate it when you're right," she said.

"I know you do." Ronnie chuckled, refilling their glasses again. "It has to be really annoying. Especially since I have no relationship experience."

"Um, beyond annoying."

"Don't worry, I only have other people's lives figured out. Mine has always been a big mess. I only do it because I love you and you need it."

"And you enjoy it."

"Maybe that too."

"Fine, so I might not have even been into Dylan, and I'm shallow. What in the hell am I supposed to do about that?"

"I don't know. I guess you try again and try not to repeat the same patterns."

"Ugh!"

"I know, girl. This was easier when we were younger."

"The pool is so much more shallow now."

"Oh! That reminds me. I have a guy for you."

"Wait, what?"

"He's been on my radar for a minute, but you were busy with...um..."

"Dylan! You're doing it on purpose now."

Ronnie snickered. "He's an acquaintance of T's at work. Nice guy. Smart and actually educated."

"Why is he single?"

"I don't know yet. I imagine it's because he's from Europe somewhere. He hasn't been here super long. I think it's worth finding out."

"What do I have to lose at this point? I'm willing to meet him."

"Let me text T."

Ronnie gathered her phone in one hand, still cradling her wine close in the other. Even with no knowledge about this new prospect, his mere existence calmed Emma's nerves. A sliver of hope in the black abyss of failure Dylan's neglect had created. If she could focus on the next, maybe the last would not be so deafening or damning.

Emma sat quietly while Ronnie tapped and swiped on her phone, allowing the conversation to cool in the room and embracing the fleeting neutrality she found in her mind. Ronnie's phone chimed several times.

"It's done," Ronnie said.

"What's done?"

"The fix up."

"What? Already?"

"Yeah, he must be at the game night. But he's in, down to meet you at your leisure."

"Well, that was fast. Makes me feel better. Now I don't even have to think about Dylan."

"Exactly. Screw him."

Emma's phone sang out from her abandoned purse. She rose to fetch it.

"Terrence didn't give him my number already, did he?"

"Absolutely not. That's your decision to make."

Emma grasped the phone and illuminated the screen. "You have got to be kidding me!"

"What?"

Emma turned the phone so Ronnie could read the notification.

Dylan: Hey babe, sorry I've been MIA. What are you up to?

"How do they always know? How? They vanish and only reappear if another guy comes into the picture," Emma ranted.

"Penis ESP. Once they have sex with you, they can just sense when another is sniffing around the goods."

"Such bullshit!"

"Yep."

Emma ignored the text and she and Ronnie drained another bottle.

*****

Emma woke up the next morning on Ronnie's couch. Her awareness stirred lazily inside her cranium. Her brain lay dehydrated on her skull, pushing heavily against the backs of her eyes. Her eyelids were glued to her sticky eyeballs. She found it uncomfortable to shift them or attempt to blink.

Her consciousness was abrasive. She had hidden from the pain of her hangover in the depths of intoxicated sleep. Once her perception bobbed to the surface, her nerves sent garbled messages that irritated her brain. She could taste the wine in the sharp edge of her headache that radiated from the center of her forehead; feel it in the sour flavor coating her tongue that flooded her mouth and beckoned nausea if she dared move it.

If she kept her eyes shut and held still enough, she could hide from the hangover, like a vicious beast stalking her. Unfortunately, the more her faculties roused, the more vividly the punishment enveloped her.

She blamed Ronnie.

Emma dragged herself upright. She was slouching into her own lap and cradling her throbbing head when Terrence emerged from the bedroom.

"Oh, Em," Terrence said quietly. "How much did she make you drink?"

"Good morning, Terrence," Emma said, struggling to raise her head high enough to make polite eye contact. "I lost count after three bottles."

"Your bestie is a lush," he cackled. "But you forgot your troubles, didn't you?"

"Oh yeah. After Ronnie dissected my soul, of course."

"Ronnie is good for both of those things. Except on me. No soul to dissect." He smiled genuinely, in a way that made Emma feel neutral and at ease, even in her suffering.

"Was I still awake when you got home?"

"God, no. You were already drooling on yourself. Ronnie was still up making sure none of the wine survived."

"She still sleeping?"

"You know that girl isn't getting out of bed if

she isn't getting paid."

Emma laughed. "True."

"Now, don't move. I got you."

"Oh no. I don't think I could possibly eat or drink anything. Ever again."

"Look, I have been with Ronnie long enough to have become something of a hangover expert. Trust me, girl."

Emma did trust Terrence. As he walked into the kitchen, she caught herself musing about how strangely inappropriate it was for Ronnie to end up with him, for him to remain and emerge out of her long history of disposable men. Where was Emma's decent guy? She was trying far harder than Ronnie ever had. She had played far nicer and always had her life more together. Until Justin. Wasn't she more desirable? Didn't she deserve the successful relationship more?

Terrence returned from the kitchen with arms loaded. He placed a can on the table in front of her.

"Soda, if carbonation soothes your stomach." Then a glass. "Ice water, if it doesn't. Hydration is important. Saltine crackers, if you're timid. Leftover pizza, if you need the grease. Aspirin and antacids."

"Wow. You really *are* an expert."

"Like I said, a lot of practice. Care if I watch some ESPN with you? I'll keep it quiet."

"Go for it. It's your house."

"Ha! It's Ronnie's house. She lets me live here."

"You're probably the only guy she will ever allow to do that, so you've got to be special."

"Nah, we fit, Ronnie and I."

"Can I ask you something? Would that be weird?"

"No, go ahead."

"With how Ronnie was, how did you even end up here?"

"You mean, how did I go from one night stand to partner?"

"Yes," Emma giggled. "Exactly."

"I saw Ronnie through her bullshit. There was something there, so I stayed. I imagine she stayed for the same reason. Things just happened how they were going to happen."

"Natural."

"Right, natural."

"As a guy, can I ask you what I'm doing wrong?"

"Em, I know you're unhappy being single. It has to suck. I never dated much more than Ronnie though. Not sure how much help I can be. Never played the bullshit games."

"I'll take anything right now."

"I would say you're trying too hard, Em. You want it too much. You're trying to force it."

"But how do I not try? How do I not want it?"

"I don't know, but you can't try so hard. Live your life. The rest will come."

"Um, okay."

"I told you I wasn't going to be helpful."

"No, I'm sure you're right. I just don't know what to do about it. And my head hurts."

"Maybe you should take a break from thinking about it and eat those aspirin."

Emma choked down the pills that cleaved to her

throat as the ice water frosted her mouth. She drew her legs in to press into her, hoping to calm her frothing stomach. She wrapped the blanket in her hands and drew it close and cuddled into the couch cushion. Terrence looked over at her gently once more, patting her reassuringly on the shoulder.

They both sank into the couch, losing themselves in the flashing of the flat screen. Terrence was probably actually paying attention. Emma disappeared from behind her eyes, drifting away from her sight and back into her mind. Sitting on the couch quiet and unmoving, watching some show she had zero interest in, felt reminiscent of her childhood. Something about sharing the couch with Terrence felt like Saturday mornings with Noah's cartoons. In the same way, it was relaxing not to think, to float away from the inane programming, and it was comforting to have that person beside her without having to talk or present any pretense. She found the silence comfortable.

The hangover was relentless. It persisted to infiltrate even this calm instant. Her thoughts were finally tempered with her mind instead of encased in the headache. Her emotions did not draw her stomach into her throat, yet the wake of the alcohol bound her insides in awkward and wretched knots. She closed her eyes and tried to again find sanctuary below the surface of consciousness.

"Oh honey, you look like hell," Ronnie said. She did not know if she had succeeded at falling asleep; she did not know how long she had been curled up silently beside Terrence.

"You did this to me." Emma did not even open

her eyes to respond.

"I helped, but I did not pour the wine down your throat."

"Close enough."

"You needed it. I see Terrence has been taking good care of you."

Ronnie moved closer, kissed Terrence beside her, then her footsteps moved into the kitchen.

"Are you not even hungover?" Emma whined, squinting her eyes open.

"I don't feel awesome, but I definitely don't feel like you do."

"I have to work tonight."

"That is going to suck," Ronnie laughed. "You better nap and eat some awful fast food or something. But I bet you're not thinking about any asshole guy."

"God, no. Just my own pain."

"Then the night was a success!"

CHAPTER 8

Emma sat across the table from Terrence's work associate. She attempted to sit naturally and not pick at the tablecloth spread out below her water glass. Across the table her date appeared calm. He looked directly at her sweetly.

"So where are you from originally, Tim?" Emma asked, lifting her glass to take a sip of water.

"My name is not actually Tim," he said.

"Oh? Terrence always called you Tim."

"Yes, I generally go by Tim. Americans have a hard time with my real name."

"What is your real name?"

"Tymoteusz."

"Tim-oh-tow-sh?" Emma stumbled.

Tim chuckled genuinely, drawing his fingers up to cover his exposed teeth. "That was close. Kind of. You see? You can call me Tim."

"Okay, Tim," Emma laughed, settling more into her chair, her shoulders receding from her neck. "Where are you from?"

"Poland. I grew up in Krakow. I came here for

university then got the job in Denver. I have been here since."

"Do you go back frequently?"

"All my family still lives there. I probably travel home every year or two. My parents and sister have been here once so far."

"It must be hard to be so far from them."

"They are happy for my success, and it is easy to keep in contact over email and MyBook."

"I suppose that's true."

"What about your family? Are they here in Colorado?"

"They are. My father works for the Air Force. He's down in Colorado Springs with his wife. My mother, stepfather, and my brother are in Denver."

"Are you close to them then?"

"I suppose. I mean, I mostly see my dad for holidays and events like that. I do see my mom pretty frequently. At least every couple weeks. And my brother and his family."

"Your brother has a family?"

"Yeah, married with a new baby."

"Niece or nephew?"

"Nephew. Mason is two months old now."

"You're probably a good aunt."

"I try."

"Do you want kids?"

Emma's heart stopped in her throat. The million dollar question of dating.

"I do. I want a family."

"Me too." He said it casually, nonchalantly, naturally. "So how do you know Terrence?"

"From Ronnie. She and I have been friends

forever."

"I like Ronnie. She is so honest."

"Ha! Yeah, honest she is. She brought Terrence to my wedding, so I met him years ago. He and I are pretty good friends too. Ronnie absolutely hates dumb comedy movies, so we'll go without her. Stuff like that."

"It is good to have such good friends. I have enjoyed working with Terrence."

"You do video game night with him too, right?"

"Yes. Those guys are a lot of fun."

They leisurely ate their dinner, Emma at ease. She did not notice she was answering the same standard set of questions; it felt like a natural conversation. She actually heard his answers rather than performing her checklist in her head. She took bites without gauging how large they were or how much she was ingesting.

"How is your food?" he asked her.

"Really good actually. You want to try it?"

She angled her plate toward him. He reached over and stabbed out a hearty bite of her salad. He nodded as he chewed. "What is that dressing?" he said. "It's awesome." He tipped his plate to her with a questioning look.

"Yes, please."

He carved out a small portion of his steak and lifted his fork to her. She leaned forward and bit the food off his fork.

As they exited the restaurant, Tim placed his arm around her shoulders. She allowed him to lightly rest his wrist on her shoulder, her body bumping softly into his as they walked. His touch felt

111

comfortable, safe yet without an edge, no anxious flutter.

"Which is you?" he asked as they walked into the parking lot.

"I'm right over there."

Tim took her shoulder and guided her to face him.

"May I kiss you, Emma?" he said, looking directly into her eyes.

She hesitated. Had he asked? Was this a European approach she was unfamiliar with? She smiled softly.

"Yes."

He leaned in and gently pressed his lips against hers. His arms wrapped around her and drew her closer. She leaned in and let him. Then he slipped his tongue past her lips, lay it thick and heavy in her mouth. And left it there.

Emma stood there, lip locked and stunned, unsure how to proceed. She moved her tongue against his; his remained paralyzed and near choking her. Finally, he withdrew, and she fought the urge to cough. He pecked her softly on the lips and grinned at her with lazy eyelids. She struggled to reflect the look.

"It was very nice to meet you, Emma. Can I see you again?"

"Yes."

"I will call you," he said, kissing her lightly once more and opening her car door for her.

Once Tim had retreated to his own vehicle, Emma wiped her face. She feared he had salivated all over her with his thick-tongued kiss. She shook her head, still confounded and a bit baffled.

Emma did not think on the drive home. She found herself stunned. She registered the confliction brewing in her emotions but could not identify the parts. She floated home somewhat detached. Lying in bed staring at the ceiling in the darkness, her thoughts began to take shape.

That was the best date I have been on since Justin. That might have been the best date I have ever been on. He is so relaxed and easy. I felt completely comfortable.

But I just don't feel anything else. I don't want him. He doesn't do it for me that way. I want to cuddle with him on the couch and talk, not have sex with him. I have to want to have sex with a guy I'm going to date. He's so dopey looking. Why did he have to kiss me like that? Just awful. I can't have sex with him after he puts his tongue in my mouth like a slab of dead meat.

But he's such a good guy. What am I going to do?

The next morning, Emma headed to Ronnie's before work. Terrence greeted her at the door.

"Hey!" he smirked. "Straight over the morning after the date. Is that a good thing or a bad thing?"

Emma giggled uncomfortably and did not answer.

"Hey, Em, new Will Ferrell coming out next weekend. Ronnie says she would rather chew open a vein than sit through it. You game?"

"Yeah, I'm down. Let me know what showing. I'll check my schedule."

"Hey!" Ronnie said when she spotted Emma.

"How were things with Timmy?"

"Timmy? Really?"

"Oh yeah. So how was the date?"

"It was good. I was really comfortable with him. We talked and talked like we knew each other forever. It was easy."

"But?"

"Well, there was no spark or anything. I don't know that I'm actually attracted to him."

"Ugh, Emma! Not with this spark bullshit again."

"And he can't kiss."

"Oh."

"I don't feel like I need to know how my coworkers kiss. Or whatever," Terrence interrupted. "I'm going to go find some man stuff to do."

He patted Emma on the shoulder, kissed Ronnie, and disappeared from the room.

"Okay, so he can't kiss," Ronnie returned. "Like how bad?"

"Pretty bad."

"Like tonsil swabbing? Sucking your lips? Slobbering all over you?"

"Like a dead fish in my mouth."

"Eew!"

"Yeah, he just like laid his tongue in my mouth and left it there."

"Maybe that's how they kiss in Poland," Ronnie laughed.

"I hope not. It was so bad."

"Kissing can be learned. How was the rest?"

"Like I said, it was good. It just wasn't...I felt more like I was hanging out with a friend or my

114

brother."

"So he didn't make you hot because he wasn't a creep. I like this guy already."

"Shouldn't I be attracted to the person I'm with? Shouldn't I, like, feel something?"

"Maybe in a perfect world. Things might need to develop. You expect to be in love with the guy on the first date? How many romantic comedies are you and Terrence watching?"

"We do not watch romantic comedies. Only comedies. And not in love with but I expect to feel, I don't know, something."

"Remind me how things turn out with the guys you do feel something for right away?"

"They poof."

"Uh huh."

"Why can't I have both? A guy I'm attracted to who is a good person. I have to believe that both exist."

"Because you are attracted to idiots."

"There you go, making me sound horrible again."

"You're not horrible. You're just a girl, and girls are dumb. Men want a tiny waist and huge tits on a bitch who is smart and not crazy. Women want these masculine, beefy guys who are also sensitive, emotional, and honest. The fucking unicorns of dating."

"God, I hate you, Ronnie. What do you know about dating anyway?"

"Not a damn thing. I only know the seedy underbelly, where things are actually ugly and honest. Far less bullshit in a one night stand. Give

Tim a chance. He's different than all the other guys you've dated. You can always say no if no spark develops."

"You're right."

"Good. Now get out and go to work before you really start to hate me."

"We're already there."

Emma hugged Ronnie tight. The usual mix of gratitude and irritation swelled up to her surface. The fog her date left her in seemed to have cleared, but she did not necessary like what was left. She wanted to believe the right guy was still out there, the man she thought Justin was when she married him, the man she populated into each of her long term plans and fantasies. Deep in her brain, she believed she would simply know it was him when she met him.

The more she talked to Ronnie and the more men she dated, the more doubt bloomed around that failing sprig of certainty.

After the blurred hours of work, Emma sat in her car in the dark for a long moment in her driveway, the same driveway where she stood motionless staring at a bikini. Her thinking driveway. She rested her head on the steering wheel and cradled her keys in her palm.

She thought about how nice it had been to be on a date without pretense, a date without anxiety. Tim had been genuinely pleasant to be around and made her instantaneously comfortable with him. That had to count for something, didn't it? That had to be worth pursuing, right?

She flashed back to that heavy, thick tongue in

her mouth and her libido shriveled out from under her. Could she be with someone she felt so asexually about already?

From the depths of her purse, her phone vibrated in the silence.

Dylan: *Hey baby girl, where have you been?*

"Where have *I* been?" she said to the dark and empty car.

Emma tapped the message field and let her fingers hover over the keyboard. Did she want to type out what she was actually thinking? Did she want to play dumb and act like it did not matter? Did she want to see him again? She could not pretend he did not disappear; she could not let that be acceptable.

Emma: *Where have you been?*

Dylan: *I'm sorry. I had some shit come up.*

"Some shit? What shit?" she said, again to herself.

Emma: *K.*

Emma rolled her eyes and heaved her body out of the car. Her flesh felt heavier. Her head became weighted and compacted down on the rest of her. She did not want to walk; she did not want to hold her phone. She only wanted to collapse on the couch and bask in the gentle glow of trashy television until she had to be up early for work.

Her phone buzzed again in her hand as she unlocked the door.

Dylan: When can I see you?

Emma: I'm working two jobs tomorrow.

Dylan: Come over when you're done.

"Why would you possibly want me to come over to your house?" Emma now spoke to her dark and empty residence.

Emma: Meet for coffee when I get off at Happy Beans before I head to Call Solutions. 2 pm?

Dylan: See you then.

***

Emma stumbled into Happy Beans blurry-eyed and exhausted as the sun pierced the sky outside. She fumbled her apron over her head, juggling her purse and keys clumsily between hands. Gladys greeted her from behind the counter, smiling at this ungodly hour as always.

"Well good morning, Eminem," Gladys's voice boomed in the waking shop.

Gladys was a hearty woman Emma estimated to be around her own mother's age. She had been working in Happy Beans since before Emma had to add a second job to pay their mortgage. She was as much a fixture in the establishment as the coffee machines that lined the counter and had more personality than all the college-aged staff combined.

"Morning." Emma tried to move her mouth through the weight on her tired cheeks. "How are you so impossibly peppy every day?"

"I have an IV of espresso in the back. Late night last night, sugar?"

"Not really. Just worked, as usual. Went out to dinner the night before."

"All work and no play. Oooh, was it a date? You know I need my updates on your dating soap opera."

"Oh girl, I have updates for you. Don't you worry."

Emma stashed her belongings in a locker in the back and joined Gladys behind the counter to open for the day.

"New guy?" Gladys asked, practically salivating over the answer.

"Yes, new guy."

"What happened to pretty boy? Dylan."

"He disappeared. Then reappeared. Texted me last night. He's going to come by before I head to the call center."

"Disappeared? Why? I thought you two were dating."

"So did I. He said he had some stuff come up."

"Stuff without an explanation?"

"Apparently."

"You better ask him today."

"That's the only reason I agreed to see him. Just to know. I'm fine making an effort, but I can't

119

handle the poof."

"Absolutely not. If they're interested, they're interested. Who is the new suitor?"

"Tim. Well, his name isn't really Tim. That's what he goes by?"

"Huh?"

"It's some Polish name I can't pronounce. He moved here for college. He works with Ronnie's boyfriend."

"So he's smart and has a real job."

"Yes, he does."

"But?"

"I don't think I'm attracted to him."

"Honey, it was a first date. You got to give the boy some time. Let him grow on you."

"That's what Ronnie said."

"You know Ronnie and I see to eye-to-eye."

"Yeah, I know. He's a really bad kisser."

"That will do it. You can train that puppy, though. See what happens."

"Yeah, I'm going to."

"What are you going to do about Dylan?"

"I don't know yet. I'm going to see when I talk to him today. He was more than a good kisser."

"Yeah, the pretty, dumb ones usually are."

"It's not fair."

"Welcome to life, sweets."

Gladys unlocked the door for the first wave of zombified commuters to shamble into the shop. Emma let her thoughts dissipate, focusing on the monotonous rhythm of taking and fulfilling orders for espressos, double chai lattes, caramel macchiatos. She let herself become the work and everything else become background noise, and the hours disappeared in a blur.

Emma high-fived the Maxwell twins when they came behind the counter to relieve her shift, matching fraternity brothers who existed in perpetual hangover. If they did not have nametags, Emma would have never been able to distinguish Brody from Ryan.

Dylan had already appeared in the shop and seated himself at a table by the windows. Emma went to change out of her uniform and collect her things from the back.

Gladys, with her apron slung over her shoulder, gathered Emma up and swallowed her in a hug, the same way she did after every shift.

"Oh, darling, if I had sons, I would set them up with you. Unfortunately, my husband only makes girls. Three bat shit crazy girls."

"Just like their momma," Emma joked. Gladys gasped and swatted at her playfully with her apron.

"Good luck today. Don't worry, you'll find your way. Trust your instincts. Stop thinking so much and trying so hard. The rest will come. And if that pretty boy decides not to play nice, you send him to me. I'll fix him up with some coffee with the special ingredient."

"What's the special ingredient?"

"Poison. Don't no one mess with my babies."

When Emma emerged, Dylan was still seated at a table against the window, sunlight spilling over him. She was glad he had selected a location far from the counter. Not that the Maxwell twins would have any interest in eavesdropping on her dating drama, but she would feel more comfortable if it was not a possibility.

Dylan looked up at her. Their eyes met, and she flushed at the contact. Her chest tightened with a pull at the base of her stomach. A blur of how he tasted, the way he felt on top of her, the heat from his mouth, his fingertips along her skin flashed over her nerves. This was a spark; this was attraction.

He poofed. He poofed. He poofed, she repeated in her head, trying to dislodge her consciousness from her physical response.

Dylan stood as she approached the table. The smile snaked seductively across his face. His eyes turned up seemingly just for her. He reached out and snagged her fingertips in his, dragging her forward to gently press his lips to hers.

With no dead fish tongue.

Emma resisted the electricity ascending the vertebrae of her spine, shoved back against the flutter below her ribs. She strove not to imagine him giving her that same look naked like the last time she saw him.

He. Poofed.

She pulled back and sat down across from him, hardening her face.

"How was work?" he asked, sitting down.

"Good. Busy. Weekdays always are."

"When do you have to be at the call center?"

"Couple hours. I have to be on the line by the time all the normal people get off work. I usually nap in my car in between."

"But instead you're having coffee with me."

"Yep."

"Speaking of, let me order us something."

While Dylan ventured up to the counter, Emma struggled to compose herself. When she thought about Dylan, there was nothing besides tinges of anger, irritation, detachment. When she looked at him, she wanted to like him. She wanted him to be The One. They would make such beautiful babies. She needed Ronnie beside her now, analyzing and cataloging his every flaw right into her ear.

"So what shit did you have happen?" Emma asked after Dylan rejoined her at the table.

"Oh, just some family shit. My brother broke up with his girl. It was a mess, pretty dramatic. I had to help him move out quickly. Then I had to keep him drunk and distracted for a couple days, you know."

Are there no phones where your brother lives? Is it a black hole of cell service? Could you have not told me this? she thought as she listened to him.

"How is he holding up?"

"He'll be all right. She was a bitch anyway."

One of the Maxwell twins approached with their drinks. "Black coffee here. And a double shot, just like you like it, Eminem," he said, placing the drinks in front of them.

Emma raised her hand for the obligatory high five and glanced at his nametag. "Thanks, Brody."

"Got you. Brode and I swapped tags. I knew you couldn't tell us apart."

"Pretty sneaky for frat boys." Ryan chuckled and moved back to the counter.

"Did your coworker just call you Eminem?"

"Yes. An unfortunate nickname."

"How did you get that?"

"His brother Brody busted me dancing to one of Eminem's songs. Like full on white girl feeling it. Then my name starts with Em, and I'm white. It sort of stuck. Everyone here calls me that, even my second mom, Gladys."

"That's hilarious."

"If you say so."

The conversation died for a moment over their steaming beverages. Dylan looked calmly at Emma, still with that curl in his lips.

"Dylan, I have to ask you something."

"Okay, shoot."

"I want to know what we're doing here. I thought we were dating. Then you, like, disappeared for a couple days, then reappear like nothing. So I'm not sure what's happening."

"Oh." Dylan sat up straighter in his chair, leaning back from her and retracting his arm back to the other side of his coffee cup. His eyes shifted around. "We never had the relationship talk."

"I know, and that's why I'm asking. When we started hanging out, you said you were looking to settle down, to be in a relationship."

"Yeah, I did say that."

"I thought things were going well between us. When you brought me around your family, I guess I assumed we were going in that direction."

"Yeah, I could see that. You're really awesome. I like spending time with you. I just don't think I'm in a relationship place right now. I have a lot going on with work and my brother and all that. I don't think I could really commit."

All the air went out of Emma's lungs from the

impact. Her mind started to buzz, her thoughts whirring. Suddenly, she could not hear anything else.

In the encapsulating silence, something flared in her. Looking at Dylan's unaffected and unattached face, heat stretched out through her limbs, embodied her fingertips. Her digits itched. She thought about the scalding hot beverages she could pour over his beautiful, misleading face. He would not be flashing that gorgeous grin when she doused him with steaming coffee then bashed him in the head with the pot until he stopped moving.

She pushed out her seat and walked out the door.

The sun blinded her as she walked to her car, attempting to hide the tears brimming in her eyes behind the dark lenses of her sunglasses. If she made it across town fast enough, she could still sneak in a car nap before her next shift. She could shut out the world, slip in the dark layer beneath reality, and pretend Dylan did not happen.

Crawling defeated into her seat, she pulled out her phone to share her pain.

Emma: Dylan is out.

Ronnie: He reappeared?

Emma: Poof. Wanted to see me today. Turns out he doesn't want a relationship.

Ronnie: WTF.

Emma: Yeah. I'll message you after work.

The sun beat down hot and unforgiving on Emma as she slept in her reclined driver's seat. Roasted dreams writhed under her skull, causing her eyes to dart rapidly below their lids. She breathed heavy and thick with her fingertips wrapped around the edge of the seat, sweat pricking through the pores at the perimeter of her hair.

Her phone alarm shattered the depths of her shallow sleep.

Emma groaned and tossed her hands over her face, shielding the heat of the sun. She did not want to open her eyes. She did not want to walk into the building. She wanted only to sleep in an empty blackness where she did not have to work every hour and fail at dating every spare minute.

The alarm sang out again, mocking her, beckoning her.

Without opening her eyes, she shifted the seat up to bar retreat back into the recline. She ground her fingertips into her eye sockets until stars burst out of the darkness, shook her head hard, and forced herself out of the vehicle.

***

"Hey, Emma," Brendan said, walking into the breakroom. "Oh man, you look tired. You okay?"

Emma looked up from dumping coffee into a large mug to see the ugly sympathy on his face.

"Yeah, I am definitely tired," Emma replied. "I was napping before this shift. Still waking up I think."

"Well, that's because you work eighteen jobs."

"Unfortunately. Have to keep paying for my mistakes, I guess."

"Speaking of, how's that new guy going?"

"Add him to my ever-growing list of mistakes."

"Oh no, what happened this time?"

"Well, I'm awesome, but…"

"The 'you're awesome but' speech again?"

"Yes, again. Apparently, I misread the signals of spending a bunch of time together, telling me he wanted to settle down and have a family, and taking me to meet his family as being in a relationship because he decided that's not what he wants. And I'm awesome…but!"

"I'm sorry, Emma. I really am. Where do you find these winners?"

"I clearly have super awesome taste in men."

"Male coworkers, obviously. Male friends, of course. Men you date? I'm starting to think you might suck at that."

"I know I suck at this. And any time I have doubts, whoever I am dating makes sure I really remember."

"It's okay, Emma. You're really awesome. But—"

"I will fucking stab you with that plastic knife over there."

"Whoa! So violent. I was just telling you how awesome you are." Brendan moved to walk out of the breakroom. "But!" he called over his shoulder, disappearing into the cubes.

Emma could not help the grin, however brief. She gulped down half her mug and returned to the phones.

127

CHAPTER 9

"Holy shit, girl. You look like absolute hell," Ronnie said, greeting her as she pushed through the door into Emma's house.

"Thank you, Ronnie. You sure know how to make me feel better. I worked one job. Then Dylan tap danced all over my bruised little heart. Then I worked a whole other job and now I'm here."

"Just a bitter shell of a person."

"Pretty much."

"Have you eaten?"

"I don't want to."

"Bitch, we are not doing this again. Don't let these assholes starve you out." Ronnie placed a hand on her hip and glared at Emma.

"Fine," Emma sighed heavily. "Get the ice cream."

Their spoons clanked and scraped against the bowls while the two ate their ice cream, Emma slow and with resistance. Each time she looked up from her bowl at Ronnie, Ronnie cast a stern glare and gestured toward the food, the way Emma remembered her mother doing when she was being defiant at dinner. As always, it was pointless to fight. She choked the ice cream down, swallowing full mouthfuls to get it over with.

"So Dylan is another douchebag," Ronnie said.

"Pretty much."

"I'm sorry."

"But you didn't like him."

"I didn't think he was going to be the guy. I don't think you truly thought he was the guy either."

"Probably not. I got ahead of myself again, wanting to be back on track."

"Ems, there is no track. The things you want will still happen."

"Sure, they will. I can't have a family while I'm single."

"There is always the turkey baster option."

"Consider that Plan B."

"Noted. See, you don't need a guy. Worst case scenario, you go with Plan B."

"I don't just want the kid, Ronnie. I want the family."

"I know you do. I still think that will happen. Only maybe not as fast as you want it or with the type of guy you think you want."

"Because I want jerks."

"You said it."

"I'm only quoting you."

"Emma, I don't think anything is wrong with you. Any guy would be lucky to have you. I do think there's a bit of damage up here." Ronnie tapped her temple. "I think some hang up is causing you to pick guys who will eventually go badly."

"You would know self-sabotage best."

"Exactly."

"How am I supposed to change who I am attracted to?"

"I don't know, Emma, but I do know that if you keep picking these same idiots because they get you wet, you're going to keep ending up here. Over and over and over."

"Eeew, Ronnie. You want Tim to be the guy."

"Timmy seems like a great guy. I do like Timmy."

"Fish tongue."

Ronnie let a burst of laughter escape. "Sure, fish tongue."

"I don't think I'm attracted to him. I like him, and I like spending time with him, but I don't think I like him like that. The awful kissing kind of killed anything."

"I get that. That's fair enough. Bad kissing is awful. Total buzz killer. But do you think that after this bullshit with Dylan and the like, it might be worth trying to develop something with Timmy? Ultimately, kissing can be taught. Boys can be trained."

"I don't want to train anyone. Why can't I just find someone I actually like? Am I supposed to fake it with this guy I'm not into?"

"Absolutely not. I would never tell you to fake something. Try to go in with an open mind. Date him, get to know him, see if anything grows."

"To hell with it," Emma said. "What else am I doing?"

***

Emma lay in the tangled sheets of Tim's bed, fighting off the tears. Frustration was hot in her ducts, and she blinked back wildly to keep it contained. The shower was running in the adjoining bathroom. Still she did not want to fall apart when he could return at any moment. He whistled in the shower in post-coital bliss.

Emma gritted her teeth and flipped onto her back, staring up at the textured ceiling, which warbled behind the water in her eyes. The clenched, unconsummated energy twitched in her muscles, and the stifled blood flow of a failed orgasm dissipated uncomfortably. Of fumbling nowhere in the neighborhood of an orgasm. Her cheeks still felt moist from his sloppy kisses. When his tongue did move, it plunged for her tonsils, near gagging her as he clutched her close. A thin ache lined her inner thighs from his jackrabbit rhythm.

Somewhere between exposed and unsatisfied, she fell despondent in the strange limbo between. How many times could she try this? When would he notice that she did not match his enjoyment? He seemed so elated to be inside her, like a giddy teenage virgin, that he scarcely noticed her muted moans and unenthusiastic responses.

She did not know how to tell him he was not ringing her bell. Ronnie made it sound so easy to inform him he was an awful lay. When Emma looked into Tim's excited puppy-dog eyes, she could only let him shove his tongue toward her esophagus.

She *wanted* to feel something for Tim. Half the heat in her tears burned from her own failure. He was perfect on paper. Educated, employed, funny. He treated her well and made her feel comfortable, so comfortable that he reminded her of her brother. Yet his appearance did not elicit even a tingle on her nerves. His touch steadily started to beckon a flinch under her skin.

What is wrong with me? Emma thought over and over again.

The thought echoed in her head repeatedly until it became a mantra and then until the sounds began to lose meaning. It recurred until it simply dissipated into silence. In that fraction of peaceful black, Emma drifted off to sleep.

***

"Good morning," Tim whispered in her ear as he slid his naked body next to hers. He wrapped his arms fully around her and pulled her close. The warmth of his body heat felt pleasant, and Emma curled into him. It felt good to be held. Slowly, his hand caressed her back, rhythmically sweeping lower. He swirled his fingertips over her hips, migrating steadily south toward her thighs. Emma reached down and tangled her fingers in his.

"I'm kind of sore from last night," she lied. "Do you mind if we wait?"

"Not at all," he said.

Tim freed his hand from hers and vigorously cupped her breast. Emma fought the urge to let her eyes roll over in their sockets. She pulled his arm around her, pressing her head into his chest until his heartbeat put her back to sleep.

***

"Good Lord, woman! You look like hell," Gladys sang out as Emma pushed her way into Happy Beans.

"Why does everyone keep saying that?"

"Maybe because it's true. Maybe because you're working yourself to the bone."

"Maybe."

"Tell me what's wrong."

"I have a problem, and I can't really talk to Ronnie about it because I already know what she will say, and what she says isn't working."

"Well, you know Ronnie and I are usually of a like mind."

"Yeah, I know."

"Tell me anyway."

"So I've been dating Tim for a few months now."

"Right, the European engineer."

"Yes, exactly. I'm trying to make it work, but I do not feel anything romantic for him. And the sex is just so bad."

"A puppy can be trained."

"Yep, that's what Ronnie said."

"See? Like minds. Sex is part of a relationship. Is there nothing redeemable about being with him?"

"Tim is great. On paper, he's absolutely perfect. I'm comfortable with him. I like spending time with him. But…"

"You don't feel anything."

"Right. And I don't know how to make myself."

"Oh honey, you can't make yourself."

"There's just no spark."

"The spark is a load of crap."

"Damn it! Ronnie again!"

Gladys laughed. "When I met my husband, I couldn't stand him. The man drove me insane. There was no spark between us unless you count my desire to punch him square in the nose. We worked together back then. He was persistent. Gradually, I got to know him. Slowly, all that hate changed. We made our own spark. Been married for a lot of years now. Good years and bad."

"So I should keep trying with Tim?"

"That's not what I'm saying, Eminem. All I am saying is the spark is a myth, but only you know how you feel. If you feel there is nothing, there might be nothing."

"The guys I do feel something for turn out to be awful."

"Well, sweetheart, that's a whole other issue. My opinion, you're hung up on something that won't let you really give this guy a chance. That's only my opinion."

"Great. Now I'm even more confused and feel even worse about myself."

"Never feel bad about how you feel. There are no laws in the mind. You can think and feel whatever you want inside yourself. Things only become good or bad when you turn them into actions. Feel how you feel, and eventually, you'll figure out what it means."

Emma sighed and slumped down on the counter. "Thanks, Gladys."

"Don't know that I helped."

"You didn't," Emma said with a chuckle.

***

Tim pulled up outside Happy Beans to pick up Emma after her shift. She balled her apron up in her hands and gulped as she reached for the handle. She took a deep breath and forced a smile as she eased in.

"Hello, beautiful," Tim said, buttered in his thick accent. He touched her hand and placed a gentle, tongue-free, dry kiss on her lips. "How was your day?"

Emma beamed genuinely at the affection. "It's always a good day when I only work one shift."

"Emma, there's something I wanted to talk to you about," Tim said as he navigated the car back toward his house.

"Sure."

"I was thinking we should go away, take a quick holiday for the weekend. I've never been to any of the ski towns here. Breckenridge or Aspen."

The flashing thought of an entire romantic weekend caught in Emma's throat. She nearly choked on the idea of the hours of faking her way through lackluster sex, moaning halfheartedly beneath him. Imagining it, the grimace contorted her face before she could catch it. From the way he stiffened in the seat beside her, he had seen it.

"Emma, tell me the truth."

"What do you mean?"

"If you're not into this, just tell me."

"It's not that."

"Emma, it's okay. You can just tell me."

"I don't know what's wrong with me," Emma said, dropping her head into her hands. "I like you, and I like spending time with you, but I don't think I feel the same way you feel about me."

"So I'm really awesome, but you're not into it."

"Oh my God," Emma breathed.

"What?"

"*I'm* the douchebag," Emma whispered into her hands.

"What?"

"I'm really sorry, Tim. I wanted to make this work."

"Look, Emma, I would rather you be honest with me. I want to be with someone who truly wants to be with me."

And that's what you deserve, Emma thought. *Only, it's not what I deserve.*

"I'm sorry, Tim."

"It's okay, Emma. How about I take you home?"

"Please."

It made Emma feel worse that Tim responded so reasonably. She envied how easily he could accept her rejection, how it made no impact on his self-worth, how he was able to know what he wanted and accept she was not it. She was not a failure to him the way all the men in her past were to her. She found him more attractive then, and that made her even more frustrated and lost within herself.

What am I doing?

The thought repeated in her head until Tim's headlights receded from her driveway.

Emma did not use a light in the house. She shut out the light with the door and embraced the darkness, letting her fingertips linger on the cool surface on the door for a long time, somewhat at a loss as to what to do. Her first instinct twitched to contact Ronnie; however, she did not want to hear what Ronnie had to say, did not want to hear how she had squandered the one decent guy.

She already knew.

She could not always run to Ronnie. She was alone, and in the dark after Tim left, she felt like maybe it was where she needed to be.

CHAPTER 10

The months after Tim passed like a monotonous blur. Something about rejecting him, and more his calm acceptance of it, lingered in Emma. She lost herself in the anonymous revolution of identical days.

A heavy hollowness weighed in the pit of her stomach. Different from the betrayal and the heartbreak, different from the embarrassment and the regret, different from the disappointment and frustration. The hole in her stomach grew deeper, extending out below her, where hope used to be.

As she drove between jobs and sat on the couch in front of mindless television, Emma was plagued by cyclical thoughts.

I am going to die alone. I am never going to find someone. I might as well go pick up five cats from the pound and get a fuzzy bathrobe and some slippers. There has to be something wrong with me. Justin didn't want me. Justin was having sex with some bar skank while I was working to pay off his debt or at home alone. Still alone. Always alone.

None of them want me. They use me then disappear. I am awesome, but there is always something better. Why couldn't I want Tim? Tim wanted me. Tim was a good guy. But I'm too broken to want Tim. I am disgusted by the one decent guy I could get. I want the ones who do not want me and do not want the ones who do want me.

I am going to die alone because I am crazy and damaged. I am never going to have a family. I am never going to have a baby. It is going to be me and my cats that probably won't want me either.

On some level, Emma knew that the ideas were half-crazed and desperate, mostly depression talking. At the same time, some thread of truth rung off her bones. She could not wrap her head around why dating was so difficult now. It had not been challenging when she met Justin. Though she did not date extensively, it came easy. She had plenty of opportunities while she was married, which she, unlike Justin, declined. Other people got divorced and into new relationships. People her age were onto their third marriages by now.

What was wrong with her?

After whirling around the drain of depression in her mind long enough, Emma would either retreat into sleep or plunge headlong into work. In either case, she strove only to quell the thoughts and focus on anything else.

She unenthusiastically brought a forkful of noodles to her mouth. Ronnie no longer had to coax and guilt her into eating; still the food in her mouth was tasteless. She absently noted the smooth texture of the noodles, the heat of the sauce, while the physiological reaction was muted, detached. Her limbs felt heavy when she moved, only matched by the weight of her skull and her eyelids. Every cell in her body was weighted and stripped of the motivation to fight gravity.

Ronnie's gaze pressed on her cheek as she chewed then trailed her next bite.

"Ronnie," Emma said. "What?"

"Are you okay, Em?"

"Yeah, I'm fine."

"Are you sure? You are not yourself at all lately."

"Yeah."

"Emma, if there is one thing I know, it's depression. And you are terrible at hiding your emotions, especially from me."

"Yeah, I'm sad. And angry. And frustrated. And lonely. And about a million other things. But I'm sick of talking about it. It doesn't change a damn thing. I'm trying to focus on anything else right now. Take a break from all the dating bullshit."

"So is that working out for you? Are you not thinking about it or beating yourself up over it?" Ronnie raised her eyebrows and sipped from her wine.

"Of course not."

"Weird. It's almost like you suck at all of that."

Emma laughed into her spaghetti, the one dish Ronnie was capable of cooking.

"Emma, it's okay to be depressed. It's okay to be sad and pissed and all of those things."

"I could have sworn I said I didn't want to talk about it anymore."

"Yeah, but you're still thinking about it, so let's get it out there."

"Aren't you sick of hearing it yet?"

"Yeah, so that's why I'm going to help you fix it so you can shut up about it for real."

Emma giggled again. Ronnie was relentless.

"Well, if you insist."

"Why are you sad?"

"I feel like the answer is always the same. I'm sad because I'm divorced and alone."

"Angry at Justin and the string of assholes after. Frustrated at the dating bullshit. Lonely and turning on yourself because you're the common factor."

"Yes, all of that. Thank you, Ronnie! Hearing it again makes me feel *so* much better."

"Oh, some venom. We're finally getting to the angry stage."

"So we know what I feel; we know why I feel it; now what? How do I make it stop?"

"You don't."

"What do you mean I don't? What the hell does that mean?"

"You can't fight it, Emma. That's not how depression works. Resistance, denial, all that shit only makes it worse. This is your life right now. All the anger and sadness and whatever won't change what it is."

"Holy crap. That is even more depressing. So what am I supposed to do? Give up on everything I want and deal with this bullshit life that I don't want."

"No, that's not what I'm saying."

"That sure sounds like what you're saying."

"Let me try to explain it another way. Your marriage to Justin was always going to end. Maybe he was going to cheat on you, like he did. Maybe you were going to get fed up with his bullshit and decide to leave him. Maybe one of you was going to die. In all scenarios, it ends."

"Still waiting for the less depressing part…"

"Emma, I spent a lot of time in therapy. You remember what a mess I was when we were young, right?"

"Oh yeah."

"I wasted all those years, all that youth being fucked up. I can't have that time back."

"We're not that old, Ronnie. It wasn't that much time."

"Still. Let me try to save you some time by sharing what I learned."

"I've been to therapy too."

"Yes, as a child. Apparently, to stop hitting kids in the head with pipes! Thanks for keeping that from me, by the way. And for your parents' divorce. You haven't gone as an adult with these problems."

"Okay, Ronnie. Hit me."

"When I was dealing with my father dying, the most comforting thing became knowing that all things in life end."

"That doesn't sound very comforting."

"Wait for it," Ronnie chuckled. "All of it is just chapters along the way. Right now for you, this is merely a chapter. A very shitty chapter, but a chapter that will still pass. Everything in life changes, one way or another, eventually. Instead of being miserable trying to get out of this chapter or

142

thinking about other chapters, live it, knowing that it will eventually end, and there will be new chapters after it."

"Well, shit."

"A little less depressing, right?"

"Maybe marginally?"

Emma sat stunned for a moment, her mind reeling around the book imagery Ronnie's belaboring of the chapter metaphor conjured up, tangled around the sharp edges of the reality Ronnie threw back in her face. She wanted to tell Ronnie to go to hell. She wanted to cry again. She wanted to not talk about it, like she had said.

She hated the words, but she hated more that they were true. How was she supposed to accept this chapter? How was she supposed to sit by and be alone when all she wanted was a family?

Emma set her plate on the table. She could no longer shove the tasteless food into her mouth. Somehow, she felt even heavier. She wanted to close her eyes so she did not have to see Ronnie, so Ronnie would stop telling her things she did not want to hear, so that all this reality she was supposed to roll over and accept would fade into the darkness. She would prefer her nightmares tonight, the garish exaggerations of this unfortunate chapter.

"I'm sorry, Emma," Ronnie said quietly. "But you do need to hear this."

"That is what you say every time, but it doesn't make it hurt less."

"We aren't guaranteed happiness, Emma. The happiness we get is fleeting, random, and surrounded by bullshit."

"You really are making me want to kill myself right now."

"No, no. That is exactly why you have to suck any enjoyment you can out of life. When you get something good, fucking love it."

"You sound like a self-help book."

"Ouch. I am serving as your therapist here, and technically, paraphrasing my own therapists."

"I just want to be there. I want to skip all this crap and have my family."

"There is no 'there,' Emma. Just like there is no spark. Those expectations are making you miserable. While you may not want the life you have right now, it's the one you have, so you have to find a way to not be miserable in it. Exactly like those years you wasted with Justin. You don't get them back."

"So what do I do now?"

"I can't tell you what to do. That's the point. You need to find something that makes you happier. Focus on anything else that brings a little joy to your life so you're not simply shambling through the dark days until Prince Charming miraculously fixes everything."

"Holy shit. I sound like a twit."

"Uh huh."

"Eeew."

"Uh huh. You should know from Justin that some guy is not going to fix this for you. Your happiness is in you. Your life is under your control."

"Jesus, I'm such a mess. How did I become such a mess?"

"Conveniently, you have all this time to now figure yourself out. I don't think you got to do that before you got married."

"No, I married Justin and thought I was done. I figured I had the husband and was going to have the house and the family and that my life was all figured out."

"Exactly."

"I am an idiot."

"No, you are a girl."

"How the hell do you know all this?"

"I'm crazy. I should bill you for the gold mine you are saving on therapy sessions right now."

"I don't think I ever appreciated your bat shit crazy until now."

"The more you know." Ronnie laughed and lifted her glass.

"So I should figure myself out before I try dating again."

"Did you even listen to any of my ridiculous rambling?"

"So I should forget about dating?"

"Emma, I swear, I am going to murder you with that fire poker over there."

"Hey, I used to fantasize about killing Justin with our fire poker while we were splitting up."

"I'm surprised you didn't do it."

"He would have deserved it."

"Maybe that's what would make you happy! Cold-blooded murder."

"Oh! That's what I'm supposed to do. Find something that makes me happy."

"Ding! Ding! Finally. Now can we please eat

this food, drink this wine, and watch something stupid on TV?"

"Yes, please."

Emma pulled the plate back into her lap, noticing that it did not feel as laborious as when she had abandoned it. She might have even tasted the spicy bite of marinara as she chewed her next bite.

***

Snow fell in large, fluffy flakes during Emma's drive home from work the next night. Rolling slowly through the streets of her neighborhood, she listened to the snow pack down and crunch under her tires. Her headlights carved through the vacant roads where snow had begun to heap on top of parked vehicles. With her neck tight and her feet whining from standing so many relentless hours, Emma thought about flannel pajama pants, hot tea, and starting a fire in the neglected fireplace. With her trusty fire poker.

She turned onto her own street and started to creep toward her driveway, her house rising so dark and empty in front of her. The accumulation of snow on the roof made the windows look drooped and despondent, the blackness pouring from every opening heavy and consuming.

The loneliness swelled out from the pit of her stomach, inflating her chest, pressing uncomfortably against her ribs. Thoughts crawled on the edge of her mind. She should be coming home to a family. She should not be working so many jobs and hours. She should have someone to take care of her. She should not have to be alone.

Should. Should. SHOULD.

Emma pulled the car to a stop with the headlights reflecting back against her garage door, fat snowflakes dancing lazily in the beams. She gripped the steering wheel and squeezed her eyes shut tight.

Something to make me happy. Something to distract me.

Emma burst through the front door, flinging snow in behind her. She chucked her purse, apron, coat, and marched up into her bedroom, stripping her clothes as she ascended the stairs. She forbade thoughts, throwing a wall between the back of her mind and the commands she issued to her body. She rifled through her drawer, tossing out a heap of clothing onto her bed.

Thermal tights under running tights, warm core shirt under a long-sleeved tech shirt, topped by a running jacket. Two pairs of socks, flip top gloves, a neoprene headband, and a beanie. She tugged her headlamp over her head and anxiously laced up her running shoes, pulling her traction spikes on over the soles.

The world was silent outside of her cavernous home. The sound of her door slamming echoed across the street, and each crunch of her footsteps lingered in the night air.

I really am crazy.

The thought managed to sneak across her mind before she leaned forward into her run.

The ground compacted underneath Emma with every stride, as if the Earth vanished under her feet.

Even over her music, she could still hear the smoosh of the snow, feel it reverberating up her calves. The fresh, powdery snow slowed her pace. She became hyper-aware of each movement, of the texture of the ground beneath her shoes, the snowflakes striking and piling on her shoulders and the top of her head. Wayward flakes clung to her eyelashes.

As she breathed, her exhalations plumed in the light of her headlamp. She ran through the swirling clouds feeling like a dragon. The steady flow of snowflakes passed in front of her, stealing her light and shielding her sight from the world around her, blurring past her like stars in a science-fiction movie.

Encompassed by quiet, she plodded past each peaceful looking house in her neighborhood. She was the only person crazy enough to be out in this weather at night. The clouds hung low, hugging the Earth and insulating the wind. The air between the flakes was crisp and sharp and silent.

The cold spoke to Emma on a cellular level; her body felt at ease with the chill. She felt special to be the only witness to the calm dusting, the way the weather was changing the world around her. The snow bit on her toes through her socks, on her fingertips through her gloves, on her exposed nose and cheeks. The heat radiating from her core had her sweating despite the frost.

As the miles disappeared behind Emma, she lost herself. For a blissful second, her mind became impossibly blank. She only watched the snow, commanding her legs to move and her lungs to breathe. She tugged the earbuds from her ears to immerse herself in the peace she found in the snowfall, a peace she so desperately wanted to feel below her heart.

Stride, stride, cloud of breath. Stride, stride, cloud of breath.

There was only the rhythm of the run and her secret rendezvous with the night.

When Emma arrived at her house, the snow on her had started to melt. The frigid dampness seeped through her layers. Her heartrate subsiding, her internal furnace kicked off, and she was able to appreciate the full chill that had penetrated her skin. When she peeled off her layers in front of the bathroom mirror, large red splotches spread over the surfaces of her bare body. The patches were cold to the touch, an odd contrast to the dried sweat also on her flesh. She scalded her skin in the shower and made that fire and hot tea.

Dozing off on her couch later, Emma finally had a smile on her face.

***

Emma ran the next day. And the day after that. Every time the house seemed too empty or the hours felt too lonely, she ran again. Four miles, seven miles, ten miles. The distances felt shorter and shorter with repetition. Gladys asked her each day when she was going to start running half marathons. Or full marathons.

The skin on Emma's feet withered and died in an endless rotation of peeling blisters and sluffing

149

callouses, different pressure points from each pair of running shoes she bought. The murderous underwires from her bras rubbed holes in her chest then fully escaped to stab her. Injuries to match where the clasps of her bra had worn a permanent hole on her back.

Emma's body was perpetually sore. By the time the muscles recovered from one run, she was adding more miles to a new route. She found some perverse comfort in the pain. When her thighs raged against squatting at work, she found an unnatural sense of accomplishment, the way being sore from sex would spark a pleasant flashback. Back when she had sex.

With an obsessive amount of running infused into her work-laden routine, the days and weeks dissolved less laboriously. On some days, Emma even felt like she might have discovered a way to be okay in the now. Or okay enough.

After another double shift, she stumbled in the door to die on the cushions of her couch. Without any ambitions of running, she dumped her things by the door and collapsed. Her phone chimed from her purse across the room. Grumbling, she dragged herself reluctantly back to collect the wretched device.

Ronnie: I have something to tell you.

Ronnie: And I'm telling you over text because I don't think you're going to react well, and I want to let you deal with it however you need.

Ronnie: I won't take how you feel personally.

Emma held the phone to her face anxiously, waiting for this catastrophic news. What could Ronnie have to tell her that she had to tell her like this?

Ronnie: I'm pregnant.

Emma dropped the phone. It bounced off the coffee table, disappearing onto the floor. Her hand remained frozen in front of her face as if she was still holding it. Her mouth hung ajar as she breathed heavily through it, hot tears tracking down her cheeks. She struggled to form thoughts.

Without thinking, Emma changed her clothes, put on her shoes, and slammed out the door. She ran hard away from her house, like she was never coming back.

CHAPTER 11

The muted, steady cry of the newborn filled Ronnie's apartment.

"Could you please stop getting skinnier while I am stuck over here with a bowl full of jelly?" Ronnie said from the couch, surrounded by baby wipes, diapers, and a nursing pillow.

"Could you please not have a baby while I am all alone and desperate for a family?" Emma responded.

"Fine, fine. Touché," Ronnie laughed. "Are you ultra marathoning? I know you're upset about this baby thing, but Jesus, Emma. You're going to run yourself to death."

"I'm not upset, Ronnie."

"Shhh! You can be happy for me and upset for you. I know the difference, and it doesn't bother me."

"No, I am not ultra marathoning. Just running myself not miserable. I'm going to do a half marathon this spring."

"Awesome! You are one crazy bitch."

"You should start running with me. Baby recovery."

"Oh no, thank you. I am only running if something is chasing me. Or to get the wine. How I miss wine!"

"You can't have it now because of the breastfeeding."

"Eh, I can have it, kind of. I can't get good and drunk like I want because then I give the baby drunk milk and that makes them stupid or something." Ronnie giggled and winced.

Emma cradled the tiny fussing child against her chest, rocking him into sleep. A tumultuous confliction of emotions raged behind her skin, rapping against her ribs as if reaching out to the baby. Josiah was beautiful, more beautiful than Emma could deal with. She could not discern between her swelling affection and her infectious envy. She only knew that she felt so much she thought she might implode into a swirling black hole in Ronnie's living room, sucking in this perfect new little family.

"Are you okay?" Emma asked Ronnie.

"No. I just gave birth. Aside from being ripped in half and being stitched back together, I am having these lovely cramps that feel astoundingly like contractions, and my poor nipples are cracked and bleeding and stick to the inside of my bra so I have to rip them open every time that tiny monster is hungry. Which, by the way, is always."

"You make motherhood sound so magical."

"I'm sorry. It's reality. I haven't slept in four days and my body feels completely destroyed."

"Don't sugar coat it for me."

"I never do. Hey, you should appreciate all the good things about not having a baby. Like an unstitched vagina or blood-free nipples."

"Gross, Ronnie."

"Exactly, Emma. Fucking gross. Welcome to my new life."

Terrence strolled in with a full water cup for Ronnie. He handed her the giant handled mug embossed with the hospital logo and looked to Emma. His eyes looked heavy and sunken with sleep deprivation, a delirious smirk played on his lips.

"Do you want me to take my boy from you?" he asked.

"Absolutely not," Emma replied, holding Josiah closer to her chest.

"You're never going to see that baby when she's here," Ronnie said. "Make sure she doesn't slip him in her purse on the way out."

"Yeah, Ronnie might appreciate the sleep without him, but I'm not letting this little man out of my sight."

Emma hated how happy and loving Terrence's features formed when he looked down at the miniature child. She hated that she could sense the unadulterated bliss they were suppressing around her. She hated that she had to feel anything about herself while holding Ronnie's child. She wanted to simply be happy for them. She wanted to be anything other than choking on the bitterness and jealousy that felt so unnatural to her.

Josiah stirred in Emma's arms, writhing his tiny

body and pressing against the swaddled blanket patterned with different colored baby footprints. He opened his mouth in a silent cry that dissolved back into sleep. His body temporarily relaxed and went slack before he tensed again, this time emitting a sharp, muted cry. Clumsily, he shoved his wrinkled fist against his cheek.

"Ugh, he's hungry again," Ronnie whined.

"Don't you dare give him to her," Terrence said, swooping in and lifting the baby from Emma. "I'm getting my ten seconds with him to change his diaper. One day you're going to want more than the boob, my man."

While Terrence changed Josiah, Ronnie positioned the nursing pillow on her lap and plucked her breast from her shirt. Emma thought she heard the rip when Ronnie pulled her nipple away from the fabric. Ronnie's breathing stuttered and she grimaced. Terrence stood and lay the baby across the pillow. Josiah immediately rooted around against Ronnie.

"Oh, I don't want to do this," Ronnie said, gathering her breast in her hand.

She flinched as Josiah latched on, breathing out in sharp, stuttered breaths. Terrence sat beside her and let his hand move up and down her back slowly until she opened her eyes again.

It was a beautiful new family moment, and Emma only felt like an intruder.

"That does not look pleasant at all," Emma said to shake the awkwardness.

"It's not," Ronnie said. "I'm starting to question my decision making. I said I wanted to have kids, right?"

"I believe those were your exact words," Terrence replied.

"Are you sure you didn't trick me into this?"

"Like I tricked you into being with me."

"You clever bastard! Seriously though, I'm not sure about this kid thing. Can I return him?"

"Ronnie!" Emma squealed.

"I don't think you want to return him to where he came from," Terrence said.

"God, no. The delivery was bad enough."

"I have decided to try online dating," Emma announced.

"Wait, what?" Ronnie said. "Surely not because of this thing." She looked down at Josiah, suckling away.

"Ronnie, be nice to your baby. You love him."

"More than anything, but I can also appreciate that he might be trying to kill me."

"Stop being a baby," Terrence said. He kissed Ronnie on the cheek and moved to the kitchen.

"You push a baby out of your body then tell me that, Terrence! Okay, Emma, so online dating? Really?"

"I've got to try something. I can't do nothing besides run and work. I need to be more proactive."

"Is this because I had a baby?"

"No, not entirely. I've been thinking about it for a while."

"Since I got pregnant?"

"Get over yourself, Ronnie. I just don't have anywhere to meet someone. I don't date anyone from my jobs, and all I do is work or run by myself.

Nothing is happening organically. I've been divorced for four years now. I've dealt with it. I've done my processing. I've become okay by myself. Now I need to try something new."

"Sounds sane and reasonable enough. Oooh, I never did online dating. Can I live vicariously through you while I'm trapped at home with a newborn baby?"

"I guess. You can help me through the whole process, especially vetting the guys. Do you want to help me set up my profile?"

"Yes!"

"What are you doing tonight?"

"Um, let me see here. I'm nursing a baby. Then, later, I might nurse a baby again. Followed by more nursing of a baby. And finally, waking up to nurse a baby."

"Think you can squeeze me into that tight schedule?"

"Josiah can deal. Or I can nurse at his beck and call while we set up your profile. You know, one of those—damn it! I wish I could drink wine while we do this."

"I'll drink wine for two. I will take that bullet for you."

"Aren't you sweet? So what site are you using?"

"I guess we decide that first. There are, like, a million of them. Marcia at work told me that some of them are understood to be exclusively for hooking up."

"You mean I could have been picking up random guys on the internet without ever having to go out?"

"You could if you were still single."

157

"Man, that would have been a cakewalk! But the number on my headboard might have easily quadrupled, so perhaps it's for the best."

"Yeah, you surely did not need any help ho-ing it up."

"Watch it! My son can hear you. Mommy was only kind of ho, Josiah. Temporarily."

"Uh huh. You spin that story however you want. Why don't you tell him how you brought his dad to my wedding to bring you drinks and be your one night stand?"

"Silence. I'll cross that bridge when we get to it."

"At least you didn't have a daughter."

"Thankfully! I have too much bad karma coming to survive a daughter."

"Guess you better not have another to be safe."

"Or because growing and having a child was horrible."

"Yeah, either way. Okay, shall we bust out a laptop?"

"Yes. Mine is on the kitchen table."

While Emma went to retrieve the laptop, Terrence returned to the living room. "What are you girls plotting on now?" he asked.

"We are writing Emma's online dating profile. You want to help?" Ronnie replied.

"Online dating? Not my strong suit."

"Dating was not your strong suit."

"Oh really? I managed to con you into dating me when you didn't even want to date. That is some Jedi master shit right there."

"He's got you there," Emma laughed. "T, maybe I should have you write my profile. Make me appealing to guys who aren't assholes."

"Hey, I said I could Jedi mind trick Ronnie. I did not say I could manage to weed out the assholes from my gender."

"Details."

"I am going to steal my son," Terrence said, scooping up the snoozing baby, "and I am going to teach him how to play some quality first-person shooter. I got to start him young so that he can get paid to play video games for a living. You girls sit out here and concoct whatever sales pitch you need. You can call me in for final edits."

"Fine, fine. Happy gaming," Emma said. She sat beside Ronnie and powered on the laptop.

"Okay so how do we pick a site?" Ronnie asked. "I only know about the ones they advertise on TV and barely, because who still watches commercials?"

"I know to stay away from Fish of the Sea and Humpr."

"Humpr? Seriously? That's subtle. Ah, I was a hoochie before my time. These hoes today are just lazy!"

"Matched.com seems legit. Then there's eCompatible, but I've heard that it is like a million questions that take forever and costs a lot."

"Do they all cost?"

"eCompatible always costs. The other sites have different levels of membership starting with free."

"You have been thinking about this."

"I like to do my research. Should I start with free?"

"I think you should pay."

"Why?"

"Because I'm willing to bet that people who are looking for random hookups are not going to pay for the service."

"Good point. Spoken like a true retired ho."

"Watch it. I don't have to help you. I could go back to my vampire baby. Okay, no. I have to help you."

"Matched.com's basic membership is $30 a month. That seems reasonable enough. That's, like, $1 per day. I could stomach that."

"Then that's where we start."

"I'm going to need our wine now."

"You're going to have to get it yourself because my reassembled ass is not hobbling to the kitchen for alcohol I have to watch you drink."

"Whew, someone is bitter!"

"You're messing with my booze here."

"No, I plan to drink your booze. In front of you."

"I'm sorry I had a baby, Emma! Have I not suffered enough?"

"Not yet," Emma chuckled, pouring a huge glass of wine. She sniffed it mockingly and took a long, exaggerated sip. "Ahhhhhhh! So refreshing."

"Yeah, fuck you. Just fuck you. I hope you date an endless string of creeps."

"No you don't."

Ronnie sighed. "Fine, I don't. But let me sip that wine."

"Sip."

"Yes, sip. Ahh, that is refreshing. You think he would sleep long enough for me to pound a glass?"

"No. Now focus. The first thing we need to come

up with is my username. Crap. What should my username be?"

"That's a harder question than it should be."

"Right."

"You don't want to use your real name because that's putting your real name out on the internet for any creeper, which I imagine there are many on such a site."

"Exactly."

"It's your first impression, so you want to grab attention and entice them to read more."

"So it should be something I'm interested in or something I'm looking for."

"Can it be NoAssholesAllowed82?"

"I feel that might be a little too direct."

"You know me. That's how I roll." Ronnie thought a moment. "What about something with running?"

"I do love running, but do you think if I do something fitness related, I'll only get a bunch of roided out jocks?"

"Eew, possible. Hmmmm."

"Why is this so hard? This should be the easy part."

"Maybe we're overthinking it."

"Me? Never!"

"How about Overthinker69?"

"Now you're just being an asshole."

"PutABabyInMeNow?"

"Shut up. You are cut off from the username decision."

"YourBabysMomma?"

"I hate you."

"You like to read a lot."

"Do I want to sound like a geeky bookworm?"

"It couldn't hurt for you to attract someone smarter. Don't make me itemize the morons on your headboard."

"Fair enough."

"How about SexyB00kw0rm?"

"Seriously, you're done."

"The RealSlimShady?"

"Just fuck you."

"EmOnTheRun?"

"Hey, that's not bad."

"See, I'm not done."

"I like that one. Username, check. Now a profile picture. Holy hell, how do I pick a picture?"

"Find your sluttiest MyBook picture and slap that on there."

"I am trying to not attract douchebags, remember?"

"Right. So we need hot and pretty but also tasteful. Something that says, *I don't put out on the first date but I want to bear your children as soon as I know you're not an asshole.*"

"More or less, yes."

"Soccer mom with cleavage."

"Why did I agree to your help?"

"Because you can't be trusted left to your own devices."

Emma opened a new tab on the laptop. "Okay, here are my MyBook profile pictures. What do we think?"

"Your current one has you holding Josiah. Don't use that one, it would be confusing. Like, is this your baby? Do you come with a baby? Why are you dating when your baby was born yesterday?"

"Right, okay."

"Where's that one when you did the race up in Aspen?"

Emma clicked through the blur of her own face until the fall leaves filled the screen.

"Yes, that one," Ronnie said. "It's before the run, so you look pretty and not like a hot, sweaty mess. You also don't look all made up like you're trying too hard. It indicates you enjoy running but is not a picture of you running. Shows you out in the beautiful Colorado scenery."

"We have a winner."

"So you have a name and a picture."

"Now, into the meat." Emma leaned forward and took a long chug of her wine, looking at Ronnie out of the side of her eye as she gulped. "The first section is what I'm looking for."

"You get a wishlist?"

"It would appear so. Interested in? Men. Looking for? A relationship. Wants kids? Yes. Income preference? Wow."

"Bitches be shallow. Is there a height preference?"

"Yes."

"What are you going to do? Because you definitely have one."

"I do."

"Are you willing to narrow the pool of already limited guys?"

"That would make me a shallow bitch, right?"

"Um, yeah."

"Okay, no height preference."

"Yay! Look at you growing."

"Look at me desperate."

"Not desperate, reprioritizing."

"Tomato, tomahto."

"You can get really specific on what you want, can't you? You can basically design your perfect guy."

"Yep."

"Then you just have to hope that he actually exists on the internet. And if he says he exists, you have to hope that he's not lying to you to trick you. Or is actually a woman. Or a geriatric pervert with wifi."

"These words of encouragement are so helpful."

"A hoochie before my time."

"Now, all about me. Age, height, blah blah blah. Body type. What should I put here?"

"Let me see the choices. Um, athletic. While you are slender, you are no toothpick with all that running. I think athletic."

"You don't think they'll expect some cut up, toned girl then?"

"That's their problem. You think they are putting an accurate type in there?"

"Probably not."

"On the internet, a keg becomes a six-pack."

"I wanted to try this online dating thing, right?"

"Yes. Just like I wanted to have a baby."

"Crap. Now I need a bio."

"What is that? A free text field?"

"Yep. All about me."

"Give it to me."

"What?"

"Give me the computer. I'll write it up."

"No thank you. I don't need you ho-ing me out."

"Emma, give me the laptop."

Emma squinted and reluctantly passed over the computer. Ronnie turned the screen away from her and curled up, clicking away on the keyboard. Emma sat expectantly beside her, watching her type words she could not read, waiting to see what dreadful concoction was brewing on the page.

"Baby!" Ronnie hollered at Terrence. "We're ready for final edits!"

Terrence emerged from the hallway with Josiah slung across his forearm, still dozing. "You girls come up with some good, man-catching material?"

"I think so. Let me read you her bio," Ronnie replied.

"Which I did not write," Emma said.

"Ahem," Ronnie started. "I am an active and fun-loving Colorado girl. When I am not working, you will see me running in any weather. I also love to spend time with my friends and have a close relationship with my family. I am looking for the right person to share my life and start a family with."

"Nice, babe. I think that works. I would reword the close relationship with family part though, could be read the wrong way. Otherwise, really good."

"Holy crap," Emma said, stunned. "Even I liked it."

"See?" Ronnie said. "Trust in me. Now we have a bio. Post this profile!"

Ronnie passed the computer back to Emma.

Emma looked over all the information once more then clicked the button and sent her dating dreams out onto the vast internet. She shut the computer and put it on the coffee table.

"Download the app to your phone," Ronnie said.

"You think I'll get messages that quickly?"

"I have no idea. Hence the app on your phone to tell you."

Emma lifted her phone and navigated to the app, installing it to her device. After she tapped in her new account credentials, she looked surprised at the notifications.

"I already have messages," she said.

"They are hungry," Ronnie replied. "What do they say?"

"'Hey baby. You have such a beautiful body. Message me back.'"

"Eeew, pass."

"Agreed. Okay, I decline this message. Why am I declining this message, it asks. Not interested. Okay. Next message. 'Hi there. You look like a nice and fun girl. Message me back if you would like to get to know me better.'"

"That wasn't as bad. Pull up his profile."

"He's cute. Wait, doesn't want kids. Decline this message. Why? We're not a match. Oh, I have to write a message. Um…I am looking for someone who wants a family. Good luck in your search. Okay. Gone. Oh wait, I have ten matches to go through too."

"So people message you and the site also gives you matches?"

"Based on the similarities in our profiles, I

guess."

"Let's process these matches then. See how good this site is."

Emma and Ronnie curled up beside each other on the couch, drawing their knees up in front of them and balancing the phone between them, the tiny screen illuminating their faces.

"Hold on," Emma said, lifting her wine glass. "I need a drink. A big drink." She took a long gulp. "Oh wait. Here, let me take one for you too." She took an even longer drink.

"You are such a bitch."

"I'm about to be a drunk bitch. Okay, here we go. First one."

"Look, it's a kid picture."

"It says here that he doesn't have any kids. You're right, it is confusing. Like, who is this kid? Family? Friend? Random kid off the street? And why is this kid in your dating profile picture?"

"To kick women who want kids and have a biological clock banging off the wall right in the uterus."

"Ah, yes. Clever play."

"You want to message him already, don't you?"

"No. Moving on. Next."

"Oh. My. God. Is that a bathroom selfie lifting his shirt? Of course it is! He doesn't even have a six-pack!"

"Let's read the profile."

"Absolutely not! This is literally like the douchebag calling card profile picture. Next!"

"Fine, fine. Oh wait, now he's cute."

"He *is* cute. Simple picture taken by someone

else, meaning he has friends or a stranger trusted him enough to do him a favor. Outside in the mountains so he's not a video game troll. Scroll down."

"Ah, shit."

"What?"

"He's undecided on kids."

"Skip him."

"It says undecided. Maybe he would change his mind."

"Like Justin? Yeah, no. Skip."

"Fine. Probably should be sure this time. Next!"

"It's a meathead."

"Be nice. He's a personal trainer. Divorced, definitely wants kids. Likes to work out, obviously."

"His profile lacks grammatical errors."

"That's not exactly high on my priority list."

"It should be. So do we like him?"

"Yeah, I think we can keep him. If I like him it tells me to wink at him. Winking."

"What happens after you wink?"

"I believe he either ignores me, winks back, or messages me directly."

"That sounds complicated."

"Here's another outdoorsman."

"With another mountain picture. I like it."

"He is very into biking. Look at all these cycling pictures. He's kind of short though."

"Five feet seven inches is not short. You are just a picky Amazon. No discounting based on height while I'm sitting with you."

"Yes, Master. Winking."

Emma raised her glass and drained it, feeling the nerves in her forehead haze. Ronnie watched her enviously from the sides of her eyes. Emma set her empty glass on the table and pulled the phone closer. Ronnie stood up and hobbled into the kitchen, walking slow and wide in an awkward limp.

"Holy shit," Emma said.

"What?" Ronnie hollered.

"I already have seven new messages, eleven winks, and twelve new matches."

"Ugh, this is already exhausting."

CHAPTER 12

Emma sat in the restaurant booth, perched awkwardly somewhere between excitement and anxiety. She gripped her fork and tapped the metal softly with her index finger then punctured vegetative bites of her salad. Emma was uncomfortable eating on dates, as if her food choices or the way she ingested would suggest something unsavory about her. She was equally unnerved if she abstained and simply observed her date eat. She caught herself critiquing his meal selection or how he chewed, asking if she could live with the sound of his mastication for the rest of her life. She compromised to eat small and light. Perhaps he would assume she was conscious of watching her figure, which was fine. More, it would pacify the nervous quease in her stomach without aggravating it.

With a mat of leaves rocking between her molars, she looked up at Andrew, or Drew as he insisted she call him. Drew filled the opposing booth with wide shoulders and pectorals that rose up in his athletic polo shirt. His dark skin pulled taut across his skull, with only the minute hints of wrinkles near his eyes. The meal in front of him was divided into a very deliberate macro ratio, heavily slanted toward the lean protein yielded by his grilled, flavorless chicken breast.

Drew was clearly very conscious of watching *his* figure.

Drew looked up from pulling the knife across his chicken and smiled at Emma. Despite his rigid, toned exterior, his face was soft and warm, spreading effortless and wide across his high cheekbones and illuminating his eyes of such a pale brown they blazed orange. Emma experienced a jolt in her center at that grin.

The spark.

"How long have you been a personal trainer?" she asked.

"Since my divorce," he replied. "After my wife left me, I decided I had to get out of the desk job and do something I could get pumped about, something I loved. I kind of dove into the gym."

"At least it's a healthy outlet and you love it. How long have you been divorced?"

"She left me about a year ago. We've been final for maybe three months now. You're divorced too, right?"

Three months??

"Yes. Four years now."

"Wow. And you're still dating? You are so hot and seem so awesome."

"Yeah, I had some bad experiences and took a break."

"I'm sorry. I hope this time is a better one."

"So far, I have no complaints."

Drew flashed that smile again, and Emma's mind swooped clumsily around her skull. She reflected it, hoping blood was not flushing her cheeks.

"What do you do, Emma? Your profile didn't really say."

"I have a couple jobs. I work as a barista at Happy Beans. I also work on the phones at Call Solutions. Sometimes I pick up shifts at The Taproom."

"Wow. That's a lot of jobs. Why do you work so much?"

"My ex accrued a lot of debt for us, and I still live in our house."

Emma did not want to talk about Justin or all the ways he had ruined her life. She hated that she could not answer inane backstory questions without invoking him. He haunted her relentlessly though she had not seen his face in years. He was with her on every first date because he was the reason they were necessary.

"I guess you don't have a lot of free time for the gym or anything then."

"Not really. I do run a lot though."

"Really? That's impressive. I can't stand running. I haven't ever been able to force myself to do it. I like lifting."

"I hate weights."

"Looks like we are the perfect balance then."

Emma quietly began to hope so.

***

172

The next morning, a sly smirk still played on Emma's lips as she walked into Happy Beans. As always, Gladys was already singing to herself behind the counter.

"Good morning, darling. You look risen from the dead. Is that actually a smile I see?"

"Maybe."

"What could possibly drag you out of the perpetual dumps and put a grin on that gloomy face?"

"I had a good date last night."

"A what? You're back on that bandwagon?"

"Yeah, I decided to try online dating."

"Oh honey, I know Ronnie having a baby before you was hard on you, but the internet is full of creeps and perverts and stalkers. You have to be careful."

"That's not what it's about. Didn't your daughter meet your son-in-law online?"

"That is not the point. She got lucky. He's not that much of a catch anyway. You didn't let his hand in the cookie jar the first night, did you?"

"Gladys, of course not. I just met him. Besides, giving up the cookies hasn't been working out so great, so I'm going to try holding back. We just had that spark."

"Ah, so he's pretty then?"

"Very pretty."

"Oh, Lord."

"I have two more dates on my day off."

"With him?"

"No. New guys."

"You have three different dates in one week?

And two in one day?"

"Yep."

"How are you going to keep them all straight?"

"I have no idea."

***

On her day off, Emma stood in the bright morning sun. She shifted her weight from leg to leg, shielding her eyes with her hand in addition to her sunglasses. The Colorado sky was a crisp blue, allowing the sun to pierce vividly through the thin air. Emma leaned against the chain link fence watching the steady stream of people trickle in from the parking lot with their hands tangled in leashes and excited dogs bouncing around them.

Finally, one figure appeared to be walking toward her.

"Emma?" he asked from behind sunglasses.

"Rick?"

They smiled at each other and shook hands. Below Rick, an energetic puppy wound Rick's legs with the leash before attempting to claw up Emma's leg.

"Who is this?" Emma asked, squatting down to meet the dog.

"This is Bruno."

Bruno frantically bounced up at Emma, lapping excitedly at her face and twirling in tight circles under her hands. His white coat was speckled with brown spots to match his face and ears.

"How old is he?"

"About two. I got him after my divorce. You

know, keep a plant alive, then get a pet. Keep a pet alive, then date."

Why am I the only one who has been divorced so long?

"I thought that was rehab."

"Are they so different?"

"Not at all."

Rick was older than he appeared in his pictures. He was shorter than Emma, his eyes cresting around her chin, which immediately doused her attraction. He had a lean and compact body. According to his profile, he was an avid cyclist, and he looked the part.

They broached the dog park fence, and Rick liberated Bruno from his leash.

"Is it weird to go on a dog park date without a dog?" Emma asked.

"Technically, you can count Bruno as a part of your date. Would you like to hold the leash so you feel like less of a poser?"

Emma laughed genuinely. Bruno darted out ahead and circled back to lick Rick's hand as they meandered in laps around the park.

"So I know you like to bike," Emma commented.

"Yeah, I bike everywhere. As long as the gas guzzling trucks aren't running me off the road."

"What else do you like to do?"

"I just like to be outside. Bruno and I are working on hiking all the fourteeners in Colorado."

"That's mountains over fourteen thousand feet, right?"

"Yeah."

"How many have you done?"

"Six so far."

"That's awesome. I always wanted to hike Pikes Peak. My father lives in Colorado Springs."

"Pikes Peak is a fourteener. I haven't done that one. Maybe date two."

Emma grinned. "Maybe."

Bruno wandered less enthusiastically, slapping his nose against Rick's hand for attention. He looked up at his master expectantly.

"I think Bruno might be a little bored of the dog park. Do you want to hike around a little more?" Rick said.

"Sure."

She looked down at her flat, unsupportive shoes as Rick pulled the leash from his back pocket and attached it to Bruno's collar. Bruno, animated again, wagged his tail, his tongue sprawling out of his mouth.

The gate clinked behind them as moved out of the dog park, the sun vibrant against the trees and dusty colored rocks. The park poured out in front of them, climbing up toward the foothills. The light was beginning to roast her exposed and unprotected skin, the heat climbing into her cells. Rick let Bruno lead them, which he did more calmly than Emma would have anticipated for his puppy demeanor. She assumed from so much practice on 14ers.

"You have four sisters?"

"Yes. Four."

"Oh wow. How was that?"

"Traumatic."

Emma choked on her giggle.

"I love all my sisters very much. They are

176

different, beautiful, and brilliant people."

"Naturally."

"But they are absolutely insane. I mean, like, certifiably crazy. Puberty nearly killed us all, including both our parents. Girls are ruthless too."

"You don't have to tell me."

"I was right in the middle, and I managed to get beat up or manipulated and played by the older and the younger set. Between all the periods and boyfriends and breakups and PMS, it was a madhouse."

"Well, you can say periods and PMS without squirming, so you're ahead of the game."

"You say ahead of the game; my ex-wife said emotionally ambivalent."

"What does that even mean?"

Rick stopped walking and faced Emma. "Thank you!"

In the momentary break, the pain points in Emma's feet started to throb. The hot burn of blisters budded on the pads of her feet and her heels. The sun also began to write in red along her shoulders and she was sure her nose.

"I don't mean to cut the date short," Emma said. "I did not wear the correct shoes for hiking, and I think I'm starting to get a little pink."

Rick rolled his wrist over.

"Oh wow! It's been three hours since we left the dog park. How did that happen?"

"I don't know," Emma laughed.

"Let's call this a date so you can go soak your blisters and aloe your shoulders. I'm sorry I kept you out here so long."

"No problem at all. It was great to meet you."

"You too, Emma."

When they ambled back to the parking lot, Rick gently took Emma's wrist and let his lips brush her cheek. The gesture was pleasant; Emma only wished that she had felt any kind of rush at the touch.

She limped through her door, gently detaching the shoes that felt embedded into her aching feet then chucked them away from her. Even her legs were starting to stiffen from the unexpected hike. She hobbled up the stairs and into the shower, the warm water igniting the kiss of sunburn at her edges. She washed the salty film of sweat from her skin and wrapped in a towel to search out her most comfortable pair of heels.

***

"You go bowling in heels, girl?" Jamal said to her as they stood in line at the bowling alley.

"I have socks in my purse for the bowling shoes, so technically I'm wearing heels *to* bowling," Emma replied.

"You look good in them either way."

"Thank you."

Emma blushed, heat rising in her cheeks. Jamal lifted his chin and let his eyelids drape slightly when he complimented her. Something about the way his speech changed made Emma's chest flutter like a moth trapped in a lampshade. When she looked at him, her blood swelled at his perfectly symmetrical face.

The rolling sound of colliding pins moved through the room around them. Emma followed Jamal to their lane, holding her issued shoes as lightly and as far from her body as she could discreetly. She held her stride as gracefully as possible, even as the blisters shrieked each time she put her weight on a foot. Her knees threatened to wobble and abandon her.

This is the last time I do two dates in one day, Emma promised herself.

She walked up the lane, cradling the ball to her chest, hoping she disguised her limp as she moved. Stepping forward and leaning to draw back the ball back sent tiny shockwaves over her tender nerves. She winced and heaved the ball back, sending it bouncing down the lane. Her ball meandered along the board, disappearing into the gutter.

Emma tucked her hair behind her ear. "I might be completely terrible at this."

"That's okay. I will happily watch you be terrible at it."

At the sly smile on Jamal's lips, Emma tensed again. She wanted to skip this bowling date. She wanted to climb into his lap and stick her tongue down his throat. All the chemistry and attraction she did not feel when Rick pressed his lips to her cheek, she felt in spades when Jamal merely looked in her direction.

"I'm kind of in between jobs right now. Surfing my brother's couch at the moment. I was an oil tech at a tire place before. What do you do?" Jamal asked.

"I have enough jobs to share. I work as a barista,

at a call center, and I also pick up shifts as The Taproom."

"Damn, girl! That is a lot of jobs. How do you have time for anything else?"

"I don't really," Emma laughed.

"But you're here." Jamal leaned the slightest bit closer to her.

"Yes. I made time for you."

The flirtation between them was palpable, as if Emma could reach out and run her fingertips along the tension. That pressure on her chest caused the rest of the world to haze. The sounds of the bowling pins moved farther away, and time swelled into the moment.

Emma basked in it, a dumb grin playing on her glossed lips, until the realization rippled across her consciousness. It started as an uncomfortable familiarity, something bristling at the edge of her blurry euphoria. It had been blissfully amnesic for that split second when she wrapped up in the way he angled his chin toward her with interest, the way her heart flapped against her ribs when he looked at her.

This was exactly the way she felt when she tumbled off sanity for Justin.

The instant the thought took form in her brain and reached its horrific hand back into her memory, drawing up the wretched recollection of how blindly and fully she loved her unfaithful husband, nausea slammed into the back of her teeth. She struggled to hold back the sensation and keep the wince off her face. Jamal talked slyly from the corner of his mouth. Emma could no longer hear his words or anything else.

Her own voice rose from the hum buzzing in her skull. *This is not Justin. He is not Justin. You are just another damaged divorcée. Calm down. Keep your clothes on tonight and calm down.*

Emma swallowed her panic like a thick, burning lump down her throat. She drew her face back up and let the sounds of the world pour back through her ears. The overwhelming tension between them and the distracting flutter in her subsided. The bowling alley leveled out below her again, and she continued the date with her faculties unearthed.

***

As Emma climbed into her bed that night, exhausted but alone, the montage of her whirlwind of first dates flickered behind her eyelids.

She drifted off thinking, *This online dating thing might not be so bad. I can do this. I can find someone doing this.*

CHAPTER 13

"Come on, spill," Ronnie said, bringing a slice of pizza awkwardly to her mouth over the nursing baby in her lap. "I've been waiting to hear about these online dates all week. Let me live vicariously through you."

"Why would you want to live vicariously through my dating?" Emma asked. "You never wanted to date. You hated dating. You adamantly avoided it."

"This is true, but presently, my nightly date gets milk drunk, pukes on me, and passes out. Frankly, I don't remember what it's even like to want sex much less have it. So you can appreciate that a little distraction from the dreary routine of motherhood would be lovely."

"You make it sound so awesome to be a mother."

"It is awesome, I swear. Some of the best moments of my life so far. But holy shit! It is so daunting, and I think I might suck at it."

"You don't suck at it."

"We'll see. No mom talk! I like to pretend I am still an adult person of my own under this boob pillow and the smell of diapers. Dating report, now."

"How do you want them? Chronologically? By ranking?"

"Let's go chronological so I don't automatically disqualify them because you ranked them high."

"Yes. Thank you so much. First was Drew, the personal trainer."

"The meathead."

"Right. We went out to dinner. He's a nice guy, recently divorced too. He's super into fitness."

"Obviously."

"I was definitely attracted to him. We had that…attraction right away."

"You wanted to say spark."

"No I didn't."

"Yes you did. Continue."

"Next was Rick, the cyclist. We went on a dog park date."

"A dog park date? You don't have a dog."

"That part *was* kind of awkward. The rest wasn't. I was comfortable with him. We talked for hours. We ended up hiking around for hours after the dog park, talking about our families and everything."

"He sounds promising."

"I don't know. I wasn't attracted to him."

"He was the short one, wasn't he?"

"No. Well, yeah, he is shorter than me. Things felt more platonic with him. I was comfortable, maybe too comfortable. There was no…flutter."

"No spark."

"Call it what you want. Then last, I went bowling with Jamal."

"Okay." Ronnie waited for Emma to elaborate. "And…?"

"And what?"

"What do you not want to tell me?"

"What do you mean?"

"I mean you sparked with the meathead, and you were platonic over the dog-lover, but nothing for the last guy? What do you not want to tell me about him?"

"He was hot."

"You think I'll think he's probably an ass?"

"Yes, that. And…"

"And?"

"It made me stupid."

"Stupid how?"

"Stupid like with Justin."

"Whoa! Okay. How do you mean?"

"I started to flutter and float, and consider jumping into bed with him and imagine a whole future without knowing him at all."

"Jesus, Emma."

"See? This is why I didn't want to tell you."

"No. Look, you caught yourself. You saw what you were doing. I assume you did not jump on top of him or elope overnight."

"I did not."

"Look how much progress you've made! You didn't need me to tell you anything. So tell me about this Jamal."

"He's hot. And charming. And unemployed. And

living on his brother's couch."

"Oh wow, what a winner!"

"I know. But again, I'm really attracted to him. I have trouble ignoring that. My head is saying, hell no. The rest of me…"

"We know what your head is saying; we know what your vagina is saying. What are your guts saying? Your instinct?"

"I don't know. When I realized it felt like it did with Justin, I almost puked."

"That seems like a clear sign."

"I don't want to toss anyone aside who reminds me of Justin. I loved Justin. What happens if I love someone else? Do I run because it feels similar?"

"That's a good point. I don't know how you'll be able to tell."

"I'm thinking I will give him a second date just to see."

"Fair enough. What about the other guys? Do they get second dates?"

"I would have no issues seeing any of them again. I don't think things with Rick would work out, but I'm willing to give it another date."

"How do you feel about all this?"

"I'm not sure. I was worried about this whole online dating thing. I thought it was going to be a series of creeps, but all these guys seem decent so far. I feel like I could do this, like this maybe could work."

"Then here's to hope."

***

Jamal met Emma in the parking lot of the apartment complex. As soon as Emma saw him emerge from below the green exterior stairway, she knew he had probably spent as much time assembling his ensemble as she had. He had donned a crisp plaid shirt with the first two buttons undone to reveal a glimpse of a shining chain against his dark skin. The front of his shirt was tucked behind a modest belt buckle, and the cuffs of his dark jeans were gathered behind the popped tongues of immaculate white basketball shoes. Another chain and a thick watch sparkled on his wrists.

Emma was aware what all the signs were telling her, but he looked so recklessly appealing. She detected that familiar sway in her reasoning, as if a portion of her thought process had dissolved beneath her, the way the entire bowling alley had faded into the background on their last date. She snatched the trailing end of her waning composure. She knew what was happening; she had done this before. She was being dazzled by the peacock, blinded by the spark.

Keep it together, Emma. He might be a dick. Okay, he's probably a douchebag. But he might not be. He is not Justin. You're only going to go on this date, keep your pants on, and find out. Mostly, keep your pants on.

Emma gathered her purse and stepped out of the car to meet him. When Jamal saw her, a wide grin made his face even more attractive. Emma's heart thumped against her ribs. Her body heat rose a single degree, bringing warmth to her face, the nerves in her skin arching toward the surface.

Keep your pants on.

"Hey girl," Jamal said as they met each other beside the car.

His attentive expression moved slowly around his face, practiced. Emma could feel the effect working on her as a blush climbed into her cheeks.

"Welcome to my new digs." He led her back toward the building from which he had emerged.

Within the first few steps, he reached back and found her hand. At the touch and warmth of his skin, Emma's knees locked, then wobbled. Grinning, she grazed her cheek with the fingertips of her other hand.

She loved the feeling, the way the weight that had been crushing her for so long since that one soggy bikini, felt alleviated. The pressure of the pain and the frustration became obscured by the excitement in her flesh. The relief was intoxicating and less about Jamal himself and more about it not being about Justin or even about what might be wrong with her.

Jamal opened the front door of his apartment and led her inside. A few pieces of furniture emerged from stacked boxes.

"You are officially the first person who has been in my new place, and you are exactly the person who I want to celebrate with. You can see I am still unpacking and getting settled. I thought we could order some Chinese food and throw on some Netflix. You know, break the place in," he said.

Did he just say break the place in? Surely, that was not a line meaning to christen the place.

Emma sat down on the couch. The entertainment

system was, in fact, unpacked and completely assembled across the coffee table. Priorities. The couch rumpled under her weight, flexing in its faux leather fabric. The material was crisp and unforgiving beneath her. She tucked her purse under the table and sat awkwardly on the cushions.

Jamal ordered their Chinese food on the phone with his thick, even tone, then dropped himself onto the couch beside her. He placed himself so close to her that the cushion angled, rolling her into him. He lifted his arm to invite her into his chest. Emma smiled, looking down, and remained upright.

"Have you seen this one?" he asked her, gesturing at the screen with the controller. "Zombies."

"No. I know everyone ever is obsessed with this show. Guess I just haven't had the time."

"With your fifteen jobs? Weird. Do you want to check it out? I'm willing to watch it from the beginning."

"Sure. I've always been curious."

"Decided then, but there's a cost."

"A cost?"

"Yep. Every time someone gets eaten by a zombie, you have to give me a kiss."

Emma looked down again, hoping the flare of heat did not show on her cheeks. Jamal's arm hovered around her a moment, gently guiding her against him. Once she flicked her eyes up, he gave her a heavy look, then his eyes wandered down to her mouth. He leaned forward and pressed his lips against hers. The warmth from his face brushed against hers. She closed her eyes and found a strange silence in his kiss.

A rush surged on Emma's nerves at the physical contact. Her mind fell quiet when her body focused on him. Below the tug of her instincts and the bliss of the distraction, another sensation writhed. She found his arm around her both pleasant yet confining. His kiss felt skilled and enticing, but too fast. Although she wanted him, a panicked suffocation sat beneath that desire.

Emma took a deep breath and sank against him and stare into the flashing screen.

"So he wakes up from a coma in the middle of the zombie apocalypse?" she asked.

"Pretty much."

"Wow. That might be the worst thing ever."

"Definitely. Especially when you're trying to run from zombies with your ass hanging out of a hospital gown."

"I would think that is the least of his worries."

"Sure, he has to figure out why all these zombies are trying to eat him and what has happened to his family, but no one wants the giblets dangling loose while battling the undead."

The doorbell interrupted a very tense standoff with gasping and clawing corpses. Jamal paused the show with a zombie mouth spread wide, cheek rotted away to reveal stained teeth. He spread the takeout cartons over the coffee table and handed Emma a set of chopsticks. He sat back down and reengaged the show.

"Is it weird to be chowing down while watching people get torn apart by zombies?" Emma asked after she finished chewing.

"Nah. I mean they're chowing down, why shouldn't we? Speaking of, that is one dead guy. Kiss."

With lo mein still rolling among her molars, Emma pressed her greased lips shut and quickly against Jamal's. While the zombies feasted on the television, they matched the sounds as they dug into the Chinese containers.

Emma's brain detached and climbed more into the post-apocalyptic world in the show with each passing scene. She noticed Jamal's tightening clutch and her reduced personal space. She chose to ignore that he held her like Justin once had.

Her eyebrows drew toward the bridge of her nose. Her forehead compiled on top of her brow slowly. She did not think it was the suspense of the looming zombie horde crawling across her face. Something felt off the longer she remained tangled in Jamal and gave him the quick kisses prompted by the plotline. This was the affection she had been longing for each cold night in her dark, empty house. While she sat alone on her couch. When she set her hand on the shifter in her car and no one was there to hold it. The gorgeous man she required was holding her exactly like she used to love. However, somewhere beneath the pleasant hum on her nerves, it felt stifling.

What is wrong with me?

Blood sprayed across the screen and Emma closed her eyes to forfeit another kiss.

This is what I want. He is the one I wanted. It just feels so rushed, so hollow. It feels like Justin.

With his name on the folds of her brain, it hit

her.

It feels like lies. But his lies or Justin's? Am I ever going to be over him?

With Jamal's face so close to hers, the emotion welled up in her eyes. The frustration roasted from the pit of her stomach down her extremities. She felt trapped, restrained by Jamal's contrived affection and bound by Justin's transgressions and damage. She wanted to shed her skin in a pile on Jamal's uncomfortable couch and run a screaming, bloody mess out of the unpacked apartment.

Breathe. Just breathe, you psycho. You can't have a family if you don't move on. You have to move on. Jamal is not Justin.

When the ending credits of an episode scrolled, Jamal lifted the controller and froze them in place.

"Intense, right?" he said, releasing her from his side embrace and sitting forward.

"Super intense. They just kill off everybody, don't they?"

"They definitely do. Don't go getting attached to any characters."

"Whoa! Spoilers."

"I didn't say anything. Yet. Hey, I realized that I haven't given you the full tour."

"The full tour of your one-bedroom apartment?"

"Yeah. Here, let me show you."

Jamal stood and snagged Emma's fingertips in his, dragging her gently behind him.

"This is the living room, obviously," he started. "You've already seen this room. Over here is the kitchen. Well, it's back there among the boxes somewhere. It's pretty tight. I don't cook much, so

191

that shouldn't be a problem. It will get the job done. Down the hall this way is the bathroom, which you have already also seen. In this closet is the washer and dryer. And this is my bedroom, where all the magic happens."

Emma stifled a choke in her throat. Jamal released her hand and sat down on the bed in front of her, patting the vacant space beside him invitingly.

"Why don't you come over here and check out this mattress?"

Emma held her breath to not laugh and flexed her eyelids hard to prevent her eyes from rolling around their sockets.

Okay. Maybe he is Justin.

Emma shook her head as the apartment door closed behind her. She discovered that her head continued to sway in dazed confusion when she sat down and slipped her key into the ignition.

Why am I surprised? Why the hell am I shocked? He's a hot jerk. And he acted like a hot jerk. Just like I knew he was going to. I knew he was going to throw me some pathetic, cliché play the entire day. I still sat there. I still wanted him to be the guy.

On her drive home, Emma did not know if she was shaking her head at his ridiculous line or the fact that she had stayed there long enough to hear it.

***

"At least you didn't sleep with him," Ronnie said as she unloaded the baby from the car seat in Emma's living room. "Old Emma would have sat right down and checked out that mattress." Ronnie let a giggle ripple out from her chest.

"Shut up," Emma said. "I mean, you're right. Old Emma would have married him."

"*Did* marry him."

"Whatever."

"So you're growing. That's a good thing. There's progress. Now pour me a half glass of that wine. I can't have you drinking alone."

"Ronnie with a half glass. Who would have ever guessed?"

"Can it."

"I feel like I'm never going to find the guy."

"You only started this online dating thing. You've only been on literally one weekend of dates. You have to stop trying so hard. You can't *make* someone the guy. What about the other two?"

"Rick."

"The dog park guy?"

"Yeah. He just kind of vanished. Like at the end of the date, he said he wanted to go out again. We messaged a little bit back and forth, never set anything up. Then poof."

"You don't want yet another poofer."

"No. I wasn't super into him, so I'm kind of letting him go."

"So there's the meathead?"

"Yes. Drew."

"What's happening with him?"

"He actually messages me pretty consistently. He has even called me after our date. We're supposed to go out again. I have to get my schedule tomorrow and see when I can actually squeeze in a date."

"Ah. See? One is still in play. How long is this three job bullshit going to last?"

"As long as it has to I guess. I can't pay the mortgage with one job, and there is so much debt from Justin."

"Why don't you sell the house? File for bankruptcy? Something."

"No."

"Why not?"

"I don't want to. This is my house. I made this my house after Justin insisted we get a new one. I love this house. I wanted to have my children in this house. And the debt is my mistake too. I let him charge all that stuff on cards in my name. This is my mess. I want to get out of it myself."

"That's admirable, sweetie, but shouldn't there be some kind of pain point, a threshold where it's not worth teaching yourself a lesson? You could start over with a bankruptcy. Your credit wouldn't be any more worse off."

"No. I'll get there on my own."

"I believe you will, but how are you going to have any sort of life, meet any sort of person, and have a relationship if you are working so much you don't even have time to sleep? Especially when you refuse to date anyone you meet through your three jobs."

"I don't know."

***

The weeks dating Drew passed steadily and uneventfully enough for a cautious optimism to bloom somewhere beneath Emma's depression. One small leaf arching up into the darkness above. She did not find him underwhelmingly platonic like Rick, nor did she find him blatantly empty like Jamal. Somewhere between a good guy she should have been attracted to and a gorgeous man who would only rip her heart again, she gently hoped Drew was the compromise between them.

Each week, Emma contorted between her schedules to carve out a brief window for a date that did not occur when normal people would be sleeping. She concealed the dark circles of exhaustion beneath her energy drink infused eyes with makeup and smiled wide with anticipation when they met at the gym after his shift for protein shakes or caught an evening matinee action movie or when he made her flavorless macro driven meals in his condo.

Gladys knew him by name rather than a random identifier, though Ronnie referred to him as Meathead. He had been in the picture long enough for Brendan to ask about him while he filled up his coffee without Emma having to tell him how Drew had vanished and she was trying something else new. Hope grew in her like a cancer, and she became comfortable enough in the idea of him to promote him to the next level.

Meeting Ronnie and Terrence.

"Why are you so goddamn nervous?" Ronnie cackled as she watched Emma meticulously arrange and rearrange the table.

"Because meeting you guys is a big step, and I'm scared to hope it will work out. This time around, the guy needs to get along with my friends. I don't want to have to have two separate lives again."

"Aw, I'm so flattered!"

"Don't be a bitch."

"I'm not. Stop cleaning. No one's house is this clean and organized. At this point, you need to sell him reality."

"I clean when I'm nervous."

"I know. Stop it. It is just a casual dinner with friends. There is a baby here for Christ's sake."

"I think I am more nervous about this than I would be taking him home to my mom or to Noah."

"That's because your mom and brother won't tell it to you like I will."

"Exactly."

"Breathe, Emma. Just breathe."

"Em, if he makes you happy, we're going to like him," Terrence said. Both Ronnie and Emma shot him a look of sharp disbelief. "Fine, if he makes you happy, *I'll* like him. Ronnie will do, you know, whatever the hell she wants."

The doorbell echoed through the house, and the three froze. Emma grew rigid, and her eyes widened. She moved to twitch toward the door when Ronnie stepped in front of her.

"Look at me," Ronnie said. "Take a breath and relax your eyes a little bit. Better. Okay, now go."

Ronnie and Terrence were giggling behind her on her walk to her front door. Drew stood on the other side holding a small bouquet of flowers and a bottle of wine. His normally enticing grin stretched more strained across his cheeks, mild panic igniting his eyes.

"I didn't know what to bring," he said as Emma guided him into the house. "I'm not sure why; I'm nervous tonight."

The tension in her face dissolved by half. Her posture relented and allowed her shoulders to descend from their clutch beside her earlobes.

"I'm so relieved you said that. I thought I was being ridiculous."

"You talk about them all the time. It's, like, worse than meeting your parents."

"That's what I said!" Emma whispered so Ronnie and Terrence could not hear them.

They both laughed, authentic smiles gracing their cheeks. Emma took his hand more confidently and led him through her house into the kitchen. They walked in to Ronnie holding Josiah against her chest while Terrence leaned in to pretend to eat his belly. The blob-like infant faintly registered the attack and tried to muster a grin in response.

"Guys, this is Drew. Drew, this is Ronnie, Terrence, and this is Josiah," Emma said.

"Hi. It's really good to meet you guys. Emma talks about you guys all the time," Drew said.

Drew moved around the counter and shook Terrence's hand firmly while looking him in the eye. Then he turned to Ronnie. She shifted Josiah to liberate a hand to meet his. Drew even took a second to crouch down to Josiah's level and greet him individually. Emma nodded approvingly behind him, a rush of relief swelling beneath her skin.

They sat around the table. Terrence took Josiah from Ronnie and balanced the infant on his thigh in front of his plate. Emma moved to the oven to extract the steaming dish of homemade macaroni and cheese. The aroma of the meal instantly consumed the room, became palpable in the air.

"I know, it's not in your macros," Emma joked as she dropped a scoop onto Drew's plate.

"That's okay, I made sure today was a cheat day. This looks like a great way to cheat." He took in the food then beamed up at her.

"So, Drew," Ronnie said between bites, "do you watch what you eat and macros and all that as part of being a personal trainer, or are you working toward another goal?"

"When I was married, I got kind of fluffy. When I got divorced, one of the first things I wanted to do was cut weight and tone up. That's how I started on the personal training thing. It allowed me to focus on fitness. When I'm preaching that kind of eating every day, it felt right to be practicing it myself. Then it kind of became habit. I have also started looking into competing."

"Like bodybuilding?" Terrence asked.

"Not any Arnold Schwarzenegger level, but yeah."

"What is the appeal? Is it the aesthetic appearance you are going for or is it the competition?" Ronnie asked.

"I guess part of it is that I do want to look a certain way. I mean, a bodybuilding competition is about how you look. More than that, though, I think I want the challenge, the goal to focus on."

Emma watched Ronnie watching Drew as she slowly flayed him into pieces with her seemingly innocuous questions. The questions sounded so gentle, appeared conversational. Emma knew from experience that she was lifting one layer of him with each answer acquired. Emma recognized the coldly analytical look on Ronnie's face while she attempted to glean the interpretations whirling below the stoic surface.

"So what do you guys do?" Drew asked.

"I'm a mechanical engineer," Terrence answered.

"My wife worked at TechServices." Drew paused. "Ex-wife," he corrected. "What about you, Ronnie?"

"Let's not talk about the soulless, boring work I do. Between that and the delicious dinner, we'll all be asleep at the table."

Josiah writhed in Terrence's arms, arching his tiny back and clumsily mashing his fists at his eyes. His cries began softly then quickly built, undermining the conversation. He rocked his tiny head back and forth, mouth wagging open.

"Uh oh, Momma," Terrence said. "Looks like he's hungry."

"He's breathing, so he must be hungry. Let me nurse him real quick, and we can take him home to bed. Emma, do you mind if I use your room to not make it super awkward for us all?"

"Sure," Emma replied.

When Ronnie came back down the stairs, Josiah was already snoozing in her arms, milk drunk. Ronnie tucked him into his car seat.

"It was nice to meet you, Drew," she said after slipping on her coat.

"Yeah, man, nice to meet you," Terrence echoed.

"Thanks. Glad to meet both of you." Drew shook Terrence's hand once more.

Emma pressed her palm to the door as she closed it behind them, her chest swelling with reckless elation. The smile stretched at her cheeks as a portion of the hole in her stomach contracted, making her a little less empty, a little less consumed. In that brief victory, she nearly felt normal. She tried to temper her grin before facing Drew.

His face reflected hers. Without contemplation, Emma simply walked forward and plunged into him. She wrapped her arms around his neck and dove into his kiss. He reacted fiercely, reciprocating the hunger in her touch. She paused and pulled away from him to catch her breath and guide him upstairs.

***

"Tell me what you think," Emma said to Ronnie the next day.

Ronnie sat at one of the tables at Happy Beans to synchronize with Emma's break. She held a steaming cup of decaffeinated tea in one hand and a bobbling Josiah in the other.

"I liked him." Ronnie looked down briefly and set down her cup.

"But?"

"But I don't think he's over his divorce. He called his ex his wife. He's focused on superficial pursuits to find meaning for himself. I think he's still floundering and recovering, which is fine and completely natural, but I worry that means he isn't quite ready for what you want."

"Ugh, I don't want to hear that. I really like him. I had this feeling last night that this could work."

"So you slept with him."

"Yeah."

"Hey, I could be wrong. I only had dinner with the man."

"You're never wrong."

"This is true, although there's a first time for everything. Don't let my judgement sway you. Just be cautious. Keep it in mind."

"As if I could keep anything else in mind right now."

Emma's chest deflated beneath her. She worried that Ronnie could visibly see her shrink back down into the darkness as the weight of the depression spread over her again. She had wanted Ronnie to tell her how amazing she thought Drew was, how he was not a douchebag, how he would work out great for Emma.

It's only her opinion. She doesn't know him. It could still work. He could still be the guy. What does Ronnie know?

She already felt the doubt beginning to coil around her heart, felt it infiltrating and poisoning the edges of her thoughts.

When Drew arrived at her house after her shift, she stripped off her coffee stained uniform and pulled herself on top of him as if she had not talked to Ronnie at all.

***

Two weeks later, Emma rested her head on Drew's swollen pecs as they reclined on his couch. The weight of sleep was pressing on her forehead, making her eyelids heavier. She had already worked six shifts in the first four days of the week, only sneaking a handful of hours in her bed. Her body was weary, her cells chanted in sedative unison. She tried to concentrate on how nice it was to bask in his attention rather than how comfortable she was laying against him, how easily she could slip off to sleep on him.

"So I was thinking," Drew started, rousing her from the edge of her subconscious. "My family is having this big barbecue. They do it every year. Kind of like a family reunion, more a party for my grandparents' anniversary. Do you want to come with me?"

Emma tried to conceal the fact that she had stopped breathing.

The family. The next step.

She restrained the smile threatening to break across her face and instead restrained her lips pleasantly. "I would love to."

"It's next month. Do you think you could get off all of your jobs?"

"Yeah, with that much notice, should be no problem. Just let me know the date and the time."

"Awesome!" Drew pressed his hand a little tighter on her shoulder.

"That's great that your family gets together every year like that."

"Yeah, they stay pretty close. There always some sort of drama, of course. Usually my alcoholic cousin. Or my aunt fighting very publicly with her third husband, assuming she's still married to the guy. Crap, I'm making us sound all ghetto."

Emma giggled. "No. Well, maybe a little. All families are drama though."

"It's crazier the more family you have together."

"I imagine."

"Are you close with your family?"

"I'm super close to my mom and my brother. I don't see my dad as often, mostly on holidays. We had a rough time when my parents got divorced and were never close after that. My extended family is far away. My dad's side lives in Massachusetts. Since I don't see him often, I don't see them much either. My mom's side is up in Oregon, but she kind of had a falling out with her sisters."

"Massachusetts and Oregon. How did you end up out here in Colorado?"

"Both my parents came out here for college. My mom went to CU in Boulder, and my dad went to CSU in Fort Collins. They actually met at a football game. After that, the rivalry was always big in our house."

"That's an awesome story. They got divorced?"

"Yeah. I was still in elementary school. My brother was in junior high. My dad cheated, and it was a big neighborhood scandal. I remember them fighting a lot before they finally split, and we moved with my mom."

He doesn't want your ugly mom! She's just a fat dumb slut, and nobody will ever want her again. She's going to die alone. Just like you!

Emma shook the young voice out of her mind.

"Man, that's rough. I'm glad I didn't have kids when I got divorced. My wife wanted kids. I always thought we would have kids together. I wasn't ready right away. I was distracted. And then she wasn't happy, and everything unraveled."

"Yeah, me too. I've thought that a lot actually. I wanted kids. I still want kids. Maybe it was a good thing I didn't have them with my ex."

"Getting divorced is so hard. I'm still trying to figure out how to deal with it. I can't imagine having to do all that while worrying about how it is affecting my kids and trying to figure out who they live with and who gets holidays."

"That definitely would have been harder. I try to remind myself of that. Do you still want kids after getting divorced?"

"I definitely want kids. I could see myself coaching baseball or basketball."

"I could see that too."

Emma closed her eyes and nestled tighter against him, letting the smile fully uncurl across her face.

His family and kids. I think he's the guy.

Something in her flinched at the vulnerability in solidifying the idea, yet such a tranquil warmth bloomed out of the dark hole below her stomach that she refused to fight it, rejected the idea of tempering it.

He was taking her to meet his entire family and he wanted kids. That was all that mattered.

In the echoes of everything Emma wanted to hear, Drew managed to become even more attractive to her. She angled her face up to his and let her hand wander around the back of his neck.

She guided him into her and kissed him deeply, letting her lips part to invite him in. Drew kissed her back, somewhat punctuated, then eased back.

"I'm sorry, babe," he said. "I have a long boot camp session crazy early tomorrow. Do you mind if we crash tonight?"

Emma stumbled over the rejection. It collided with her forehead and sent the blossoming heat retreating back into the darkness inside her. Clenching her teeth, Emma swallowed down the rigid feeling of outrage.

He's tired, and you are falling asleep on him. It's fine. It doesn't mean anything.

"Sure."

She curled up against his muscles and jumped off the edge of her mind into sleep.

***

Another five shifts passed in the next three days. Feeling like the hollow shell of a person, a machine mechanically executing practiced movements, Emma poured the coffee; she picked up the phone; she poured the beers. Repeat. And repeat.

When she pulled up into the parking lot of the restaurant, she cast her eyes up to the rearview mirror to check her appearance. She looked tired. Ronnie and Gladys would say she looked like hell. She smoothed her hands over the top of her hair then fluffed it from underneath. She ran her finger under her lower eyelashes to clean up the settled liner and mascara, blinking several times in an attempt to widen her eyes. Squeezing in time to see

Drew was worth missing a little sleep alone.

She found him already folded into a booth under the neon of the window signs. She grinned at the unsuspecting back of his head. It felt good to have someone to meet, to feel the hints of a future spread out before her.

"Hey there," Emma said as she slid in across from him. "Were you waiting long?"

She reached across the dinner table for his hand. Drew stiffened. His fingers did not entwine hers as she was accustomed to, instead remaining stiff and frozen. Drew did not meet her eyes. His eyes darted around anywhere else to avoid her eye contact. Emma thought of having coffee with Dylan the last time.

"No," he replied, his voice thin and awkward. "I just got here."

Emma retracted her hand and sat up straighter against the back of the booth. "What's wrong, Drew?"

"Um, well...Emma, we need to talk."

Emma's heart seized dead in her chest, the last beat echoing through her now stunned mind. She curled her hands together, wringing them in her lap. She did not want to look up at him.

"Oh yeah? What about?" She knew where *this* conversation went, even as unexpected as it was. She already knew her lines.

"Emma, I don't really know what to say. I don't know how to tell you."

He stopped for a moment, and the silence between them became thick and nauseating. Drew looked anywhere that was not at Emma. She gnawed on her bottom lip and waited to hear it.

"Look, Emma, I like you. I mean you are really awesome, but…"

"But," Emma whispered.

"But I just don't think I'm ready for all this. I thought I was. I really did. I especially thought I was with you. But I don't think I can be in a real relationship right now."

Isn't that what you asked for? Isn't that what you were on Matched.com for? Isn't that what you told me you wanted?

"When we got to the idea of meeting my entire family, it just felt, I don't know…too real."

That was YOUR idea! That was what YOU wanted! Too real? What does that even mean?

The thoughts screamed through Emma's head. She remained quiet in the booth across from his stuttered excuses. Without noticing, she had reached up and wrapped her hand around the steak knife on the table. Unknowingly, she clenched it harder and harder until the color fled from her knuckles and her fist quivered. She steadily started dragging the knife across the table, closer. With the handle pressed into her palm, she pictured herself plunging the blade into his temple. She imagined the tip of the knife piercing his face and disappearing into his skull. She saw blood start to obscure his wide, lying eyes.

Drew looked down at her gradual collection of the weapon and met her eyes to give her a confounded look. Emma took note of the actions of her hand and released the blade.

"I'm sorry, Emma. I really am. I didn't want to hurt you because I'm still wrapped around my wife.

Ex-wife. Please, say something."

"What is there to say?" Emma's voice was soft yet sharp. She cast her eyes hard to stare into Drew's one last time and see what Ronnie saw. Then she imagined plunging the steak knife through his head again. She would drag the blade back out to feel the teeth bounce in another language along the wound. Her hand searched along the table to find the handle again.

A waitress ambled up to their table and loosed a scrap of paper and pen from her black apron. "Hello there. Are you guys ready to order?"

"No," Emma said coldly, staring into Drew. "I was just leaving."

***

Emma had not even bothered to change her clothes after retreating home in defeat, the ones she had spent the better part of half an hour selecting for what she thought would be another date with Drew. She wished she had not invested so much time and care into staging her own dumping.

You're awesome BUT. You're awesome BUT.

The line echoed over and over in her brain until her skull throbbed against her ears. First in Drew's voice, then in a throaty symphony of the procession of other men who had uttered the same cowardly sentiment.

I'm so awesome I'm going to die alone.

Emma wanted to burn her clothes to obliterate the aroma of that cheap diner and the scene it conjured in her mind; she could not bear to part with a pair of jeans that were so flattering. Even if, ultimately, no one would appreciate them. She surrendered to the cradling neoprene of her running tights and sports bra, hoping to forget the composed version of herself.

She slipped on her running shoes, the beaten cushion of the sole contouring around the familiar shape of her foot. She pulled the laces tight until the shoe firmly hugged her socks. Then she plunged her earbuds into her ears and increased the volume until she could no longer hear her own thoughts.

Emma ran past her pace. The first mile vanished without her registering it. She scarcely reconnected with her body until her wheezing breath and throbbing body heat recaptured her attention. She forced a deep breath and dialed back to a more familiar stride.

One, two, breath. One, two, breath.

Her pounding heart served to consolidate her mind. The ravaging, desperate thoughts collapsed into the exertion. She was the run; she was the music beating against her eardrums; she was the anger pumping her thighs faster than her cardio could support.

I'm awesome, but he's a damaged, divorced asshole. I'm awesome, but he doesn't want to have sex with me anymore. I'm awesome, but he's embarrassed to bring me to his huge, happily married family. I'm awesome, but I'm not as good as his wife. Ex-wife! I'm awesome, but he doesn't want me. I'm awesome, but no one wants me.

She scaled the hill ahead of her, stretching her strides longer to abbreviate the pain of the incline.

Her breathing struggled against the gravity pulling her backward. She dug deep into the anger infecting her, wrapped her brain around it, and poured it as fuel over her muscles. She puffed between taut lips and scrunched her face to match her fists.

Emma reached the summit of the hill, the acidic adrenaline pouring over her nerves. She flinched against the burn and stopped to grab her knees. She closed her eyes and let a shriek bellow out from the darkness in her belly, the sound resonating against the houses around her before she realized she had released it.

She glanced around to make sure no one had witnessed her outburst. Then she sprinted home even harder.

CHAPTER 14

Josiah planted his small, fat palms on Emma's coffee table, sidestepping to trace the perimeter of it. Ronnie looked down at her glowing phone and did not seem to notice, yet Emma stared in strange amazement as the child that had been a sleeping blob in her arms now moved across her living room.

"Is he supposed to be walking already?" Emma asked.

Ronnie locked her phone and stowed it in her pocket.

"He's not walking," she said. "He's traveling."

"What's the difference?"

"For it to be walking, he can't hold on to anything. He has to take steps totally on his own. When he is holding onto something, it's called traveling."

"Isn't it too early for that too?"

"Nah, nine months is pretty standard as I understand this milestone bullshit."

"Milestone bullshit. You sound so proud, Momma."

211

"I know. I sound like a horrible mother. You have to remember, I work from home. I saw him do this for the first time. Then every time after. Now I have him traveling all around my chair and over my legs all day long while I'm trying to work. So yeah, it's a little less amazing. So here I am, scrolling social media on my phone while my smart, beautiful baby is doing something adorable, and I look like a neglectful asshole when all I want is fifteen seconds when I don't think about what he's doing."

"Wow. Sorry, I hit a nerve."

Ronnie cackled. "Now I sound like a bitter, resentful housewife."

"I suppose you are arguing you are none of these things."

"I'm either none of them or all of them. And hey, I am not a housewife. I work from home."

"So you're a housewife with another job."

"Pretty much. Maybe I should be a housewife. Terrence keeps saying he'll be a house husband. I only have to make enough money for him to quit his job, and he'll stay home with the kid."

"There you go."

"Doubt I'll be making my salary plus his cushy engineer salary any time soon."

"Yeah, not likely."

"So how is the new job?"

"It's good. Really good."

"Do you think you'll like it?"

"I think so. Mostly because it's the one job instead of three, and it has a normal set schedule where I can have nights and weekends off."

"I bet. That has to be liberating. You might even get to, I don't know, *sleep*. Or have a life."

"I wouldn't even know what to do with either of those."

"I'm sure you will figure it out."

"Speaking of that, I've been thinking." Emma hesitated. "Maybe I should give online dating another try."

"Seriously? I mean, won't you have the time to meet a guy in real life now?"

"Where? At a shitty bar?"

"No. Maybe one of those million races you're always running or your run club."

"Trust me, runners are not there to pick people up, they are there to run. They are thinking about running."

"Well, whatever. Do you want to go back online? Haven't you heard about the Don Juan killer?"

"The what?"

"The Don Juan killer. Do you not watch the news?"

"When the hell would I be watching the news?"

"You use the internet, don't you? Social media?"

"Apparently not enough."

"There's a local serial killer who is knocking off young girls, and the cops think he's using online dating sites to select and lure his victims."

"How have I not heard about this?"

"Because apparently you've been living under a rock since Drew crushed you."

"Ugh. Let's not talk about Drew. Or any of them."

"While you were taking your hiatus or whatever, this guy has been offing girls just like you. Do you actually want to go back and do that all again?"

"I have to. I don't want to be alone. I want a family. The only way to do that is to date."

"And you think online dating is your best approach? Even with a serial killer in the mix?"

"It's the most realistic. And I didn't give it a full try last time. I mean, I answered a good number of messages. I don't even think I told you about all of them."

"You left shit out? Well, hell. Tell me now!"

"These were all while I was dating Drew. I had the stage five clinger."

"Oh yeah? What did he do?"

"We chatted very basically, and he was all over me. Like, I felt like he was picking out our house and china patterns. He messaged me constantly, made me feel like I was the only person he interacted with."

"Scary."

"Yeah. I stopped answering him, and eventually he went away. Then I had a guy who messaged me and didn't want kids. I told him that was a deal breaker and he gave me some story about how the profile must have autopopulated that because he definitely wants kids. So he changed his profile and everything."

"Oh, and I'm sure he meant it."

"I was not buying it. Oh! And I got recruited by a pimp."

"By a what?"

"A pimp. This nice, funny guy starts messaging

me. We talked back and forth for days. I liked him; we seemed to click. Then he started talking about how clients would just love me and how I could make so much money with him. Once I finally figured out he was a pimp and trying to recruit me, I flipped out, and his profile disappeared."

"Oh my God! How shady! That all sounds horrible. Why would you want to do it again?"

"I only went on dates with the first three guys. I thought doing the paid account would eliminate the guys using it as a front for hookups. I mean, why would you pay money to lie? That, apparently, wasn't enough."

"Clearly not with the clinger, the profile chameleon, and the pimp."

"I think I need to go all in and try eCompatible."

"You *have* been thinking about this."

"We both know it's almost all I think about."

"True. So how is eCompatible different?"

"It costs more. It's also more involved. There is like some lengthy personality or compatibility test. Then I think you can only contact people they match you with, and there's some whole long process to that."

"So hopefully all that weeds out the assholes using it as a front for hookups."

"Exactly."

"So back to online dating we go. You cannot get murdered by a serial killer though. Josiah needs his auntie."

"Fine, fine. No murder."

"Are we writing a new profile?"

"No. I won't subject you to that again."

"How am I supposed to live vicariously through you if we don't do it together?"

"Rest assured, I will keep you well informed."

"Good, because my life would be boring without my soap opera updates."

"My dating life is your soap opera. Here for your entertainment."

"You should be flattered that I invest the interest. Consistently."

"Yes. Now I feel so awesome about my life."

"Good. I'm here for you."

"Clearly."

After a few hours of being mesmerized by Josiah's baby tricks and listening to Ronnie both glow in and complain about motherhood, Ronnie and Josiah departed. With an equal mix of seething jealousy and unexpected relief at not being in Ronnie's situation, Emma closed the door behind them, basking in the heavy silence until the hollowness of the house gnawed at her.

She gathered a bar of chocolate from her pantry stash and poured a tall glass of red wine, arranging perfectly on the couch with a heavy blanket and a mindless movie babbling in the background. She curled up with her laptop across her knees as she nibbled on the chocolate and sipped on the wine. The main page of eCompatible reflected against her face mockingly.

Emma took a deep breath and a deeper gulp of wine. Then she depressed the mouse button to create her account.

***

Weeks later, Ronnie showed up on her doorstep with a bottle of wine in each hand.

"I barely recognize you without that tiny human attached to your hip," Emma joked as she let her in.

"Tell me about it, girl, but believe me, I am going to drink to forget that fact."

"Sleeping here then?"

"If only. No, I have to be home for the tiny tyrant. I made Terrence drop me off."

"Clever."

"Why, thank you. Glasses now. Stat!"

"Calm down. I'm sure you won't die."

"I might! Even if by suicide."

Emma laughed and rolled her eyes at Ronnie's morbid theatrics and fetched her the largest wine glass she owned. She chuckled at Ronnie gulping down her first glass.

"This is just sad," Emma said.

"What?"

"I mean, you always chugged your drinks. Now it's just desperate."

"See what having kids will do to you? Maybe it's not always the worst thing that you haven't had them yet. Enjoy being able to leisurely sip wine for pleasure rather than gulping down out of necessity."

"Noted. Enjoying."

"So are we online dating tonight?"

"Look at you, all up in my business."

"As usual. How is the whole eCompatible thing going?"

"Exhausting!"

"Really?"

"It literally took me three hours to complete the

personality test."

"Why? What did it ask you?"

"The same thing, over and over and over again. Worded differently. Asked from the opposite side. Asked again. Then there were all these questions that made me feel horrible about myself. I don't want to think about how I let people walk all over me or how I care what people think or how I'm sad a lot of the time. Or advertise them. I probably spent half of my time agonizing over what kind of person would be matched to my sad little answers. It honestly had me questioning if I even deserved a good match."

"Oh, Jesus. That sounds horrible."

"It was. And after those three hours, I was supposed to set up my profile."

"Wow."

"I couldn't even do it. I was too tired and depressed and feeling awful about myself. I had to sleep before I could put something remotely desirable together. I got that done and out there, and eCompatible started sending me matches."

"Does it work the same as Matched.com?"

"Not at all. On Matched, it does send you matches. Who knows how they even come up with those matches. You saw them. You can search profiles and message or wink at anyone you want. eCompatible doesn't let you do any of that. You can only see the people it matches you with based on this ridiculous personality test. So, I finish the test and create my profile, then the system starts sending me matches."

"Then you message them?"

"No! Dude, I can't even begin to explain this process. Let's see…"

"Wait, take a big drink first."

Emma took a long, slow pull from the glass. "Okay, so I take the three-hour personality test. Then I create my profile. After that, each day eCompatible sends me seven profiles that match what I'm looking for. I can then look at their profiles. If I like them, I send them three multiple-choice questions I pick from some stock list. Like, how many kids do you want? Or what is your idea of a perfect date? Whatever."

"In addition to my daily seven, I might also match what other people are looking for. So I show up in their daily matches, and they send me their own stock questions. I look at their profile. If I like them, I answer their questions and send my own."

"After the stock questions, we send our list of deal breakers, which ten things that we require."

"Wait, what? I am so confused already." Ronnie leaned on her hand. Emma recognized the weight lengthening her face and what it felt like.

"So the deal breakers are things like no racists or I need monogamy or must want kids. The absolute requirements that make or break the relationship."

"Okay, I got it. So you exchange stock questions, then you send these deal breakers. Then what?"

"If you're still interested at this point, you send three open-ended questions. You can either pick from another list or write your own or some combination of that, but the answers are free and open."

"They have to write a little paragraph?"

"Yeah."

"Nice, so you can judge their grammar and intelligence level."

"Of course you would go right there. So, same thing with the open questions. They answer and send their own. At this point, you can message each other only on the eCompatible system."

"Jesus!"

"I know! And I'm not even done. You message back and forth on eCompatible for a while, and there, you can exchange real contact info and take your relationship off the site."

"Man, they really trap you in there forever."

"And you have to remember, this is only the process for one person. I am getting seven matches a day plus questions from whoever I am a match for and is interested."

"Exhausting!"

"Right? It is literally like a second job. I am checking messages on my phone every break. When I get off work I spend at least two hours sorting through matches and answering questions. Thankfully, some guys disappear halfway through the process. Otherwise I might have to stop sleeping again."

"Are you talking to anyone out of this whole mess?"

"I'm talking to like a hundred guys, I think." Emma laughed heartily. "No, I'm somewhere in the questions with a few guys right now. I've gotten all the way to normally messaging with two, and I'm texting with one guy. We're supposed to go on a date this weekend."

"Wow, that only took a month."

"Literally a month."

"That is ridiculous!"

"It really is. Like I said, exhausting."

"It better be worth it."

"Seriously. Otherwise, I might kill someone."

CHAPTER 15

Emma sat at the table at another restaurant, the scene entirely too familiar. Plunging headlong into her eCompatible matches, she had been on so many first dates recently that she did not even want to eat anymore. No more sushi, no more Italian, no more salad, no more bread baskets. No more awkward meals sitting across from men who turned out not to be a match at all.

She attempted to shove down the preemptive disappointment welling inside her while she waited for her date to return from the bathroom. She tried to suppress the pessimism that had blossomed into a poison in her blood, telling herself she had to keep trying, she had to commit enough to ensnare her future. Every time she desperately encouraged herself, the sentiments lost more meaning. Like a word repeated over and over until the sound of it changed. Like she had been exactly here before. A strange tingle of déjà vu edged each lackluster date.

Her fingertips toyed around the cool, condensated edge of her water glass. Then she compulsively lifted it to her mouth, taking nervous sips. The parade of preceding failures danced through her mind, despite how hard she attempted to barricade them back behind her consciousness.

Her first eCompatible date had been potentially the most uninspired and awkward of her increasing experience. Bob had a minimum of ten years on his numerous profile pictures and droned on about his monotonous job the entire meal. He traveled around replacing optometry machines and self-service photo kiosks, which Emma unfortunately learned were the same technology. She also learned that she had maintained the ability to sleep with her eyes open as she once did during her high school classes.

She never responded to another message from him. Even his queries were mind numbing.

Next was Logan. Logan was, in a word, perfect. Upon seeing him, the spark splattered across her nerves, making her skin crawl with sensation. Surprisingly, she found substance beneath his attractive exterior. A gentle sense of humor trailed in his genuine and straight smile. Conversation flowed naturally between them, without requiring pretense, and the hours vanished in a blink rather than raking her slowly over each second.

With him, Emma felt it. She felt the bottom of her attraction fall out for her to plunge into the depth beneath rationality, falling helplessly. Nearly at the same moment, he was gone. Not in a poof, but in a flurry of rampant overthinking to which only she could completely relate.

He was relocating for work, and they had only started seeing each other. He told her how much he liked her but thought they did not know each other well enough to attempt a long distance relationship. The train of thought meandered on through a million possibilities, colliding dead with the end.

Emma did not want to think about it. She took another tense sip of her water.

Logan left a crater in her chest and weakened her resolve. She barely registered the two men who followed him. She only needed to know they were not the one and did not work out either. So here she sat, trying again at a first date, hoping against hope it would actually result in something, anything, else.

The longer Emma sat alone at her table, the more she questioned if she wanted her date to come back at all. It could be better if he used the bathroom as an excuse to slip out the back. That, at least, would be a new experience. No guy had done that to her. Yet. She would probably simply shrug and switch from water to something a bit more potent. Vodka instead of wine. Something that would bite back and take the edge off her reality more quickly.

What is his name again?

She strained to remember.

Rudy? No, not Rudy. Reese? It could be Reese. I'm going to go with Reese. Reese who delivers soda around town and is from Wyoming. With the younger sister who is a barista like I was. Who has six nieces and nephews and can't wait to start a family. Who plays pool competitively in his spare time.

She felt like she was reciting his eCompatible profile. How much of it had did she read, and how much did they actually talk about? Or had he messaged it to her? Was it in one of his questions? What were *his* questions? She struggled, incapable of differentiating the instances of communication, not to mention the numerous other messages from other men she could be confusing into the equation.

If he did not return, she could act parallel to her emotions. She could let the paralytic depression coating her muscles manifest in her actions. She could drop the terse, forced smirk from her face.

A headache bloomed between her eyes, unwrapping spindles of pain that snaked around the curve of her cranium. The more the unpleasant realities disrupted her heart, the heavier the ache became in her skull.

Why am I here? I should go home. Why do I keep trying?

She felt nothing for Reese. She could tell because even now she could not remember what he looked like or what he was wearing. He had made no impression on her beyond her regurgitation of the highlights of his dating profile. She could not have picked him out of a lineup.

I should just go home.

The thought kept playing around her brain, like the lyrics of a song stuck in her head.

If he hasn't left me first.

Again, she hoped that he had removed himself and liberated her. Again came the tug of impulse to hop up, sling her purse over her shoulder, and vanish out the door. That gaping chasm below her stomach, the depressive pit in her center, weighed her down, pinned her to the seat. The duality and entwinement of hope and desperation paralyzed her.

She became utterly dependent on the moment to reveal itself in one direction or the other. She had to know for sure if he was the one.

Reese emerged from the hallway in the back. He grinned at her, and Emma remembered that he was attractive enough. The consistent turmoil receded, disappearing back down into that hole to resurge when she was next alone.

"Sorry," he said as he sat down. "I drink too much water when I'm nervous, and I might have gotten here early."

Emma giggled, pulling her fingers back from her own water glass.

A young waitress bubbled her way up to their table with her pen and small pad already in hand. "Are we both ready to order?" she asked with a pleasant grin.

"We have been," Reese said.

His voice had thinned and become tighter since he apologized about his water drinking. His posture mirrored the change in his voice and he now sat rigidly across from her. Emma squinted and tilted her head at him.

"Um, I will do the Cobb salad please," she said, "with vinaigrette on the side."

"Sounds good," said the waitress. "And for you, sir?"

"I want the steak, but listen closely. I want it medium rare. I mean I want there still to be pink in there. If it's not bleeding a bit, I will send it back. I also want the fries, but I need them to be crispy. If they're not crispy, just bring me a salad with ranch. You got that?"

Emma recognized the tension that now infected the poor waitress's smile. She kept the grin on her face seamlessly. Emma knew how it felt to hold it while gnawing at the soft inside of the cheeks. She knew the waitress was concentrating on pinching the wet flesh between her molars then letting it slip back in order to hold her facial expression steady.

Emma did not hold her facial expression steady. Her mouth fell wide, and her eyes betrayed her disgust. Fire blossomed in her chest and radiated out into her extremities. He could probably see it on her face if he was not busy talking down to the waitress.

As soon as the waitress fled the table, Reese deflated right in front of Emma's eyes, reverting back to the gentler original she had met initially. He grinned widely at her, but now Emma found the sight revolting, all the attraction siphoned from him.

"I think I was telling you about my little niece, Delilah," Reese said.

Emma stared at him blankly. A story that seemed so genuine and enticing when he introduced it now sounded hollow and false, like the forced attempt to sucker a woman who truly wanted children as she did. Everything about him was different after that vile tone to the waitress.

Reese continued to talk; Emma did not hear it.

The waitress returned to their table, balancing the two plates in her hands. Internally, Emma flinched, dreading another interaction between her date and the unfortunate waitress. Once again, Reese stiffened, glaring down at his plate as she placed it before him.

"Can I get you anything else?" the waitress asked. When they produced no requirements, she clasped her hands together. "Enjoy your meal."

"Wait," Reese said. "Let me check this steak before you leave."

Reese cut into the meat slowly and meticulously then spread the flesh with the utensils. He pressed down with his fork and gauged the juices. "Honey, this meat is not bleeding. I told you I wanted medium rare." Reese managed to infuse even more condescension into his voice.

"Sir, that is what our kitchen considers medium rare. The cook checked it twice for me. I can take it back if you like."

Reese looked across at Emma. He *had* to register the revolt in her features.

"No," he said. "This will be fine. Bring me the side salad. These fries are clearly not crispy."

Emma rolled her eyes as the waitress was as she walked away. She had been unrolling her silverware to drape her napkin in her lap then stopped and deliberately placed them on the table beside her salad plate.

"Excuse me," Emma said without looking up. "I'm going to run to the bathroom."

She snagged her purse behind her and secured it over her shoulder. Each step away from the table felt like a relief. She marched very deliberately to the bathroom and placed her palm on the door. Then she looked back over her shoulder. From their table, Reese would not be able to see the front door. She left the restaurant.

Emma spent the next day in a zombiotic trance at

work. Her head was so full it was empty; she felt so overstimulated she was numb. When the distractions fell away, she registered only a revolving parade of all the dating failures now on her roster. Each punctuated with, *Honey, this meat is not bleeding.*

Dylan recoiled, dragging his hand across the table away from hers. *You're really awesome. I like spending time with you. I just don't think I'm in a relationship place right now. I have a lot going on with work and my brother and all that. I don't think I could really commit.*

She thought of how easy it was to talk to Tim, how nice it felt to be held by him. And she thought of his fish tongue flopping between her teeth. *Look, Emma, I would rather you be honest with me. I want to be with someone who truly wants to be with me.*

She saw Jamal's flawless face as he guided her into his bedroom, where the magic happened, and patted the vacant bed beside him. *Why don't you come over here and check out this mattress?*

She thought of Drew inviting her into his future and to meet his family while she lay contentedly on his chest. *Look, Emma, I really like you. I mean you are really awesome, but I just don't think I'm ready for all this. I thought I was. I really did. I especially thought I was with you. But I don't think I can be in a real relationship right now.*

Logan's perfect voice, *I just don't think we've been together long enough to try long distance. I really like you, but I don't see it working. I wish you all the best, Emma.*

She thought of Rick, short and lean, who had

hiked off into obscurity.

She thought of the monotonous torture of Bob's droning about his mind numbing job.

She thought about Reese behaving abhorrently to the waitress. *Honey, this meat is not bleeding.*

And all the other men who disappeared into the faceless, repetitive blur. The ones she had forgotten. The ones she had never even met. In the end, here where she was alone, they all revealed themselves as the same.

She wanted to pick up something heavy and bash it against each of their skulls. She wanted to smash and hit until bone gave way and brain matter leaked out. She wanted the blood to pour down until they became unidentifiable, until they felt the way the ragged edge of her soul felt where the sinking hole in her stomach began.

With the memories echoing in her skull, her head swayed side to side. The thoughts pulsed so strongly she shook her head. Her mind could not wrap around her reality.

It cannot be this hard. It cannot go like this for everyone. No one would get married! People would only get pregnant by accident! Why is it so hard for me? What did I do to deserve all of this? I think I deserve to be happy. I think I deserve someone and a family. Why am I the only one who believes this? It's not fair for it to be this hard.

Her inner monologue raged, yet her tongue swelled with inactivity. She worked silently, tapping values onto the keyboard, reformatting the spreadsheet, avoiding conversation at every opportunity. The longer her molars rested on top of each other, the more it felt like they had fused together.

Maybe it would be better if I never talked to anyone again.

The depression and disappointment permeated every cell, making her heavier by minute ounces. Even her blood flow slowed, uninspired to keep her living. That seductive, strong current in her brain drew her toward sleep; the siren song beckoning her to escape her waking life into the shapeless darkness of twisted dreams.

Unfortunately, she could not sleep at work, and so relentless was Ronnie that she would not be permitted to retreat home either. She could never craft an excuse that would convince her, neither the truth nor any lie she might concoct.

Emma closed out her shift and moved mechanically to her car. The trees and street signs slipped over her windshield. Her eyes processed the moving shapes in front of her and responded accordingly; she did not see a thing. Her brain segregated her functions with autopilot and allowed her to fixate on that deep and welling chasm inside her.

When she walked into her house, she abandoned everything at the front door and dove face-first into the welcoming cushions of her couch. Her consciousness might have abandoned her body before her full weight depressed the fabric. Instantly, the darkness swallowed her, where her mind felt heavier yet her soul felt lighter.

***

Emma woke up to Ronnie's voice as she set her purse and keys on the coffee table, dropping them deliberately. The sound shattered Emma's retreating sleep.

"Did you come home and pass out on the couch?"

The light had dissipated in the house, trailing in gray tones out the windows. She must have been asleep for a chunk of time, though she had both only closed her eyes for an instant and been swimming within her grim mental mirror for years. She struggled to disentangle from the thick and sticky strands of the sleep still cleaving to her perceptions like tar. From Ronnie's expression, it must have outwardly appeared as quite a struggle.

"Oh, honey, was it that bad?" Ronnie asked.

Emma planted her face down in the cushions. "Yes."

"What happened with this one?"

"He was a dick to the waitress."

"Really?"

"Yeah. Like a complete dick. From the start. The first time he talked to her. Dick."

"Oh shit."

"Yeah."

"Great way to earn points with someone who spent decades in customer service."

"Exactly. He was fine before that. Nothing special, no epic spark or anything. He was even kind of cute and endearing about drinking too much water when he was nervous."

"What did you do? Did you awkwardly stick it out in true Emma fashion?"

"No! I left."

"You what?"

"I got up, went to the bathroom, and left."

"You ditched out on him?"

"Yep."

"Seriously? I don't believe it."

"It happened."

"Look at that. Starting to look out for yourself."

"Yeah, well clearly no one else is going to."

"That's what I'm saying! I'm so proud of you!"

"You're proud of me for getting up and walking out on a date without saying a word?"

"I'm sure you said you were going to the bathroom."

"You might be a horrible person."

"I'm definitely a horrible person, and I would have preferred if you'd gone off on him in public, particularly in front of the offended waitress. But baby steps."

Emma laughed out loud, a fraction lighter. At least she was growing as a person by Ronnie's standards, not that it was paying off with anyone else.

"So what's next? Another date? Another break?"

"Those are my only two options, aren't they? I'm not sure."

"What does your head say?"

Emma gestured wildly. "To hell with it! Give up!"

"What does your heart say?"

"Keep trying. You have to find him."

"Polar opposites, as always. What do the guts say? Always go with the guts."

"I don't know what the guts say. Some blend of the two."

"That's not helpful at all."

"Tell me about it. I have another couple dates lined up from eCompatible, neither that I am excited about. I don't know if I should go ahead and try them anyway or say to hell with it."

"Yeah, hard to say. And I can't tell you what to do."

"Can't you? I'm sick of making these decisions that blow up in my face. Wait, haven't you been making my decisions since my divorce?"

"*Guiding*. Guiding your decisions," Ronnie giggled. "Very different."

"Fine. How would you *guide* this decision?"

"Honestly, as me, I would say to hell with it. I would do what I constantly tell you to do: live my life, make myself happy, and hope things ultimately fall into place." Emma rolled her eyes. "However," Ronnie lifted her finger, "as you, knowing you as I do, you will need to go for it. You have to know if one of these guys is the one."

"Damn. You know me too well."

"It's a curse, I know."

"What if I compromise between my heart and my head?"

"How so?"

"What if I went on the dates I already have lined up, then assuming they suck as much as all the others, I let it go for a while? No new contacts, no endless messages and questions."

"Damn eCompatible."

"It's like a full time job! I work all day long then

come home and spend half as many hours combing through matches and asking questions and answering questions and trying to keep guys straight when I message back and forth. The whole time, I just want to quit. I want to give up. By the time I get to the date, there's been so much virtual foreplay I've lost interest in the guy, *if* I can even remember which one he is."

"I think it's a fair compromise. A little bit of both, just like your guts. And you get to quit that eCompatible bullshit."

"Why can't I have a bang buddy turn into my baby daddy?"

"Oh honey, that is an unintended art. Only the most elite of hoochies can pull off such an accidental transition."

"Clearly, I am not that skilled."

"Clearly. You will just have to do it the old-fashioned way."

"The old-fashioned online dating way."

"You know, whatever."

"Two more guys. Two more scheduled dates. I can do this."

"You can do this. After so many, what's two more?"

"Right. What's two more?"

***

The next morning Emma was in her car heading west. Although she was not quite sure where she was headed, she was wearing her running shoes and the mountains were beckoning to her. Trail running would be something new, an additional challenge to distract her and snap her mind firmly back within her flesh.

She picked a park close enough to civilization. She wanted to run, not hike, so she needed to stay in the lower elevations. A challenge was one thing; brutal hills were quite another.

The gravel crunched under her shoes when she stepped out of her vehicle. It felt good to step away from the machine, to retreat from the road and disappear into a slice of wilderness. The park was unfamiliar to her; the trail would forge new paths in her mind and muscle memory. She simply started jogging and followed the line of dirt that carved through the plants.

Trail running did present a new series of challenges. Her mind was continuously engaged. She could not coast as she did street running; she could not rely on the terrain to be even and expected. She was forced to run with her eyes downcast, perpetually gauging and judging the grade and angle of the trail and protruding rocks. The muscles in her calves flexed in new patterns to steady her stride over the varied surface.

All that focus afforded her no time to think, to overanalyze, to lament. Her experience reduced and simplified to not falling over or rolling her ankle. She even forgot to synchronize her breathing with her strides. She only concentrated on making steps against the pull of the grade and proper footfalls among the rocks.

The day was perfect, the weather beautiful. A thin, warm breeze caressed the sweat on her skin.

The sun matched the heat she brewed in her exertion. She forsook her usually blaring music to hear the wind against the leaves and the scrape of her shoes on the trail, finding tranquility in her own panting breaths.

Another sound wafted on the breeze to her. It started faintly, low enough for Emma to think she imagined it amidst the shuffle of her own movements. It persisted and built on itself as she crested a small hill. Mixed in the tones was the gentle trickle of a stream. She dropped out of her run to silence her footsteps and strained her hearing, quietly moving toward the stream.

The sound rang out again, and Emma's guts flinched. She could not identify the noise; it was completely alien to her, but her body knew to be alarmed. She thought it was an animal, the way the yelp was not contorted or contained into anything that resembled a word. It was forced, strangled. And desperate. It was the desperation that reverberated in her and set her nerves on edge.

Your dad is my daddy now. He doesn't want your stupid mom anymore.

Emma heard Jeremy Davies's child voice again climb out of the back of her brain. Her heart stopped beating.

She's just a fat dumb slut, and nobody will ever want her again.

She's going to die alone. Just like you!

Why did she keep hearing him? Why did his stupid, immature insults keep surfacing in her mind at random times? He had not graced her thoughts in decades; why did he play at the edges of her brain now?

Another outburst echoed from the rocks and snapped her back to the trail. She wandered off the path in pursuit of the sound, her muscles tense and senses on edge. Each yowl sent a wave of fear blended with curiosity trembling down her skin. She reached the bank of the creek, which had methodically carved its way down between two rock cliffs. The sun peered down into the crevasse, blue sky and spotted clouds peeking through.

Emma caught sight of the antlers first. They moved against the rocks as the wounded deer released another bellowing shriek. The way the deep *baaaaaaa* echoed off the miniature canyon walls made Emma think this was what it must sound like when lambs were slaughtered. The creature must have plummeted from the crest of the cliff. For a deer to not be able to run from an injury, it must have been severe.

Having identified the sound, Emma's anxiety faded. Each time the buck yelled, it became expected. She moved closer until she stood beside the large beast. The deer took notice of her and stared at her calmly with wide eyes. Emma caught her own reflection in the large, dark orbs as she stood intrigued by the injured creature.

She was sure that the buck had broken his back. While he was able to move his head to survey Emma, his legs fell limp from his large trunk, and the hind two contorted at an extreme angle. The buck kept his dark gaze fixed on Emma, blowing heavy breaths out of his nostrils. Then he released one more muted and sad whine.

Emma did not think. She climbed slowly up on the large boulder that had cracked the deer's spine, his large eyes following her. She stood above him and tightly gripped an antler in each hand. She stared back into his gaze and took a deep breath. Then she launched from the boulder. Her fall twisted the deer's neck. It snapped when she landed back on the dirt beside him.

The life receded from the buck's large black eyes.

She stood beside the body of the creature for an instant, running her fingers along the stiff hair on its now contorted neck. She hesitated in puzzlement of herself then hopped back over the creek and jogged steadily back to her car. She did not know what to think; she was surprised to find she was not thinking at all.

In the heat of the sunshine pounding down on her, in the rhythm of the scrape of her strides against the path, her mind tumbled backward, effortlessly sidestepping out of her present.

She smelled the stale, dusty air of the basement in her parents' house in Colorado Springs. The aroma filled her sinuses so potently she felt like she could taste the particles swirling around above her. If she looked toward the window, Emma could see the small pieces of dirt dancing against the sunshine. The concrete and unfinished walls made the sounds of their footsteps and voices echo strangely back at them. Emma always thought it felt like being in a dungeon.

"You might as well just kiss me now, Emma,

because we're going to be family." Jeremy Davies' voice was high and relentless, piercing at her brain and making her neck bristle. She resented her dad for letting him come over to play so often.

Jeremy stood shorter and rounder than Emma, his pale skin flushed in splotches to match his ginger hair. He rocked back and forth on his heels as he talked, swinging his arms, with a sucker stick hanging out of his mouth. The sticky and sugary film drizzled out onto his cheek.

"No we are not, Jeremy! I already have a mom and a dad."

"Yes we are. My momma told me so. She told me your dad is my daddy now. He doesn't want your stupid mom anymore."

"That's a lie, Jeremy!" Emma shouted, pushing him back off his heels. "My daddy would never want your ugly mom!"

"No, he doesn't want your ugly mom! She's just a fat dumb slut, and nobody will ever want her again."

Emma did not want to, but she had started to cry. Hot, angry tears streamed down her cheeks. Her little fists balled up and quivered at her sides.

"You big baby," Jeremy mocked, picking himself up off the floor. "She's going to die alone. Just like you!"

Jeremy's voice died when she silenced him with the pipe. The sound of the impact replaced it, bouncing against the basement walls.

***

Two nights later, Emma wiggled her toes in her heels in the bar parking lot. The familiar thoughts moved over her mind.

What the hell was he thinking? What am I doing?

She scrolled through her phone.

Mark: Hey beautiful, I'm really looking forward to finally meeting you tonight!

Reluctantly, Emma opened her car door and toddled across the cratered parking lot, wobbling on the height of her heels.

CHAPTER 16

The lights of oncoming traffic pierced through the night and into Emma's eyes. She did not see them. She did not see the lines on the road steadily pulsing beside her car. She did not see the gentle curve of the road as it wound downward. She simply navigated, detached. The shifting and bumping in her trunk had gone quiet long enough for doubt to infect her mind.

She had not killed that guy. She could not have. It was merely a very vivid fantasy. He had left her in the parking lot after he said his heart was not in this.

You know, my heart is just not in this.

The anger flared up over her disbelief.

Yeah, I killed him.

Emma steered the car toward home. Something twinged in her guts, telling her that she should not go there, that she should run, that she should drive and keep driving until Mark had decayed down to a pile of bones in her trunk. She allowed her mind to veto her instincts. She could not up and run without

242

preparing. She would not get far enough for Mark to even begin to stink.

The key is not to panic. That is how you get caught. If you panic, you get caught. He had it coming. Now you just need to calm down and get away with it. Think. Think fast but think.

She took a deep inhale through her nose until the crispness of the air made her nostrils tingle. The metallic odor of the blood covering her sent ripples over her senses. She let the breath, warmed by her heat, spiral out of her lips. Her chest deflated, her shoulders slumping as she released an iota of her tension along with the breath.

On the darkness of the highway, Emma was alone, encapsulated in the black. In the silence, she could forget to classify her victim as company. When she abandoned the speed and the isolation of the lanes and the streetlights invaded her capsule, the muscles in her back gnarled up and curled toward her spine. She gripped the steering wheel tightly, her palms slipping in the blood still wet on her hands.

She perched on the top of her pelvis, hugging the steering wheel the way her aging mother did. The road assaulted her through the windshield at such a harsh angle. Her breathing became tight and restricted, her heart pounded in her ears, her eyes stretched wide. Every nerve under her flesh arched into high alert and overstimulation.

When the garage door rumbled down over her and stopped with a thud on the cement, a layer of fear uncoiled from around her heart. She had made it home; she was hidden within her garage. She breathed out heavily and sat, still clutching the steering wheel, until the light clicked off. She even sat frozen and paralyzed for a few long moments in the darkness.

If I don't step out of the car, it's not real. If I don't open the trunk, I can't know that he's actually dead. Right now, he's that cat in the box that is both alive and dead. If I stay here forever, he's both alive and dead, and I am both guilty and innocent. Or if I leave the car running, I die with him. Ronnie would probably be the one to find us when I didn't answer for a couple of days. She would probably have Josiah with her. She would find this moron in my trunk and would not even be surprised. Am I even surprised?

She reached down and flipped off the ignition. She was not going to die for this random guy, just like she was not going to die for Justin. Once again, she was going to figure it out, reinvent herself, and find a way to deal with her new and unexpected circumstances.

The sound of her heels against the floor echoed through the dark as she fumbled along the edge of her car and splayed her hands out in the darkness until she found the light switch. She mentally inventoried additional locations she would need to bleach out his blood. Everything she touched, every single thing she came in contact with since the punch.

She slipped her heels off and abandoned them beside the door into her house. She would be so sad to see them go. They were one of her favorite pairs—tall, red, and striking. The concrete bit coldly at the soles of her feet as she reluctantly moved back toward the still cooling vehicle.

The garage was largely vacant. Most of Justin's possessions had occupied the garage. The house was predominantly unchanged from when he left. The garage was where his absence was visible. Perhaps that was why Emma had forsaken the space completely after he left. She had not depressed the garage door opener since his departure, parking in the driveway even in the snow. She did not want to see the emptiness inside her.

In the far corner, sheets of drywall leaned against the wall. Tools, folded strips of plastic, and other supplies heaped in a haphazard pile of true Justin style. Emma would have almost found comfort in the idea that Justin abandoned the remodeling project because he left, but the home improvement accoutrement had resided forgotten in the corner even before his infidelity was born.

Justin never committed to anything.

More rage blazed up from that aching hole at Emma's center. It was Justin's fault. It was all his fault that she was here.

Why couldn't he have just loved me? Why couldn't I have just been good enough? Why couldn't we have just had a family and been happy and normal? Instead, he's having sex with some bikini-clad cocktail waitress, and I'm about to dismember my date.

Emma moved toward the trunk with purpose, fueled by the heat brewing in her belly. She noted all the blood smeared over the rear of the car and took mental notes on what to clean. She pressed the trunk release button and the lid slowly ascended.

Mark appeared as a puddle of bloodied flesh, his mess of limbs collapsed flat. His mouth hung ajar, relinquished by lax facial muscles. One arm fell across his face, obstructing his remaining eye. Was he dead? He looked dead. Emma leaned in deeply, bringing her ear beside his body.

A shallow rasp crept up to her.

Of course, he's alive. No one dies from keys to the eye.

She stood up out of the trunk, tiptoeing her way across the cold garage floor. The cement was so chilled it felt wet beneath her toes. She took elongated strides to leap her way to the supplies in the corner. She grabbed the stack of plastic sheets and spread them out over the length of the garage floor. The thin layer of plastic managed to dull the cold slightly. She coated every inch of the floor in the opaque layer, including behind the trunk of her car.

When satisfied that she had accounted for every scrap of floor, she walked around to the trunk to heave Mark out. She loomed over his body, puzzling for a moment. It had been difficult enough to tip him into the trunk in the first place, with gravity on her side. The prospect of dragging him out seemed far more daunting.

If I'm going to kill someone, I'm going to have to figure out how to manage the body.

As the thought wandered calmly over her mind, Emma managed the perspective that she might need to be worried that she was so calm and nonchalant in the situation. In merely the course of this one evening, only since the assault with her keys, her mind began to feel foreign to her. Through the chaos, she managed to note her thoughts forming in unfamiliar patterns and her emotions responding unexpectedly. She did not have the time to be concerned, so she could only register both how different and how natural it all felt.

She reached in and grasped Mark's ankles, tugging them awkwardly up and out of the trunk. His legs dangled limply over her bumper, shoes swaying gently as she jostled him. She pulled his feet downward and let her grip climb his pant legs, guiding his lower body out, again relying on gravity to do the work. When his hips crested the bumper, his body plummeted in kind. Emma groped to slow his descent. Mark crumpled in a sickening squash onto the floor.

Man, I'm glad I put the drop plastic everywhere.

Mark's body collapsed unnaturally. He piled on top of his own bent legs, his arms draped awkwardly over his torso. Although a muffled moan spilled from his mouth onto the concrete, he still did not move.

"Fuck," Emma breathed. "I guess I'm committed."

She moved over to the tools and retrieved a hammer from the top of the pile. She tested the heft in her hands, bouncing the murder weapon in her palm. Suddenly, everything felt more deliberate.

She took a deep breath and brought the hammer into the back of Mark's skull. The crack echoed against the garage walls, and something about the noise sounded familiar and comfortable to her. A jolt of unmatched excitement rocked her. She sneered broadly and happily when she brought the hammer down once more.

When she stopped, Emma listened. There was no rasp, no groan. Only silence. She pushed his shoulder to unearth his face from below his now dented skull. Emma had never seen a dead body before. When she laid eyes on what remained of Mark now, she did not need to check a pulse to know he was gone. His lone eye sat disturbingly wide and unfixed, appearing milky in its flatness.

Emma thought of the deer.

She suspected regret and guilt should be swelling over her chest, yet the emotions surging through her at the sight of her victim were unexpected, uncharted.

I did this.

It was power behind those words, pride. Not shame.

I am capable of ending someone's life.

The smile was wholly inappropriate on her lips, but she could not deny how naturally it appeared. She was relieved that no one was here to witness her giddy confrontation with her sin. She reached up with her bloody hand and forcibly wiped the devious grin from her face, noting she would need to later scrub that cheek.

Focus. Get rid of the body.

Emma ripped herself from basking in the sight of her dead date. She bent over and wrapped her fingers around both Mark's wrists, his skin already surprisingly alien. Whatever made flesh living and human had bled out of him when the hammer

248

snuffed out what was left. She held tight and leaned back, finding she was no match for his body weight. Her grunts bounced off the walls.

She released Mark's wrists and his hands fell, slapping against the plastic. She could not drag him, so she stepped over his heaped body and shoved at him until he splayed onto his back, then she dug her hands under his hips and pushed until he flopped onto his face. She rolled him over and over until he spread out over the space where Justin's car was once parked.

She could never manage the corpse whole. She needed it to be in smaller pieces to be able to transport it.

"Well, Mark," Emma said to the body, "let's see what your heart is really into."

Emma did not have an expert level knowledge in tools. She only knew that a saw would cut through skin, muscle, and bone. It did not have to be neat where he was going.

She moved to strip the bloodied clothes from the corpse. She grasped first at his shirt, contorting his arms in inhuman angles behind his back, attempting to wrench the fabric free. Sweat beaded on her forehead as she struggled. Without his cooperation, undressing him was more challenging than wrangling Josiah into pajamas.

"Screw this," she mumbled. "I'm cutting them off."

Emma fetched a pair of scissors from the kitchen and chopped lines through the fabric, ripping the articles of clothing open and off his body.

To think I would have wanted to strip him for sex

a couple hours ago.

She tugged off his boxers.

Good thing I didn't.

She spread out the now naked body in crucifixion pose and fetched the Sawz-All from the pile of tools, figuring it would not be loud enough to arouse the suspicion of the neighbors through her garage door.

I'll start somewhere simple. The wrist is probably the smallest.

She plugged in the saw and flipped the switch, buzzing it to life in her hand. The vibration of the blade reverberated up her arm. She pressed down into Mark's still cooling flesh and braced it into position. Then, without hesitation, she plunged the wiggling teeth into his skin.

The blade was more motivated than Emma expected. It ate through the wrist ravenously and did not hesitate until it met the bone beneath. Emma grinned again as she held his arm tighter and pushed down harder on the saw. Then the hand fell disconnected onto the plastic, and a new blood pool formed.

The hand looked different separated from the body. More dead and less human. Her brain wanted to tell her it was an intricate and lifelike Halloween decoration. The thought slipped over her consciousness and she had to reach out and poke the still spongy flesh to remind herself that, though cold, it had been part of a person.

A thread of surreality wove through her perception, allowing her brain to wobble along the line of sanity she had always considered hard and rigid. Dancing on the edge now, she appreciated how flexible and fluid it felt, like standing ankle-deep in murky waters.

She wanted to pick up the severed hand, slap it a high-five, and laugh her brains out. She wanted to curl into a ball and weep until she had completely dehydrated herself. She wanted to burst out of her garage and run barefoot in the dark until her feet were bloody stumps. She wanted to call Ronnie and confess. She wanted to drag a blade across her own throat and just end it all.

The humming of the saw in her hand brought her back from the mental precipice and grounded her against the vibration of the nerves in her body. She cackled, the sound startling her as it echoed off the garage walls over the buzz of the saw.

"This is so ridiculous," she whispered. "How did I even get here?"

Justin, she thought again.

"Enough of that bullshit."

She bumped the hand aside, rolling it over itself, and stretched out the nubbed arm. She plunged the blade into the inside of his elbow, cringing at imagining how sensitive that flesh was living. She moved slowly and methodically, first carving down through the skin and muscle, then bearing the teeth of the saw down through the resistant bone. She segmented the body at each joint until it was light, manageable pieces and a cumbersome torso.

A sea of blood had formed beneath her work, spreading out and pooling far across the plastic floor. Emma was kneeling in it when Mark was finally in a pile of pieces.

Exhaustion crept into her body below the adrenaline pumping hard through her system. The task ahead was so utterly daunting. There was just so much Mark to get rid of. Chunks of body, gallons of blood, and everything into which it had come in contact. However, prison loomed as a very undesirable alternative. Though potentially she would have better luck finding her soulmate in a women's super max facility.

She shook her head and pulled her body up from the blood ocean on her garage floor, almost at peace with her focus, shifting now to all the Mark residue splattered around her.

Her phone rang.

The mechanical singing seized her heart in her chest. Her brain forgot the normal, scripted response to such a sound. Her eyes rattled frantically in her head while she desperately scrubbed her hands against her pants and clawed for her phone.

"Hello?" she said, straining for normalcy in her tone.

"Emma? Are you okay? You never texted me after the date!" Ronnie practically yelled into the phone.

"What if the date had gone super well and I was sleeping with the guy right now?"

"Come on, I know you better than that. This Don Juan killer shit and breastfeeding has me all paranoid."

"Relax. I'm fine."

"Wait, why do you sound so funny? Are you in a parking garage or something?"

"No. I'm in my garage."

"What? You haven't been in that garage since the divorce. Why in the hell are you in there?"

"The date did not go well."

"Jesus. How bad did it have to be for you to go in there? Why would you go in there?"

"I guess I'm wallowing little."

"I'm coming over."

"No, Ronnie. I'm fine. I needed to be depressed for a while."

"Are you sure? Are you okay? You sound funny."

"I'm fine. I'm about to head to bed anyway."

"Okay but I'm coming over in the morning."

"No, Ronnie. I'm going to go for a run in the morning. Clear my head. Probably a long one. I will come over for dinner, if that's okay."

"You have me worried, Emma. You don't sound okay."

"Trust me, Ronnie."

"Okay. I'll be texting you in the morning. Goodnight, Emma."

"Goodnight."

With Ronnie's voice fading from her ears, Emma resurfaced to her new reality. Just her and pieces of Mark, alone in her crime.

***

Hours later, Emma climbed behind the wheel of her car, the acidic odor of bleach eating at her nasal cavity. Her eyes burned from the smell and from the weariness lurking beneath all her excitement and agitation. Cool water droplets splashed on her shoulders from the trailing ends of her hair. The dark road in front her wound up and westward.

She reached down and brought the energy drink to her lips, the last addition to her strange midnight shopping trip. It was necessary even as the unnatural taste pooled along her jaw. Her heart did not need aid in perpetually fluttering, but her eyelids did require persuasion to remain ajar.

Daybreak fractured the night above her, the wheels beneath her crunching to the trailhead. Her hiking boots had been so neglected they now felt foreign around her toes, even as the groove of her shape still remained in the sole. She drained the obnoxiously large can into her mouth, stepping out of the car and heading back to her trunk.

She half-expected Mark's one remaining stupid eye to greet her again when she lifted the lid. Instead, what remained of Mark sat in clean and neatly packaged bags. Justin's lack of commitment had rewarded her again when she discovered he had left all of his hiking packs and backpacks alongside hers in the storage closet.

She had lined each bag with a garage bag to prevent leakage. Mark's torso, including his unimpressive penis, was shoved into her tall backpacking bag that she had used all of once before the murder. Then she had played Tetris as she stuffed thighs, feet, hands, and arms in two more large packs. She had gathered up all the bloodied evidence, absorbing the raging pool of blood in some old towels before rolling and folding and tying to trap the mess within the plastic. She removed the battery from Mark's cell phone and wrapped the pieces and his wallet in amongst his dissected clothing. She packed up the clothes and beloved shoes she was wearing, all her cleaning supplies, the cloth lining from her trunk, cramming it all carefully into three more bags. The bags each bulged and threatened their seams.

Six bags will be at least three trips.

She reached into the naked metal trunk and retrieved the headless handle of the shovel she had purchased. She heaved the torso-laden pack onto her back and gathered up the tent bag she emptied and stuffed with crime scene evidence.

Her boots on the trail scraped quietly against the silent dawn. She swung the shovel handle ahead of her in stride, allowing the end to bump along the rock with each step. She would appear like a normal hiker, backpacking out to a campsite with gear, a tent, and a walking stick.

She leaned forward against gravity and against the weight of this portion of Mark, climbing the grave altitude of the mountain path. She trudged for close to an hour, until the sun climbed out from behind the eastern edge, then she departed the trail. She wandered through scrubby grass, unearthed boulders, and towering trees until the trail was a distant memory.

She halted to scan the entire circumference around her. Satisfied she was completely alone, she dropped her bags. Mark's torso landed with a thud. He was heavy.

I should have frozen him and sent him through wood chipper, Emma mused. *That was always my favorite method in all my shows. Might have been suspicious to buy a body-sized freezer and a wood chipper though.*

Emma retrieved the spade of the shovel from the bag and reattached it to its handle. Then she began digging. She plunged the tip of the shovel into the dirt, shifted the pile aside, then repeated the action. Again. And again. And again. The hole grew deeper with each scoop, and the movement became tranquil and rhythmic. Emma disappeared into the steady sound of scrape and dump and the gentle rotation of her waist. Under the casual morning sun and a kind breeze, digging was decidedly relaxing.

She retrieved her water bottle from the pack then deposited both bags beneath the earth, falling into the equally enthralling pattern of burying the evidence. She covered the bags with the displaced dirt and meticulously smoothed and stomped it, swirling pine needles and branches over it until it was indistinguishable.

With the shovel blade in her waistband and water bottle in hand like any normal hiker, Emma hurried back to her car. She loaded her shoulders with another backpack and another repurposed tent bag, secretly hoping some homeless person had found all the tents she had deposited in the dumpster a few miles from the supercenter. If there were surveillance cameras everywhere, she wanted to create more dots to find and connect. Then she took a divergent branch of the trail and wandered off at a completely different point.

By the time she cracked her trunk once more, hunger nibbled harshly at her stomach. Again, the physical exhaustion crept up beneath her purpose. She shoved some protein bars and a fresh water bottle into the outer pockets of the last backpack and loaded down with the remaining bags. The other vehicles joining hers in the parking lot pressed her motivation to finish her work.

The sun climbed high in the clear sky above her, and Emma felt the weight of her last trip. Her legs whined at each step, reluctant to continue climbing up this mountain for a third time by a different route. She did not want to continue on. She wanted to go curl up on her couch and sleep until she did not remember any of the previous night had happened.

The broader light made Emma edgy. More hikers would be joining her on the mountain as the day wiled on. She was honestly surprised she had not encountered anyone. All her posturing and preparation to appear innocuous had, so far, been unnecessary. Only the birds passing slowly above had been around to witness her careful disposal.

"Emma?"

The sound of her own name seized Emma in a startle. She had not seen a person, not heard a sound aside from her own on her trek through the long morning. She whirled around and let her mouth dangle wide in shock and fear.

She noticed the dog first. Bruno had gotten bigger over the months, sprawling out into his own flesh and making gains on his once floppy paws. He recognized her, his tongue spilling out from his jowls in a doggy grin, tail whipping rapidly behind him.

"It is you," he said. "Rick. Remember?"

Holy shit.

"Yes!" Emma forced out, pushing a smile through her anxiety. "Rick, how are you?"

"No complaints. Bruno and I are out here as usual. Still hiking every weekend and working on those 14ers. I see you followed through on hiking more."

"I did," Emma almost laughed. "I've been recently…motivated."

"That's awesome. It's so nice to just be outside. I like to hike, just me and Bruno, so I can shake all the thoughts loose in my head. You look great, by the way."

"Thank you."

"Hey, I'm sorry I never messaged you again. I, uh…"

"Don't worry about it, Rick."

Don't say you were awesome but. I don't want to hear you're awesome but. I don't want to hear any of it. I don't have any more backpacks to put you in.

"Are you seeing anyone?"

"Yeah, I am," Emma lied. "Relatively new. I think it has a chance."

"Good. I'm glad to hear that."

"You?"

"Yeah. I actually got engaged recently. To my yoga instructor."

You have got to be fucking kidding me.

"Oh congratulations." Emma's voice fell flat despite her best efforts.

Bruno circled around Emma enthusiastically, letting his nose find her backpack. Once he caught the scent of the contents, his tail went wild, and he buried his snout aggressively against the canvas, bumping so hard he rocked Emma.

"Whoa," Rick laughed. "What do you have in there?"

Heat flushed her face and she was thankful for the direct sunlight and exertion of hiking to blame it on. She gritted her teeth and contorted her facial features into normalcy. "I packed a pretty intense lunch. Spoiling myself today. I am planning to bust it out when I get to the top. I should probably get going. I'm starving."

"Yeah, us too. We're headed back down." Rick paused. "Emma, it was really good to see you. Good luck with your new relationship. I'm so glad to hear you found someone."

"You too, Rick. Bye, Bruno."

Emma spun on her heels quickly to distance herself from Bruno's incessant sniffing. Her heart throbbed so hard she could scarcely see past it. She took long, exaggerated strides without looking back to hide the terror that must have been painted over her entire face. Her pace infused with panic as she marched up once more.

The last hole took longer to dig, a seeming eternity measured by the metronome pattern of scooping and piling.

When she tapped the blade on the closed hole, gauged it from a distance, it was done.

Mark was gone.

Emma dropped to the dirt over the final two bags in a heap, finally collapsing. She found some strange comfort in knowing part of her victim was packed into the earth below her. It felt appropriate to lay Mark to rest this way.

How much do you like hiking now, Mark?

She took a deep breath in, sucking in the thin, piney flavor of the mountain air, then leisurely ate her snack perched atop her potential success.

She came back to the trail with the shovel head once again stowed beneath her shirt, carrying the light weight of only her walking stick and her nearly drained water bottle. Her relief also lightened her. Unencumbered by incriminating bags, she felt like she could float back down the trail and fly home.

The day came full circle. The light waning from the sky, Emma returned to the city, parked in the driveway, and shuffled into her house, hoping to steal a nap before Ronnie would be beating down her door to check on her again. She had earned a nap.

***

"She lives!" Ronnie cried as she opened the door for Emma. "She doesn't answer her damn phone for half the day, but she lives."

"I told you I'm sorry. I went for a hike. A long hike."

"You told me you were going for a run. You haven't hiked in years."

"Yeah, I changed my mind. I needed something different."

"Fine. Come in. Terrence is almost done cooking."

"Thank God. If it was up to you, we would be ordering pizza again."

"Hey, you've known what this was for years. I don't cook."

"Hey, Eminem!" Terrence called from the kitchen. "I'm so glad you're here. Ronnie has been driving me crazy worrying about you since last night. Don Juan killer this, dead Emma that."

"I'm sure," Emma giggled. "Where's Josiah?"

"Napping," Ronnie answered. "He needed it. That boy is nonstop."

"That's my little man!" Terrence called. "Food's up!"

The three filled their plates and brought them to the table to dine.

"This has been more than enough suspense," Ronnie said between bites. "Tell us about this nightmare date."

Emma set down her fork and took a deep breath. "He lives down in Colorado Springs, so we decided to meet in the middle. He picked this awful dive bar right by the highway. I mean it is *horrible*, worse than the place we used to go when we were kids. So he gets there, and we decide the place is awful and pick a new place to go. I go to the bathroom, then we head to the parking lot to go to the new restaurant. All of a sudden, he up and tells me his heart is not in it, and that's it. That's the end of the date. He went home. He fucking went home."

Then I punched my keys through his eye and bashed his head in in my garage.

"Seriously?" Ronnie gaped. "His heart was not in it? What does that even mean?"

261

"Right? I have no idea."

"Baby, what does that mean?" Ronnie asked Terrence.

"I don't know. I've never said some bullshit like that."

"How did you not kill this guy?" Ronnie asked.

Emma wanted to laugh out loud. She wanted to slam her hands down on the table, shaking the plates, and chuckle until her sides split.

"I came home," Emma said, adopting a familiar and depressive tone. "I didn't even know what to do, how to feel. I think I was in shock maybe? I came home and went into the garage. It probably made it worse. It just felt right. It felt full circle to be reminded of where all this started. With Justin. So I stayed in there and cried, then I went to bed and got up and went for a hike this morning."

Hearing the depressive narrative that used to be her reality made Emma sick. How could she have sadly gone through it all before? How could she have done nothing but cried and felt sorry for herself? A smack of disgust at her former self filled her mouth, her self of two whole days ago.

"So what now?" Ronnie asked.

"Maybe you should change teams," Terrence chimed in.

Ronnie giggled and nudged him. "Shut up."

"You two should experiment together. I would be there as, you know, the control group."

"Silence, you," Ronnie laughed again. "Seriously, now what?"

"I'm done. I am *so* done."

"Like done done?"

"Yes. No more of this online dating, no more trying. I am going to focus on myself and try not to be miserable. The price is just too high for all this."

"I think that's a good idea, Em," Terrence said, chewing. "The rest will come, right?"

CHAPTER 17

Emma dissolved in the throbbing crowd of other runners, the seething mass of bodies shuttled into the start chute like cattle. She bounced between her running shoes, hopping her weight back and forth in an attempt to maintain a smoldering heat and steady blood flow against the cold edge on the air.

The pre-race excitement rolled through her in waves. Her heart pressed up against her ribs, her muscles itching frantically in anticipation. Although she tried to force the energy out through the soles of her shoes as she bounced, it continued to well under her face. Trapped in the cluster of bodies, the last minutes before the start sound dragged endlessly.

Then eternity crazed into the present and the loud beep rippled through the air. The crowd took a collective gasp and leaped toward the start line. The road became a steady stream of bobbing heads, the thunder of rubber on asphalt echoing through the morning.

Emma grounded her breathing into a rhythm timed to her footfalls.

Stride, stride, breath. Stride, stride, breath.

Months had passed since Mark. Emma had obsessively followed the news for weeks, glued to inane local TV coverage, scrolling through anything on the internet. She even frequented Mark's MyBook page, knowing in the back of her mind that her visits could be tracked online. If quizzes could tell you how many people viewed your profile, the cops could ascertain the same.

Nothing. Not even a post from a friend asking to hang out or a stupid meme with a cat on it. No news on his disappearance, only the occasional speculation about the Don Juan killer. Emma had existed in suspended animation, poised in panic as she went through the motions each day, waiting for blue-clad officers to take her away.

The ground beneath her disappeared from her perception when the second mile marker slid past her. Her body harmonized to the rhythm of her run, comforting in its monotony. After two miles, her body accepted that she was not going to stop and ceased throwing up flares of burning muscles or lungs to dissuade her. She disconnected from her flesh and existed behind it, tucked somewhere her mind could wander and trapped thoughts wriggled free.

Mark was always on her mind, the way a new and torrid lover would be. She would feel the impact of her barbed fist impaling his face reverberate up her arm; hear the wet flop of a body part falling away from the whole and onto the plastic; taste the mountain air palpable with relief after the final fraction of evidence was buried.

Her mind always circled back to that day. Each detail was branded deep into her brain, burned beyond her memory into her personality, infusing every experience after. She could not move on, and every day after felt like a hollow echo or lackluster chorus.

Stride, stride, breath. Stride, stride, breath.

The pack had thinned and spread over the route, clumping into groups of similar pace. As the fifth and sixth mile fell behind them, the sprinters began to slow, the hares walking in intervals among the steady march of the tortoises. Emma committed to her pace, devoted to a level speed, unaffected by grade or distance. Running became mindless in its consistency, liberating in its steady detachment.

The float crept up out of her warm and cycling muscles, climbing the nerves in her limbs, bumping up each rib, levitating into her consciousness to separate her perception from flesh. Her legs pumped, her lungs breathed at their measured inhales, her brain no longer required to cue or monitor them. Her body jogged on like an automatic machine, her mind released into the wild beyond her skin.

The sound of her breathing overlay the rhythmic clomp of her shoes and those of her fellow runners striking the pavement, embodying the scene with its own sense of life, as if her breath belonged to the day and the footfalls were its heartbeat.

Her eyes rolled back and forth behind her sunglasses. The vivid Colorado sun poured over the course and beckoned the heat already brewing in her belly. The colors around her amplified in her throbbing euphoria, the blue of the sky bleeding down on her, the red of the towering rocks humming.

She rode the float with practiced experience, savoring every second when running did not feel like work, knowing her wall awaited her. Her mind harmonized with the run; her endorphin level spiked, and the lightening sensation of bliss tingled over her.

And she thought of plunging her keys into Mark's eye.

The dumb look of shock on his face.

The hammer cracking his skull.

And she thought of eating a granola bar sweaty and relieved on top of his buried remains.

The flashes amplified her tranquility. She rode that justified freedom in giving him what he deserved, until her anxiety forced itself up around the peace and her heart stiffened in her chest.

No, her voice of reason called. *It was a mistake. It was not the best decision of your life. It was not a great moment. It was a huge mistake that could still land you in prison or on the lethal injection table. You don't get to smile about it. You don't get to remember it fondly. You did a horrible thing. You murdered an innocent man.*

Was he innocent? her own mind countered. *Was he innocent when he told me his heart wasn't in it to go have sex with some ex or tell his friends what a stupid bitch he had met at a dive bar? He had it coming. He deserved it. They all do. They all lie or cheat or leave.*

While the thoughts rang true against her bones,

Emma's breathing had quickened and she had leaned into a harder pace without noticing. Auto pilot became angry, and the heat rose out of her chest to bloom in her face.

She's just a fat dumb slut, and nobody will ever want her again, she heard him again.

She's going to die alone. Just like you! That small voice echoing against her skull. The sound of it inside her head made her cringe and shake it aside.

He deserved it.

The idea pounded like a mantra in her brain as the miles vanished behind her.

And I liked it.

The last forbidden thought slipped across her brain right before she sprinted to her brink across the finish line. She forgot she had felt it at all as she dry heaved past the red, blinking clock and flagged banner.

***

After a long shower of muddled, conflicting thoughts, Emma composed herself to meet Gladys for lunch.

"Eminem!" Gladys shouted across the restaurant when she spotted Emma.

The smile on Gladys's face threatened to crack her cheeks. Emma was warmed and relaxed by the genuine reception. She hurried to the table and dove into Gladys's warm, soft, firm hug. She clung to her even an extra second after Gladys released her clutch.

"You look amazing, darling," Gladys said, her fingertips lingering on Emma's shoulders as she looked her over. "Have you still been running yourself to death?"

"Of course. I just did a half marathon this morning. I also did some rigorous hiking recently."

"It shows, honey. You look much happier and more rested than at Happy Beans too. How is the new job treating you?"

"I like it. It's boring, actually, which is nice. I go in, put in my hours, and go home. I actually have time to sleep and maybe think about having a life."

"That's great to hear. We miss you though. Those twins are about lost without you."

"Those twins were lost *with* me."

"Fair enough. Well, I miss you. My mornings are not the same without your face."

"I'm sure they replaced me."

"Yes. With two largely worthless little twits."

"Aww, thanks, Gladys."

"How's Ronnie?"

"She's good, the same as she always is."

"Been keeping that little baby alive?"

"Yeah, she bitches a lot, but she does well. Josiah is adorable."

"How about the dating quest? It's been a while since I got an update on the saga."

Emma's face fell.

"That's not good," Gladys said. "Tell me. Vent to me, honey."

Emma rubbed her thumbs over her brow and took a deep breath. "Yeah, not good." The words felt heavy in her mouth, pressing down on her teeth.

"I went all in and did the whole eCompatible thing, which meant hours of personality tests then hours of matches and hours of questions and hours of messaging. It would seriously take weeks to get to emailing a guy to set up a date. I went on some dates. Most were awful, including a guy who was a complete dick to the waitress."

"Oh no!"

"Oh yes. I walked out on him."

"Good for you!"

"One guy was awesome. I thought he was the one. We just clicked, and I was into him, and he didn't poof or become some douchebag. Then he had to move for work, and he couldn't get his head around trying a long distance relationship so early on, so we ended it. He even ended it well. He was completely honest with me, no bullshit."

"Ouch."

"Very much so. You would have liked him, Gladys."

"I'm sure."

"So he was gone. I told myself that he should give me hope because I found a decent guy. Though it didn't work out for other reasons, I knew they existed and were still out there. So I kept trying. I got burned out and decided I would try the last few dates I had lined up then call it."

"Fair enough."

"My last date was horrible."

Emma wanted to tell Gladys what had actually happened to Mark. Exactly like she wanted to scream *murder* into the phone when Ronnie interrupted her cleanup. Her crime isolated her from her support system. Confessing to the women she told everything was too risky for her. And for them. Ronnie might have been able to understand. She probably would have shouldered a backpack and helped Emma dig, but Gladys would never be able to look at Emma the same with murder painted across her face. She would probably contribute an anonymous tip to the cops, for Emma's own good.

"Tell me, sugar," Gladys encouraged.

"We met at this shitty little bar. We decided the place was awful and spent a beer finding a new restaurant to go to. I went to the bathroom, and we headed to the parking lot to drive to the new place. In the parking lot, he told me his heart was not in it and left."

Left this world.

"What? What happened while you were in the bathroom?"

"I have no idea. Ronnie thinks he got a text from an ex or a booty call."

"Ah, yes, that would make sense."

"It was awful. 'My heart's not in this.' That one might have been worse than 'you're awesome but.' It's hard to tell."

"I'm so sorry, Em."

"I just don't know what I'm doing wrong. I don't know what's wrong with me that this keeps happening. I mean, I'm the common denominator, right? Something has to be wrong with me, right?"

Hot tears burned at her eyelashes, the rage climbing her chest and knocking against her breastbone.

"No, honey, no." Gladys's tone fell smooth and

thick. "This is just people. This is just dating. None of us know what we're doing. None of us really know what we want and would not know it if it walked up and introduced itself. If we do end up with the right one, it's ultimately the luck of unknowingly making the right decisions. Your life will go its way. You have to enjoy the ride."

"So what do I do?"

"Emma, you need to find things that make you happy, and accept that those things might not be being in a relationship or having a family. I'm not saying those things won't happen, but they might not happen now. There is no reason to stay miserable while you wait."

"So you want me to just let it go."

"Yes, honey. Let it go. Find yourself and be you. The rest will fall into place."

But I'm a murderer...

"I'm starting to feel like I don't know who I am anymore. Like maybe I never did."

"That's okay, sugar. Most of us spend our whole lives figuring that out. You're still only a baby. Trust me. Like I said, the rest will come."

***

The night had begun to reach up into the fading day when Gladys and Emma hugged outside the restaurant. Again, Emma did not want to let go. She wanted to embed herself into the comforting warmth of Gladys's embrace. The air felt all the colder when she did release and walked back to her car clutching her own arms.

She could not go home. She could not face the dark and the silence and the strange allure that now radiated from the garage. The ancient enticement of the fluorescent signs in the bar window beckoned from the road and she turned into the parking lot instead.

The alcohol paraded onto her taste buds with crushing intensity, causing her to squint one eye as she sipped from the straw. She highly doubted there was any soda in her drink. If there was, the ratio was terribly miscalculated, or she had lost her talent and practice for drinking strong drinks fast. That was why people came to a place like this: strong, cheap drinks. Because it was on her way home, that was why Emma was here too.

She forsook her normal practiced posture and collapsed onto her elbows on the wooden bar top, allowing her spine to hunch, and gathered herself closer into a ball around her poignant beverage. A couple of sips in, she already felt the hazing sweep of alcoholic fingers along the back of her forehead. Her nose tingled faintly, alerting her of a foreign substance dancing through her veins. She drank wine with Ronnie plenty, but it had been a long time since she had imbibed with liquor.

She hadn't even bothered to case the bar, not even wasted her time evaluating any prospects in attendance. She fixated on her purpose and kept her eyes trained on the diminishing drink in front of her and her sad, warbled reflection in the mirror behind the liquor bottles. Her reflection's eyes took on their own air, crawling into their own separate being.

The murderer.

Emma felt a strange fracture of consciousness, her nerves grounding her in the barstool, her ears placing her in the tavern. She recognized the reflection in the smeared mirror as her own, yet she saw something divergent in the eyes, something different from the self she defined, yet something she also recognized.

The murderer.

She's a murderer.

I'm a murderer.

Emma ripped her eyes away from the other's and sipped hard until air swirled at the end of her straw.

"It looks like you could use another drink," a voice said from beside her.

Emma hesitantly looked up into hopeful and expectant eyes, which were probably equally intoxicated. The man who had crept onto the barstool beside her appeared to be in her demographic. Plain but clean and neat clothes draped from his shoulders. His symmetrical face registered as attractive enough in the back of Emma's brain. She turned her head and struggled to not roll her eyes. Her reflection failed to control herself.

"I'm Geoffrey," he said, leaning in slightly closer.

"Sarah," she said curtly. She did not know why she spit out a fake name; it seemed like the right decision.

Geoffrey reached out his hand. Emma recoiled, then caught the eyes of the murderer in the mirror again, the eyes with which she did not want to be left alone. She closed her own eyes for an unnoticeable instant and shook Geoffrey's hand.

"Nice to meet you." He smiled. "How about that drink?"

"Sure. I would love a refill."

Geoffrey signaled the bartender and ordered Emma and himself a matching round. Given the look in Geoffrey's eyes, he had been enjoying the bar for a while before coming over to her. He probably had taken some preemptive shots for bravery. His eyelids drooped gently at the edges, and his wide grin hung sloppy at his cheeks. Emma picked up her drink to catch up with him.

"So what brings you into this fine establishment tonight, Sarah?" Geoffrey asked.

"Trying to unwind after a long day."

"You're too pretty to be having a rough day."

Emma noticed her reflection gagging and heaving in the mirror. She cast her gaze down flirtatiously and said, "Thank you."

What was she doing? She could not even fake an orgasm for a guy as wonderful as Tim, yet she was feigning flirtation with some pathetic barfly.

This is called self-destructive behavior. Her reflection laughed in her face. *Why don't you have sex with him then turn yourself in? Murderer.*

She could not drink fast enough. She needed a numbing layer on top of her senses. She needed to see Geoffrey through clouded lenses. Geoffrey was talking about something. She could scarcely hear him over her lack of interest and her straw suckling at the empty base of her glass.

"Wow, you were thirsty!" Geoffrey exclaimed.

"Like I said, long day."

"Would you like another one?" Geoffrey raised his hand to the bartender, who responded with a fresh round.

"You got this one since I bought the last?" Geoffrey asked without making eye contact.

Are you fucking kidding me? Emma's reflection yelled from the mirror. *What a cheap bastard! Won't even pay to get laid.* Her reflection slapped the bar dramatically and spun around on the stool, howling with laughter.

Giggling, she set her cash on the bar top while her reflection rolled her eyes hard enough to sway her hair.

Geoffrey had conveniently not driven himself to the bar, instead taking a preemptive cab. He happily offered to drive Emma home in her car. She noted that he was probably too intoxicated to drive, but she was not going to do it. The world tilted and rocked sideways with each step. She was too drunk. Might as well let this frugal moron take the DUI.

Emma did not know why she was taking him home with her. Though physically acceptable, she found him wholly unenticing. She looked at him through warbled eyes in her driver seat and tried not to wrinkle her nose.

Why am I doing this? Why am I bringing him home with me? This is what self-destruction looks like. What a wonderful victim he would make.

Her thoughts were as drunk as she was, slurring randomly and disjointed through the alcohol in her head.

Then the thought of her empty house and her devious reflection in every mirror swelled up over her brain. She could not look into those eyes and see the version of herself that terrified her. She could not listen to the echoing thoughts of the murderer inside her head. Geoffrey may have been inane and irritating, but such sensations kept her outside of her own head. She could concentrate on not liking him; she could sleep with him to not think about anything.

Geoffrey groped her before the front door was even locked behind them. He grabbed at her sloppily, his drunk kisses coating her lips in his saliva. He tasted like the drinks they had shared at the bar. Her head sloshed too violently for her to care. They wobbled and swayed in their embrace, tripping their tangled way up the stairs. He fumbled her clothes off and tossed her down on the mattress.

***

Hours later, Geoffrey snored naked beside Emma in her bed, greedily wrapping her blanket around himself and leaving her with only the trailing edge of the fabric. Emma lay flat on her back, staring through the blackness to imagine the texture of the ceiling. Her eyes snapped wide as the deafening roar of her brain crowded the empty darkness above her.

She drummed her fingers on her breastbone, trying to ground herself through the sensation, attempting to keep her churning mind contained within her flesh. Sobriety edged on her nerves, carving itself out of the sedation and back to the surface of her skin. With the disorienting weight waning from her brain, the chorus of accusations and doubts only became more deafening.

She felt nothing about the sex, unchanged by his uninspired, clumsy performance. He was cheap even in bed, fumbling over her until he seized for an instant then collapsed. He was satisfied by his own rapid orgasm and clearly gave no thought to her experience. Emma thought this lack of reciprocity should have enraged her, but he did not matter. He did not matter at the bar; he did not matter moving inside her; he did not matter snoring annoyingly beside her.

What mattered was the terrifying detachment blossoming inside her chest and how welcoming and comforting it felt. Emma knew exactly what she wanted, more clearly than she had ever discovered herself before. The clarity resonated from the black base of the hole below her stomach and rang through her entire skeleton like a tuning fork. She recognized what she needed more than when she had foolishly and wholeheartedly thought Justin was her forever.

Geoffrey drew in a sinus rattling breath beside her. She wanted to kill him.

Each time Geoffrey inhaled, Emma saw another way to kill him.

Pillow over his face.

Belt around his neck.

Shoved face first down the stairs.

Hammer to the back of the skull.

Kitchen knife across his throat.

Each morbid vision excited Emma more than any of Geoffrey's fumblings had failed to do. When he had touched her, she felt nothing, only vague annoyance. Yet when she imagined the feeling of forcing his life out of his body, her entire nervous system tingled.

She rolled her head on the pillow to look at the back of his head.

She wanted to kill him.

The mere realization calmed her entire body, silenced her entire mind. Now the only thing she could conceptualize was murdering him.

Geoffrey stirred beside her. Emma slammed her eyes shut and deepened her breath to feign sleep. He did not even look toward her. He sloppily dragged himself from the mattress and lumbered across the dark room toward the bathroom. With his back to her, Emma opened her eyes and sat up. His path meandered and strayed across the carpet, his pale buttocks glowing against the darkness. He was clearly still drunk.

Emma's mind went silent. She was done thinking. She rose noiselessly from the sheets and trailed him stealthily.

Without turning on the light, Geoffrey was unloading his bladder into her toilet.

She hesitated, hidden behind the open door, for a moment. Every fiber, hair, and cell in her body stood on complete edge. She was honed, focused. A strange blend of calm and excitement centered her. It felt natural.

Emma took a deep breath through her nose and closed her eyes, feeling the singularity of her intent draw to a focus in the center of her sight. She burst around the door in one fluid movement, shoving her palms and all her momentum into his bare shoulders. He toppled from his precarious balance at the impact and went cascading into the bathtub. He managed to crane his neck in the arc of his career, and Emma looked into his wild and disbelieving eyes before his skull collided with the tile then bounced down into the faucet.

His head made a sickening and satisfying squash with each impact. The tile produced a heavy thud that reverberated through the dark room, while the faucet edged the sound with the crack of the bones in his face. Geoffrey's body instantly went limp, his entire weight pooled chaotically in the porcelain basin.

Emma stared blankly at her new victim, feeling a placidity radiate through her chest. Placing her bare toes on the tile floor, she carefully stepped toward the bathtub, leaning forward toward the body. Then the wet sound bubbled through his demolished nasal cavity.

He was still breathing.

She took a moment to scan her eyes over the room. Then she reached her hands out to cradle the cold porcelain. The lid scraped as she removed it from the toilet tank. She wrapped her fingers around the cool material, comparing the smoothness of the painted top to the roughness of the unfinished underbelly.

She shifted the long rectangle in her hands until the short side stared down at Geoffrey's crumpled form. She lifted the lid high above her head, exhaled, and brought it down with all her force onto what remained of his face. All hints of breath stopped. Geoffrey's body adopted the deflated immobility like Mark when she had introduced him to the hammer.

Just like Mark with keys impaled into his face, Geoffrey was no longer recognizable. He was reduced to a bloody pile of unanimated flesh.

Emma reached over and flipped on the light, enlightening the blood-splattered scene. Although she nearly gasped at the sight of so much Geoffrey on the walls, her surprise quickly gave way to an inventory of future cleaning.

Holy shit. There's blood all the way up on the ceiling. I'm going to have to bleach this entire bathroom. And burn the sheets. I don't want a single cell of Geoffrey left in this place. I don't want to get rid of this much blood again. I should drain him right here before I chop him up this time.

Emma pulled a towel from the rack and wet it, swiping over her entire naked body to clear any droplets prior to stepping onto her carpet. She strutted nude through her dark house and retrieved a knife from the kitchen, then padded gently back up the stairs and opened his throat.

A waterfall of blood poured from the wound and over Geoffrey, slowly disappearing down the drain. Emma kept the knife toying at her fingertips while the body emptied. She spun and caught sight of her reflection in the mirror.

Hello, murderer. Her reflection smiled at her.

The look felt at home on her face. Something about the reflection she now saw staring back at her, naked in the bloodied bathroom, appeared more authentic, more *her* than she had ever seen before.

When she looked into those bold eyes in the mirror, she occupied her own flesh, swelling out to the edges of her skin. She was in harmony with her body, rather than an awkward occupant of it.

"So this is what I really am," she said aloud, her voice sounding haggard and dehydrated, bouncing off the bathroom walls. "This is what I want. This is what makes me happy."

The truth resonated through Emma as the blood dripped off the walls, and she felt some semblance of peace spread through the gaping black below her stomach.

CHAPTER 18

Emma basked in the soft glow of public, free internet at a library across town from her house. The screen in front of her reflected the painfully familiar colorful dating page with ads dancing along the sidebars. The sight of such a page used to make Emma's skin crawl, used to coil her chest in tense knots. Now she lounged placidly in the uncomfortable plastic chair, a strange and subtle smirk playing on her lips.

She sat in front of a blank profile, vague forms and ideas shifting beneath her scalp, teeming along her nerves. Name, the field asked.

Who do I want to be? What would I want my name to be? What name would they want me to have?

Deidra, she typed into the field. Her fingers were energized on the keys, animated by the creation of false lives.

I think Deidra is from New Orleans. It sounds like Deidra would be from NOLA. Let's see, what does Deidra do for a living? Business Professional.

That's perfectly vague.

Hi, I'm Deidra from New Orleans, and I'm a business professional.

30 years old.

Athletic build.

Looking for a relationship.

Undecided on children.

When she reached the open paragraph reserved for a bio or mission statement or whatever, Emma hesitated, tapping her nail on the space bar. A jumbled blur of every profile she had read over all these attempts echoed against her skull. Every false line, every double entendre. She began to type.

`I am a fun-loving, active girl looking for my partner in crime. I really want someone I can talk to and start a new adventure with. Message me if you want to know more.`

Emma reread her work. "Oh shit," she breathed.

She needed pictures. They could not be actual pictures of her. She needed someone who looked enough like her to be recognized at the date but not actually be identified.

She decided Deidra would have long blonde hair. She'd always wanted to be a blonde. Maybe then she would have more fun. So she needed a blonde who looked somewhat like her.

Emma opened a new tab and asked the search engine for blondes in their thirties. She scrolled through a barrage of smiling women, heavily peppered with pornographic images, until she found one that portrayed the woman far enough away to dull her features. She tilted her head from one side to the other to decide if the picture resembled her enough. Or would when she donned a matching wig.

Emma saved the file and uploaded it to Deidra's new profile. She trailed the image to a tragically public MyBook page and snagged a couple other distant shots of the blonde. Specifically, a few obscure ones with her in a group. She uploaded the stolen images as her profile's other pictures, then she released Deidra onto the online world, dangling the bait over what she knew well to be desperate waters.

Part of her felt like Deidra as she sauntered out of the library. The persona crawled up out of the back of her mind and stretched out under her skin. She decided that Deidra was fierce and confident, that she owned what she wanted and settled for nothing less, that she used men instead of being used by them. Deidra played prey while she hunted. Emma felt that bit of empowerment, that part of her swell at being taken out to play.

On her way back across town, she pulled into the parking lot of a superstore. Not her own local store, one somewhere on the way. Still feeling the curvaceous drag in her step and the extended posture in her spine, Emma walked slowly and deliberately down the torturously lit aisles. She tossed a prepaid smartphone into the cart.

She parked her cart and lingered in the clothing section, brushing against the circular racks of garments. She lifted shirts and dresses in front of her, evaluating each one in the mirror. In her mind, Deidra shopped somewhere a bit more refined, more expensive, but Emma did not have the budget to finance fancy personas. As if the men would notice the difference anyway.

She settled on pants tight enough to reveal the contour of her hips and a shirt that would cling subtly to her and allow a hint of her cleavage. Then she ambled through the shoes and snagged a matching pair of heels one size too big. She paid in cash.

With her costume supplies safely stowed in her trunk, she glided her car to the home improvement store across the shopping center. She still felt the otherness in her stride, the extra layer of personality influencing her mind. She walked like Deidra, confident and wily. She sauntered, infected with the knowledge that she was in control now.

Emma snagged a chain hoist, a bucket, many more sheets of painter's plastic, along with some paint, brushes, and rollers to sell the story. Again, she paid in cash, keeping her head down in front of the cameras and avoiding eye contact to not make an impression on any other patrons.

With one final stop for a convincing blonde wig, Emma walked into the restaurant to meet Ronnie and Josiah, feeling some blissful blend of liberated and excited. She could not wait to climb into Deidra's shoes. She could not wait for Deidra to ensnare and execute her first victim.

She arrived at the small café before Ronnie, which was never surprising. She got settled at the table with a glass of water and set up her burner phone. She kept the edge of her peripherals alert to stash the phone before Ronnie could ask what it was for. When she pulled up FishOfTheSea.com, a devious grin consumed her face at seeing how ravenously those fish were biting.

Emma caught sight of Ronnie coming past the front window of the café, juggling Josiah in her arms, and quickly stashed the phone deep in her purse.

"Hey," Ronnie said as she approached the table and dumped Josiah into the staged high chair.

"Hey," Emma replied. "You made it out. Aren't you afraid someone might see you with him and think you're a mother?"

"Don't worry. Anyone would assume he's yours, and I'm just your friend who loves food and booze too much."

"Shut up."

"How are you? I feel like I haven't seen you in forever. You're always hiking or whatever. Ever since that last awful date, you've been different."

I've determined that murdering stupid guys I date makes me happy and fulfils me on a deep and disturbing level, so I've spent the past few weeks planning and preparing for my next kill.

"Yeah, I've been trying to deal with some shit. I'm trying to concentrate on living my life. Working, finding hobbies I enjoy, trying to make myself happy."

"I see you do that without us."

I have been avoiding you because, deep down, I'm sure you are going to be able to see right

287

through to what I really am.

"I'm only trying to find my way on my own. I can't horn in on your family forever."

"Yes, you can. We're your family too."

"I know, and I appreciate that, but you know what I mean."

"Yeah, I do."

"I talked to Gladys recently, and since then, I guess I've been trying to figure out who I am."

"Gladys knows her shit. So who are you then?"

"I honestly don't think I know."

"That makes sense. I mean, how often do you think you've really been yourself in your life? You weren't yourself with Justin. You weren't yourself after he destroyed your life. You weren't yourself dating all these asshats."

"Exactly. I think it's time I find myself."

"I love it. Are you done with dating then? No more trying?"

I'm not done, but I am done with the bullshit. I am done with the searching. I'm done being used. Now I'm going to use them.

"I think I'm done. Done playing the game."

"I'm glad you've made that decision."

"Yeah, it kind of sounds like crap coming from someone in a relationship with a family."

Someone who has everything I am supposed to have.

Ronnie laughed. "I'm sure it does, but I am firmly convinced that I ended up here because I wasn't looking for anything. I wasn't trying to make anything happen. I didn't give a shit."

"No, you did not."

"I was simply me, trying to find out what made me happy. I didn't try to impress or trap Terrence because I didn't think I wanted him. Things got to happen naturally."

"From this side, it looks like you got what I wanted without trying at all."

"Life is not about getting what we deserve. We don't get to earn things. Life would be fair if shit worked like that! Besides, I told you, we somehow switched lives at some point. Married to a cheating piece of shit, me. Domestic life with the quality partner and kid, you. Not sure what happened there."

"This is a very deep conversation before we've even ordered lunch."

"It's what we do. You look great though, Em. You look, I don't know…happier, less stressed."

"I am, I think. I've made peace with it. I'm not trying to force things anymore. Maybe I won't find someone. Maybe I won't have a family."

"Don't say that. It's not like you're fifty years old."

"No, maybe it's okay though. I don't need those things to have a happy life."

"Wow, you're like the fucking Dali Lama all of a sudden."

"I have found enlightenment."

In murder.

"You got a new car. How is it?"

"I love it."

"I liked the picture you sent. Must be nice not to be so broke anymore."

"Oh my God, to not have to agonize over how

I'm going to scrape up the money for all the bills. So nice!"

Plus, I needed to sell that rolling crime scene as fast as possible.

"One day I'll have to even ride in it. You know, when we actually hang out again."

"We're hanging out right now, Ronnie."

"Yeah, whatever. So what are you up to the rest of the weekend?"

As soon as I leave here, I am going to go through all these messages on my fake dating profile and select a victim. I am going to spend some time leading him on until he's ready to meet me. Then I'm going to find some way to kill him without getting caught. Then I'm going to go for a hike.

"I think I'm going to go for a run tonight. Then relax on the couch tomorrow. Then I'm hoping to go for another long hike."

"What is up with all this hiking? I thought the running was intense, but this is next level."

I have to get rid of the bodies.

"I like the hiking. It's peaceful to be by myself, conquering the trail, pushing myself farther than the previous time. It gives me a lot of time to sort out my brain."

"Is that where you found this enlightenment?"

"Definitely."

"Whatever is making you happier, I'm glad. Keep doing it. I have missed this Emma."

"What's different about me now?"

"You look like you again, not so weighted down by Justin or what he did or trying to fix what he did. It looks like you're actually living again."

"It is good to feel like myself. I don't think I have since we were young. Like super young. When we were stupid and reckless and thought we could get away with anything."

"Back before you needed to be someone else for Justin. It's better you're out of the game anyway. That Don Juan killer is still out there."

"You and this Don Juan killer thing."

"Hey, my best friend is out on the wilds of the internet, dating strange douchebags while this guy is luring women through online dating and killing them. Plus, I'm all hopped up on momma bear hormones. Yeah, I'm going to worry, and obsessively read about him on the internet."

"So I'm confused. If he's doing this all online, how is he getting away with it? Can't his profile and all that be traced?"

"Yeah, it totally can. Like if I created a profile at home and messaged all these people, my IP address and all that would be all over it. Cops could trace it. They figure he's some kind of tech guy, probably works in computers. He's either using public internet, burner phones, or he's managing to ghost his IP address."

"He's smart."

"Oh yeah, quite the catch. Brilliant, but will strangle you by the end of the date."

"Is that how he does it?"

"Yeah, piano wire or something. He strangles them and leaves the body."

"Leaves the body?"

"Yep, he's confident. He hunts openly online, leaves the body to be discovered."

Brave guy. That must be so much less work.

"At least he's not a rapist."

"No, he offs them before that stage in the date. I guess it could be worse."

"So what have you been up to while I've been off finding myself again?"

"Terrence has had this big project at work."

"Yeah, he had to bail on the last movie we planned."

"That stupid comedy? What a tragedy."

"This is why we don't take you."

"Anyway. He's been having to put in extra hours with your good friend Timmy. It's been a lot of time with me and Josiah."

"Ah, Timmy. How is he?"

"Married now."

"Of course he is."

"Hey, he was actually a good guy."

"Yeah, I guess he deserves it. Are you pulling your hair out being full time mommy?"

"Of course I am. You know I am. I mean, Josiah is awesome. He's getting to be more fun the more stuff he can do, but he's also an exhausting amount of mischief. Sometimes at the end of the day, I want to shower, put on real clothes, and talk to other adults like a human."

"The burdens of working from home."

"I know I shouldn't complain. We don't have to pay for daycare. I know I will miss these times with him when he's older. I'll be glad I had all this time with him, but sometimes, I honestly feel like I'm suffocating. Or like I don't exist anymore. There's no more Ronnie, only Mommy here to feed you and change you and answer your every vexing whim."

"Ronnie, you couldn't cease to exist if you tried. There is way too much you in there for that. You would burn the place down before you let that happen."

"True enough. I just have to make it through this patch with Terrence's work, then I can call in my time off. Let him make up his shifts."

"Why don't you let me take Josiah? I can watch him for a few hours, and you can go do something to make you feel like you."

"That would actually be great, as long as you don't take him hiking."

"Don't worry, I won't."

Ronnie hugged Emma tightly as they stood on the pavement in front of the café. Ronnie clutched her firmly, and Emma noticed she did feel like she did when they were younger, when she did not feel the desperate push of depression clinging to the embrace.

As Emma turned the corner away from Ronnie, she let Deidra climb back into the swing of her hips, that sly smile slithering back onto her face, somehow feeling at home.

***

Deidra was definitely popular on the site. When Emma checked the trick line phone, the notification counter on the site was high—winks, likes, and messages. The fish were biting furiously. Emma grinned anxiously, trying to decide where to start.

The small phone screen was infuriating. Even

with the dating app downloaded under her phony email created at the library to establish her profile, she longed to pull the site up on her laptop. But her internet activity could be traced on her router, if it ever came to that.

She thought about the Don Juan killer who had Ronnie so fiercely fixated. She had to be smart like him. If he could fish online without being traced, if he could let the bodies get found, she could do this. She would take it one step farther. She would hunt outside her city to reduce the chances of being recognized or identified on the date.

She scrolled through the barrage of messages.

TNBoy80 said,

Hey gorgeous! Your profile really caught my eye. You look like such an interesting person. I bet we could have a lot of fun together. Message me back!

Emma rolled her eyes and kept scrolling.

NateDawg$ said,

Hey girl, do you think you can handle me? I guarantee I'm more man than the last guy who sent you here. Give me the chance to show you what you've been missing.

"Bingo," Emma said. "Hello, douchebag."

"Deidra" tapped at the touch keyboard.

I'm sure I can handle you. What do you have to offer?

Before she could even open another message, a picture of NateDawg$'s penis popped up in her inbox. Emma nearly choked on her wine when she opened the message to be greeted by a full bush of dark pubic hair bristling along an aroused yet largely unimpressive shaft.

"Oh my God," she giggled. "He did not lead with a dick pic."

Emma sat stunned with the phone frozen in her palm for a moment. How do you respond to a dick picture? Deidra was not a straight up slut. He was going to have to work harder than that.

She typed, snickering,

Calm down, big boy. How about we start with drinks?

NateDawg$ messaged Deidra both immediately and incessantly. He made it too easy. Emma constantly steered NateDawg$ away from phallic images and direct sexual references, asking him the canned litany of pre-date questions. He said he had never been married and was undecided about children. He was looking for a partner to travel with and just have fun. All his answers sounded hollow.

The next day after her morning run, Emma wandered the aisles of her local grocery store. The trick line vibrated in her pocket. She lifted up the phone and gasped, somehow surprised again. NateDawg$'s penis again consumed her screen, this time at an alternate angle in different lighting. The picture must have been snapped in another bathroom.

Her face flushed, she slammed the phone screen into her chest. Gripping her basket with her other hand, she glanced around to make sure no other customers had glimpsed the graphic anatomy on her screen.

What in the hell was wrong with this guy? Why would he think a dick picture would be enticing? It was gross.

From the privacy of her car in the parking lot, Deidra calmly replied to confirm the time and the bar they would meet at that night.

Over the course of the day, Emma slipped into Deidra's skin by degrees. When she responded to NateDawg$'s messages, she began to think like Deidra. She left Emma behind—the divorcee, the depressed single girl, the woman who tried to please all these men who left her—and crawled into the fierceness of a huntress. NateDawg$ was her prey; he just did not know it.

She assembled her costume meticulously. She tugged on the tight pants, feeling them squeeze against her legs. She pulled the shirt over her head and adjusted it until her breasts peered out appropriately. Then she dangled a necklace into her cleavage and painted her face in the practiced, contoured lines. She colored until her eyes contrasted brighter, until her blemishes vanished.

She placed and replaced the wig until it could be mistaken as natural hair.

Looking at Deidra in the mirror, she decided she had made the right decision to invest in the wig. With her tits out and her ass hugged, he would never notice the bargain tags on her clothes. All NateDawg$ would be worried about would be introducing her to his over-documented penis in person.

Deidra had a long drive on the dark highway to reach the southern city of Colorado Springs. She did not even turn on the radio, instead preferring the lines on the road whipping past her tires and the wind swirling against her windows. She became calm as she drew near her destination, focused and anticipant.

She parked in an alleyway behind and down a couple blocks from the bar, an alley Emma would have avoided traveling alone in the dark. The narrow space was poorly lit and ominous. She popped the trunk and reached inside, grasped the screwdriver, and plunged it into her back tire, the impact sending a horrible ache from her palm up into her arm. She struggled hard then ripped it back out, hearing the air hiss out. She tossed the screwdriver back on the plastic lining in her trunk and sashayed on her heels into the bar.

She sat calmly at the bar, waiting for NateDawg$. It was no surprise he was late. When he entered the bar, she spotted him immediately, tattoo art screen printed over his shirt, a flat-billed baseball cap low on his head. Deidra noticed him but pretended to be obliviously perched on the barstool.

"Deidra?" His voice was the same forced gruff tone she imagined while reading his messages.

Deidra smiled and remembered to answer to the name.

"Nate?" she responded, letting seduction creep into her lips.

"Nice to meet you." Nate extended his hand. "Damn, girl. You are prettier than your profile."

"Thank you."

Nate drew back the stool beside her and slid himself uncomfortably close to her. Deidra discarded Emma's disgust and moved in responsively. Nate allowed a flash of seeming victory to flash over his features. His eyes lingered in Deidra's cleavage even as he spoke again.

Deidra did not listen to what he was saying. She moved her head to the side and widened her eyes. She twirled the false strands of hair between her fingertips. While Nate was distracted by evaluating her body, she glanced down at his hand. A stark white line wrapped itself around his ring finger. Not the unbound finger of one never married, not the faded line of a distant divorce, the vivid mark of infidelity.

A cheater. Deidra's heart fluttered.

Nate set his empty glass on the bar in front of them, licked his lips, and placed his hand on Deidra's thigh. Emma cringed at the contact; Deidra put her hand receptively on top of his.

"Do you want to get out of here, girl?" Nate angled his chin toward her, his eyelids lowering.

"Sure. Walk me to my car?"

She laughed on the inside at the wave of confusion over his face.

Nate reached for her hand as they walked down the alley. He dragged her on her heels toward him. She pretended to waver with intoxication. His fingers groped around her waist, hooking her in close. Emma rolled her eyes behind Deidra's welcoming grin.

"Oh shit," Nate said as they approached her car. "Is that you?"

"Yeah," Deidra said. "Why?"

"You have a flat, girl. Man, that's like totally flat. Look, we can take my car and come back for yours in the morning."

"Oh no. I wouldn't feel comfortable leaving it here overnight. You think you could change it for me?"

Nate looked Deidra up and down once more. "Yeah. Why don't you pop your trunk for me?"

Deidra opened her trunk and lifted the lid.

"Why is your trunk lined in plastic?" Nate looked back at her perplexed.

"I work for a gardener. I have soil in my trunk all the time. It gets everywhere. Easier this way."

Nate accepted the lie and lifted the floor of the trunk to reveal the spare tire and tools. Deidra leaned against the cold concrete wall while he struggled to jack up the car and remove the flattened tire. She made sure to angle her body attractively for when he paused to glance back at her. Each time, she flashed him a gracious and suggestive smile, and he snapped back to work. When he turned away, she rolled her eyes or giggled silently.

At last, he loaded the damaged tire into her trunk. As he smoothed the plastic back down, she eased up behind him and fetched the tire iron from the asphalt beside the car, her eyes sweeping the alley for witnesses.

"Hey, I missed the tire iron," Nate said, his head still in the trunk. "Can you give it to me?"

He reached his hand back toward her, and Deidra raised the iron high. She took a long and deliberate breath, savoring the way time suspended as the weapon arced through the air, then slammed into his skull. The long neck of the four-pronged shape imbedded into the bone with a sickening and heavy thud. Nate's body jerked, and Deidra had to imagine the look of unadulterated shock contorting his features. His breath stumbled and sputtered, so she tugged the tire iron back. It abandoned the wound with a strange sucking sound. When she struck him again, his body fell limp.

Before he could completely collapse, Deidra used his own fall to guide his body into the trunk. When his shoulders contacted the plastic, she crouched down on her heels to gather up his legs and tuck them in after him. She tossed the bloodied weapon on his chest and grasped the package of bleach wipes from the corner of the trunk. Quickly, she ran the cloth over her hands and face and the outside of the trunk and bumper. Tossing the cloth in, she closed the trunk over him. She was still alone and unseen in the vacant alley.

The smile on Emma's face carved so deeply and relentlessly that her cheeks were fatigued from the expression. The city disappeared in her rearview mirror. She abandoned her car and the monotony of driving, allowing her body to coast on autopilot as her brain ignited and twitched over all the preparations that would need to be done when she pulled into her garage.

The plastic was already prepared. She had hung it on the walls and spread it over the floor, even under where the car would park this time. She had weighted the plastic down on the edges to avoid any sliding or rolling. She did not want to have to bleach the concrete again. The chain hoist hung securely from the ceiling with the bucket waiting beneath it. She had a new blade for the Sawz-All.

So consumed was she in walking through her disposal steps that she barely noticed the lights flashing behind her. The glimpses of red and blue assaulted her eyes from the rearview mirror. She squinted at them until she registered the police car behind her.

This is it. I'm done. I am going to prison, if not getting lethal injection.

Her heart seized in her chest and dropped like a weight into her stomach, its impact radiating up her bones. She stopped breathing as she pulled her car onto the dark shoulder of the road.

Hold your shit together. You have to hold your shit together.

"Good evening, Officer," Emma said, forcing a smile at the cop at her window.

The rotating red and blue lights painted the officer's uniform in alternating hues. The large spotlight cast hard lines over his face otherwise obscured by the night.

"Hello, ma'am," he said flatly. "Do you know why I pulled you over?"

Because I have the dead body of a creep in my trunk that I plan to dismember in my garage and bury in the mountains?

"No, sir. Was I speeding?"

"Yes, ma'am. The speed limit through here drops down to sixty-five. You were going seventy-six when I clocked you a few miles back. Where are you headed?"

"Home."

"Where are you coming from?"

"Honestly, I am trying to get home after an absolutely awful date. I met this guy at a bar. He told me he had never been married, but when he showed up, he had a bright wedding ring tan line on his ring finger. Not an old one, he was married. Then he tried to convince me to go home with him."

"That's too bad." The officer moved to look down at his clipboard.

"I've been divorced for a few years now," Emma rambled. "I've tried everything. I recently resorted to online dating."

"That's too bad, ma'am." The officer raised his pen and opened his mouth to continue talking.

"It's just been horrible. I have probably been on a hundred first dates, and they all end the same. If I like the guy, he disappears. If I'm not into him, I can't get rid of him. Most of them are complete liars, only pretending to be someone else."

"Ma'am," the officer attempted to interrupt.

"I thought this guy would be different. He said

all the right things online. I can't believe he was married! And I can't believe he didn't think I would notice that huge white line on his finger! It was probably more noticeable than the wedding ring itself."

"Ma'am," the officer tried again.

"Do men actually think women are that stupid, Officer? Are you married? Would you do that to your wife?"

"Look, ma'am, it sounds like you have had a rough night. I am going to let you off with a warning tonight, but I want you to drive safely home and obey the posted speed limits." The officer took a half step back with each sentence.

"That's very nice of you. Thank you, Officer."

"You're welcome, ma'am. You have a good night and drive safe."

The officer disappeared back behind his glaring, flashing lights. Emma rolled up her window and sat momentarily stunned. After the police car pulled past her, she rejoined the highway. Only then did she allow a loud chuckle until the sound echoed back at her from the windshield.

The plastic crunched and rumpled under her tires as she pulled her car into her garage, the door rumbling shut behind her. She exited the car and moved to the trunk, opened it, and stared down at Nate's sad, crumpled body. His eyes were frozen half open, lacking any vitality, fixed dull and muted. His skin already looked flat. His body had that alarming and unnerving stillness to it that betrayed his demise.

Emma stalled over him for several long

moments. Hoisting the corpse from the trunk was her least favorite part of the process, or dragging one down her stairs and across her house. As she struggled to wrangle the inanimate flesh, she questioned if she should exchange some runs for weight training. Her muscles were unequal to the leaded weight of the dead.

Nate collapsed into a heap on the plastic, a fall that probably would have injured him if he was alive to feel it. Emma wrapped her hands around his ankles and dragged the body across the garage, leaving a trail of smeared blood along the plastic. As his body slipped along the surface, she thought of Mark, of how much more difficult it was to move him. She was getting stronger. Perhaps, she dared fathom, she was getting better at this.

She bound Nate's legs with the chain and hoisted him up until his body dangled upside down from the ceiling. The corpse spun gently in its suspense while Emma gathered and positioned supplies. She placed the large bucket directly under Nate's wobbling head, picked up the knife she had set out, and firmed her grip around it. Taking a fistful of Nate's greasy hair, Emma wrinkled her nose and began cutting, struggling to hold the lubricated strands tightly.

The blood came spurting and pouring from his throat, pooling in the bucket below. Emma took a step back, allowing the blood to fill the bucket and avoid the extra splatter. She kept hold of the knife and crossed her arms while the corpse drained, the rhythmic sound of the blood hitting the bucket sedating her.

When the shower was reduced to a drip, Emma picked up the Sawz-All and buzzed it through the remainder of Nate's neck and divorced his head from his body. She waited until the blood stopped dripping before lowering the body and continuing to segment it.

She heaved the torso first, attempting to wrangle the smooth shape slicked in blood. She wrestled it into a garbage bag, wrapped it tightly, and wound duct tape around it. Then she set the body part aside and repeated the process with the next portion.

Once the body parts were individually wrapped, she washed her hands and fetched her new hiking bags. She could not afford to buy a new set of backpacks after every victim without arousing suspicion, so she wrapped the pieces again in clean garbage bags, carefully packing the pieces against each other inside the backpacks. She removed the bloodied plastic from the trunk and placed all the packaged remains of Nate inside.

After she gathered all the bloodied plastic, the tire iron, the burner phone with the battery removed, Nate's phone with the battery removed, her costume, every scrap of evidence associated with Nate's untimely death, she packed it efficiently into the tent bags, wrapping the bundles in clean garbage bags and taping the parcels tight.

When Emma lifted the bucket, the ocean of blood sloshed up against the side. She held her breath and steadied her body, taking small fractional steps into her house. With forced poise, she guided the blood bucket into the bathroom and sent the contents down the bathtub drain.

When she began the painstaking process of bleaching everything, she knew there was no way she was eradicating all the evidence left behind. No matter how much bleach chased the liters of blood down the drain, no matter how meticulously she scrubbed every visible crevice of her trunk, she would miss some microscopic trace.

The important thing was to never draw attention to herself. If they never traced the profiles to her points of internet access, if they never found the body, they would have no cause to scrape her drain or shine the blue light into her trunk.

Part of Emma wanted to preserve a memento of each fallen man. The keys from Mark's face. Geoffrey's wallet, a screen capture of Nate's ridiculous profile or unprompted penis pictures. She wanted the trophies to remember and relive, like the serial killers in her favorite television programs. From those same programs, she knew to dismiss the urge, to bleach, bury, or burn every single thing associated with the crime, and to vary her habits and create no patterns in the trails she might leave.

Emma crawled into bed utterly exhausted, each movement and stroke echoing on her muscles. She reeked of bleach, and she could still feel the blood on her hands.

***

In the morning, Emma packed up and went for a long hike on a new trail, three extended routes into nowhere in three divergent directions.

Her footsteps on the dirt echoed in the quiet

morning. She permitted the seduction of the rhythm in her hike and the tapping of her walking stick, her mind wandering past her path.

What am I doing? Am I simply a murderer now? Is this all what I do now?

You do what makes you happy, another voice of hers chimed in. *This is what makes you happy.*

This can't be what makes me happy. This can't be okay. I can't up and decide to start killing people and burying them in the mountains. You don't just wake up one day a killer.

Maybe I was always a killer. Maybe I would have killed Jeremy Davies. Maybe Jeremy Davies had it coming too.

A couple of bad dates are not enough motive for a killing spree.

I bet a thousand women would disagree with that. I bet a thousand woman wished they were doing what I'm doing. Finally taking control. Finally being honest. Finally not getting used and discarded.

The second voice grew louder with each step. The flimsy voice of reason, Emma's old voice, faded into the back of her mind. The new thoughts felt at home, naturally rippling over the wrinkles in her mind. Each stride up the mountain was one further step from the sad, wounded girl she used to be.

CHAPTER 19

Emma stuck out her tongue and curled it up to lick the bottom of her nose, making Josiah giggle. Each time, he gave her a look of sheer bewilderment, which quickly transformed into a simple and honest laugh that shook his tiny frame. Emma could not witness such a chuckle without bursting into her own giggles. She stuck her tongue out again, and Josiah slapped his fat palms onto the coffee table and bounced frantically on unstable legs.

She ran a hand over the plumes of hair jetting out from his head and pressed her lips into his warm cheek. Kissing his face was infectious, and she peppered his cheeks. Her pocket vibrated, and she broke away.

"You ridiculous boy." She eased up onto the couch, holding her new prepaid smartphone to her face to evaluate "Jennifer's" prospects. Jennifer's picture of a saucy redhead greeted her as she launched the app and navigated to her inbox.

TNBoy80:

Hey gorgeous! Your profile really caught my eye. You look like such an interesting person. I bet we could have a lot of fun together. Message me back!

"Very original, this one," Emma told Josiah. "I'm pretty sure I've read this exact message before."

Josiah looked at her blankly, gumming her remote.

Heavy220:

Hey beautiful. Your profile really caught my eye. It sounds like we could have a lot in common. I really like movies. Maybe sometime we can Netflix and chill?

"Now, see, Josiah, Jennifer's profile clearly states that she does not own a TV and prefers to be outside. Do you think Heavy220 even read her profile? Of course not. He looked at her pictures, thought she was hot enough, and sent her this message that has absolutely nothing to do with her. And look at this. His profile picture is a shirtless selfie." She flipped the phone toward Josiah and the child giggled. "Jesus, almost all of his pictures are shirtless selfies. He must be very impressed with his sort of six-pack. There's one at the gym, another in the bathroom, another at the beach. We got it, dude, you're proud of your body. Josiah, you have to promise me you are never going to be like these silly boys. You're going to be better than them, right?"

"Ba-ba!" Josiah shouted, arching his back for emphasis.

"I'll take that as a yes. Well, I think shirtless selfie boy is just the right match for Jennifer."

Having lost interest in her ramblings, Josiah toddled off to find mischief in her un-baby-proofed house. Emma tucked the trick line away and returned to being auntie instead of Jennifer.

***

"There's my boy," Ronnie cooed enthusiastically when she walked through the door.

Josiah abandoned his toy and marched straight to her with his arms extended and fingers flexing in and out. Ronnie scooped him up and nuzzled him.

"Aww, you actually do love him," Emma teased.

"All it takes is five minutes away to remember that. Thank you so much for giving me a break."

"Anytime. I need my auntie time too."

"What are you doing tonight?"

"I think I'm going to have a date."

"What? I thought you were out of the game."

"Ha! It's not what you think. Just meeting Brandon from my old work."

"Okay, that's definitely not a date."

"Your Don Juan killer been up to anything

lately?"

"No, I haven't seen anything lately. He must be taking a break. Smart move to not get caught I suppose. The only missing persons that have popped up have been guys in their 30s. One in Colorado Springs recently. He probably fell off The Incline or something."

"Sometimes people just leave. Who knows how many people nobody noticed?"

"True enough. I better get Josiah home. Terrence will want to get his boy time in. We'll do something soon, yeah? Maybe a girls' night or something?"

"Definitely."

When the door closed behind Ronnie and Josiah and Emma's house fell silent again, she groped for the trick line to plan Jennifer's date for the night.

***

"It's so cool that you wanted to go see a horror movie. Most girls never want to see a horror movie. They don't like the blood, I guess. And the fact that you picked a drive-in movie, old school," Manuel said after she picked him up from his house.

I could just kill him now, skip the entire date.

He was already in her vehicle. Still, part of her needed to let him play out the sad little charade.

"I'm glad you're impressed," Jennifer responded.

"What's your favorite horror movie?"

"I'm not really into movies or TV. Like it says in my profile, I prefer to be outside or reading."

"Oh," Manuel's voice struggled for an instant. "Then why did you pick a drive-in movie?"

"Because you said how much you like movies and I used to love going to the drive-in theater when I was a kid."

"Oh, well that's still awesome."

"So you like to work out?"

"What?"

"You have so many topless pictures in your profile."

"Oh, yeah. I guess. I go to the gym sometimes."

Jennifer parked her car along the last row of the drive-in parking lot with the large silver screen centered in the distance. All the other cars lined up in front of them, tall trees obscuring anything behind. The back row was strangely isolated. Manuel looked excited by her parking selection. Perhaps he thought it indicated she intended to get frisky once the sun set and the film started.

"We should probably watch from the back seat, don't you think?" Manuel said without looking at her.

Emma rolled her eyes hard. The exhaustive sigh could be heard echoing in her head.

"Sure. My front seats actually fold down, so we can see."

They settled into the less than comfortable back seat as the movie flashed on the giant screen before them. Before the trailers even poured into the feature presentation, Manuel's hand crept to her thigh. His other arm snuck behind her to circle her in closer to him. His advancements were neither subtle nor stealthy.

First time he meets me, and he's already breathing on my neck, already groping at my body.

Is this how dating is supposed to go? Am I missing something here? Am I supposed to put out and hope he isn't using me? Am I supposed to hold out some predetermined amount of time to try to convince him to care about me beyond sex?

Old thoughts rose in Emma's voice.

Too many games. Too much pretending. Acting like you don't want what you want to eventually get what you want. I know what I want now, pure and simple. I want to be in control. I want to kill them. One by one.

The movie unraveled on the screen in the formulaic horror arc. By the time the serial killer had emerged and knocked off a few supporting characters, Manuel had completely wrapped himself around her. Jennifer knew he was no longer watching the movie.

I guess I'm going to have to kill him or have sex with him at this point.

Manuel's hand slid up Jennifer's back, lifting the hem of her shirt to expose the skin above her waist. His other hand brushed along her face, angling her toward him, his fingertips moving toward her hair. Jennifer cocked her head to avoid his fingers discovering the wig, and dove into his kiss to distract him. Manuel opened his mouth receptively and squeezed around her.

Some base and destructive part of Emma wanted to follow this carnal path, to romp with Manuel in the cramped back seat of her car prior to introducing him to the trunk. As Manuel's tongue wormed through her mouth, she thought of the Don Juan killer Ronnie insisted on perpetually bringing up. She reminisced on the admiration she had for him when Ronnie said the victims were never raped. He never had sex with them, consensual or otherwise. His murderous motives were pure.

From the corner of her eye, Jennifer saw the killer stalking the poor final girl through a dilapidated house in the middle of nowhere. The music twirled on a high pitched edge, gathering all the suspense into it. The crescendo was coming.

She pulled back from Manuel, her hands against his chest.

"What is it?" he asked, mouth still pulling toward her.

"I have condoms and a blanket in the trunk."

Manuel stiffened, his hand already on the door handle. "Pop the trunk. I'll go grab them."

Manuel leaped from the car before Jennifer even pretended to reach toward the lever. She reached under the collapsed front seat to retrieve the heavy metal flashlight and pulled the handle for the trunk.

The blanket was clearly visible on the top of the trunk. Emma had made the condoms more of a treasure hunt. Manuel dove waist deep into the trunk and was clawing around through the dummy contents when Jennifer crept up silently behind him. She peered over the car at the movie screen. The killer continued to hunt the final girl. The movie fell quiet until he emerged, brandishing his gleaming butcher knife. When the soundtrack exploded, Jennifer tapped Manuel.

He whirled around to look at her, bringing his head slightly out of the trunk. Jennifer raised the flashlight high and brought it down into his face.

Even over the blaring death scene on the screen, she heard his nose collapse into his skull and all the breath heave out of his chest in a grunt. As the movie killer hacked up the last nonessential character between him and his final girl, Jennifer brought the flashlight into Manuel's face until the sputtering stopped.

She tipped and tucked Manuel into the trunk, tossing the bloodied flashlight on top of his collapsed form. She took a step back and panted deeply in the night air. Her eye caught the clear stars in the distance first. Then she checked her surroundings. The one car that had parked in the back aisle with them rocked subtly on its suspension. A thin layer of fog obscured the windows. When the transition between scenes silenced the movie, she could make out the moaning.

Jennifer thought it was safe to assume they were not paying attention to what she was doing beside them. All the other cars were in front of them, passengers most likely fixated on the screen or each other. The shield of trees behind isolated Jennifer standing over Manuel's limp body in the trunk.

She reached beside Manuel's limp feet and retrieved the bleach wipes. She bathed her face and hands and the full back end of the car. Then she dug into the bag tucked against the corner of the trunk and pulled out fresh clothes, a baggy shirt and yoga pants. The night air nipped her skin as she changed clothes in the open. She relished being alone in the back of the dark lot beside the rocking sedan.

***

Emma stood in the shower the next day, washing the crusted layer of sweat and dust from the hike from her body. Her muscles ached down to the bone, thin layers of acid still nibbling at the surface. Her body felt weighted by an exhaustion that burrowed toward the center of her skull, struggling to tug her consciousness down with it.

She pulled the handle of the faucet to bring the water to a scalding edge, drawing lines of burning heat down her skin and thickening the air she sucked into her lungs. With the fatigue in her body, Emma's mind took on additional weight to match. Her thoughts became heavier and slower, winding her down toward that aching hole below her stomach.

She had not thought about that hole for a long time. There had been no sinking pain while she was pretending to be Deidra or Jennifer or any of the other venomous women she concocted on public internet or untraceable burner phones.

Emma abandoned the steamy bathroom and curled up on the couch, cocooned in a blanket in front of mindless television. Anything but a romantic comedy where the quirky leading lady ended up with her changed and newly evolved man after they resolved their epic miscommunication.

Manuel was scarcely cold beneath the soil, but she already felt the slow itch tickle the bottom of her chest. She was aware she needed to be patient, to wait out the news, to allow her crime to cool and drift off into the past. She wanted to hunt. She

316

wanted to be holding a new trick line in her hand, messaging a new victim. She wanted to be crafting a persona and luring a deserving suitor.

She did not want to be herself, alone on her couch in a quiet house.

Maybe this isn't my cure, Emma thought, knitting her brow. *Maybe this is only a distraction.*

She permitted her thoughts to stray and meander uninhibited. Mark surfaced first, his mangled face and dead eye peering out past her fistful of keys, materializing from her memory in vivid detail. At the recollection of the damage she caused, her heart lifted. She was animated; alive. The hole at her center collapsed in on itself until she felt whole again.

Nate and Manuel tucked and folded flashed before her, limp and lifeless in her trunk. She remembered the excitement of stealing their breath while they bent into their coffins unaware. They never saw it coming. They thought they would bed her, use her, and discard her. They never imagined she would be taking something from them. A surge of power flowed at the sensation of pushing their legs into the trunk and concealing them beneath the lid.

The pulse of the unadulterated thrill of her secret, her other life covered in plastic and buried in the mountains, resonated through her. In that guilty rhythm, she felt at harmony with herself, the cells in her body in symphony with the amalgamation of personality firing inside her brain.

You are nothing but a killer. You did not find a partner or have a family because you do not deserve them. You are a killer. That is who you are, and that is what makes you happy.

Something in Emma resisted the simplicity of her truth. She was not supposed to be a killer. She was not supposed to acquiesce to murder, much less perpetrate it. She was supposed to be horrified by what she was doing, the way Ronnie worried compulsively about the Don Juan killer. She was supposed to be scraping and crying to find her partner and her family, finding a way to live the life she always wanted.

Am I the girl who I have been my entire life, or am I the killer I think I am now? Do I want a life with a family, or do I want death in the trunk of my car?

Justin surfaced in her mind, washing up on her consciousness like a piece of garbage from the depths of the ocean. She always found him at the base of that consuming hole in her person. He was the impact that had created the crater.

I should kill Justin, she thought then hesitated. *No, that would get me caught for sure. He's not worth the risk or effort.*

All roads led back to the naïve girl who fell for the idea that he loved her fully and unconditionally and that she was worthy of the life she wanted. The thought flashed over her mind that *she* was who Emma truly wanted to kill.

CHAPTER 20

Months passed quietly while Emma questioned herself. She felt like a killer in her cells while a lonely girl in her mind, and she did not know which to heed. No one missed Manuel in the news. Someone missed Nate. Scrolling through MyBook, Emma caught the story shared by a Colorado Springs acquaintance from her childhood. Nate's dumb face was in the thumbnail, again in a flat-billed hat. His wife had reported him missing.

I knew that son of a bitch was married.

The image of the stark wedding band tan line on his finger in the bar light flashed over her eyes, a familiar rage flaring behind her ribs and into her cheeks.

She did not dare click the link on her real phone. The preview text was enough to indicate that the missing man had a wife and two young children, and police had no leads.

Son of a bitch.

There was not so much as a passing mention of a missing man in Pueblo. Manuel did not appear on

319

the radar at all. Although by her own timetable she was free to launch a new hunt, she hesitated, perched on the decision between her life or the deaths of others.

Emma sat at her desk with earbuds in her ears, the colored spreadsheet expanding infinitely on her screen in front of her. She clicked and stared at it until her monitor blurred.

Elizabeth peeked her head around the edge of Emma's cube, tapping her keys on the metal frame supporting the canvas wall. Emma instantly remembered the way Mark's face concaved under the blow of her keys, the sensation of her fingers tangled within his dying wound. She shook her head to shake the memory loose and smiled up at Elizabeth.

"Lunch?" Elizabeth asked.

Eric appeared behind Elizabeth, towering over her petite frame and gently massaging her shoulders.

"E-squad lunch?" he echoed.

"Fine," Emma said, popping out her headphones. "But only if we go to Happy Beans."

"Of course, honey, I love Gladys," Eric said, tilting his head. "That old queen gives the best advice."

"I told you." Emma chuckled, following them to Elizabeth's car.

The E-squad, as Eric so flamboyantly dubbed them, sat around the small table in the coffee house, nibbling on bagel sandwiches, their oversized coffees venting steam between them.

"So this new boy," Eric said, deliberately placing

his sandwich back on the plate and folding his hands.

"What's his name?" Elizabeth asked, still chewing.

"Skylar," Eric purred. "Can you believe that? Isn't that like the gayest name you have ever heard? I feel like I've bagged myself a twink, but ironically, he's super butch. You wouldn't guess he was gay right off."

"Are you sure?" Emma joked. "Or is that only in comparison to you?"

"Hey now, bitch. I burn brightly because that is who I am. Skylar is a little more…muted."

"So how is it going?" Elizabeth asked.

"He is a daddy in the sack."

Emma cringed. "I don't need to know that."

"Yes, you most certainly do. One of us needs to be getting some action, and it surely has not been you two celibate bitches."

"Hey!" Emma said. "We would have no problem getting laid."

"Yeah," Elizabeth joined. "The problem is getting action from guys who are not assholes."

"Amen," Emma said.

"Use 'em and lose 'em, girls. That monogamy, long term relationship bull is some socially constructed slavery. Shake your shackles, and go have fun! Drop them before they can drop you is what I always say."

"So how long does Skylar have?" Emma asked.

"Until he acts shady or like a clinger. Either direction and I'm out."

"Sounds so simple," Elizabeth said, giving

Emma an exasperated face.

"All right. I have to go talk to Gladys before we head back," Emma said, rising from the table.

Elizabeth and Eric giggled as Emma walked across the familiar store to the counter. One customer stood in front of her, collecting his coffee. He wore a flat-billed baseball cap low on his brow. Emma immediately saw Nate's hat spill from his head and into her readied trunk as the tire iron punctured his skull.

Emma stopped breathing. Gladys's customer stepped aside, and Emma approached her at the counter.

"Eminem!" Gladys grinned. "I thought that was the E-squad over there."

"Will these nicknames never die?" Emma forced air back into her lungs and a smile across her cheeks.

"No, apparently, they are going to multiply instead."

"Lucky me."

"Come around here so I can hug you properly."

Gladys and Emma met in the small hallway where the counter terminated. As always, Gladys reached out and gathered Emma in deep, wrapping her entirely in her embrace. Emma breathed in to smell Gladys's sweet aroma that emanated softly below the coffee scent soaked into her skin. She momentarily collapsed into the hug.

"What's wrong, sugar?" Gladys said as they stepped back.

"What do you mean?"

"You can't hide from me, Em. That light I saw in

you last time isn't there. What happened? What's going on?"

"I'm just struggling, I guess. Still trying to find out who I am or what I want."

"Emma, you have to stop thinking so much. Everyone is trying to figure those things out. Most people their whole lives. Go with what you feel."

"I just keep thinking that I might not be who I thought I was. I might not want the things I always thought I wanted."

"Is that a bad thing?"

"It might be."

"Or is it an unknown thing?"

"It is definitely unknown."

"And that's scary."

"Very."

"You can't change who you are, Emma. You can only figure it out. Don't worry about what you think you're supposed to be or what you think you should want. Do what makes you happy, like we all keep saying. You have a limited time. You only get this one life. Don't waste time fighting yourself. Do what you want; the rest will come."

Emma smiled genuinely and some of the weight lifted from her chest.

***

That night, in the glowing light of the library computer screen, she decided she wanted to be "Eva."

Somewhat calmed and revitalized, centered with Eva's phone securely tucked in her pocket, she decided that Eva took her time. Deidra and Jennifer had been too rash, rushed through the hunt and the kill, leaving her wanting. Eva was going to evolve; Eva was going to be patient, take her time, and savor the entire process.

Before she staged her hunt, Emma capitalized on the burner phone to Google Colorado missing persons reports. She dragged her finger along the screen to catch glimpses of all the faces that had vanished unexplained. Nate's report was still there from when his wife had initially gone to the internet for help.

You are better off without him, honey.

Her heart seized in her chest when she saw Mark's dumb, muted eyes slide up the tiny screen. An unnatural and inappropriate jolt of excitement captured her at the sight of him. Her first. The unmatched thrill of crossing that line, of taking her first life, pounded.

She forced herself to divorce from the nostalgic moment and kept scrolling. She found Manuel too. The wave of memory as she rolled him into her trunk was not as strong as the thought of Mark; still, the perverse fondness remained.

I should be worried that they are reported missing. I should be worried that people are looking for them. At least one of them had to tell someone about the date they were going on. At least one of them has to have a thread that leads to me. And that is why Eva is going to be calm and even more careful.

Over the passing days, Emma let the messages accumulate in Eva's inbox. No matter what persona

Emma presented, the barrage of incoming communications always seemed identical. The guys who basically told her she was hot; the guys who would send her penis pictures and try to get away with a simple hook up; the guys who sent her novels about their backstory, including the damage that brought them to the site; the guys who did not even bother to read the profile she carefully created and crafted. The guys who were a little too desperate.

Then again, the women Emma created were not entirely unique, nor were they greatly removed from her authentic profiles. How many ways could she say she wanted to find a nice guy to settle down with? Clichés were unavoidable.

Emma tried to draw a line down her mind between her authentic self and the Eva she was pretending to be. Even as she sat in Emma's life, her mind wandered to Eva's online dating escapades unfolding on the tiny screen in her pocket.

The phone vibrated against her hip as she sprawled across the carpet with Josiah.

"Uh oh, little man," Emma said to the toddling child. "Sounds like we've snagged another one."

Emma flipped on the screen and pulled up the message.

TNBoy80:

Hey gorgeous! Your profile really caught my eye. You look like such an interesting person. I bet we could have a lot of fun together. Message me back!

"Josiah, he's back!" Emma cried.

Josiah looked up at her from his board book then turned back to the thick pages unenthused.

"This guy sends me the exact same message to every profile. He must just copy and paste it. Oh, buddy, don't worry. Auntie is going to teach you to be so much better than these idiots. Not that your mother wouldn't smother you long before you could become such a douchebag. Third time is the charm. I think we have our winner!"

Emma tapped out a reply to the lucky TNBoy80 and stowed the phone back in her pocket. She reached out and snatched Josiah up, hoisting him above her head like an airplane. He laughed and opened his gummy mouth wide, the light catching the few, small protruding teeth. A long string of viscous drool dripped from his shining lips and splattered on Emma's cheek.

"Ahhh!" she cried, plopping Josiah giggling into her lap and wiping at her face with her sleeve. "No wonder your mother says you're disgusting!"

Emma was still giggling when Ronnie and Terrence walked in.

"Oh no, Ems, did he puke on you?" Terrence slipped off his coat and shoes at the door.

"He's too old for spitting up anymore," Ronnie corrected.

"That's why I said puke."

"Whatever." Ronnie rolled her eyes.

"He just drooled on me. Like nearly straight into my mouth," Emma said.

"You were airplaning him, weren't you?" Terrence said.

"Yeah."

Ronnie cackled. "Amateur."

"Good date, then?" Emma asked.

"Yeah, this deeply disturbed girl and her horror movies." Terrence shook his head.

"Hey!" Ronnie protested. "You like horror movies too."

"I did. It was a good one. Actually got Ronnie to squeeze my hand during the scary parts."

"Shut your face. I was only holding your hand."

"Sure, sure."

"Awww, you guys are so cute," Emma joked.

"You're sticking around, right, Eminem?" Terrence asked. "We have an exciting night of Netflix, without the chilling, and changing diapers ahead."

"I wouldn't miss that for the world!"

The three fell into the abyss of Netflix, locking into a series about zombies and marathoning the episodes end to end. As the first episode flashed, Emma instantly recognized it.

"Oh shit," she laughed.

"What?" Ronnie asked.

"This is the show I marathoned with Jamal. He had me kiss him every time a zombie killed someone. Then he took me into his room 'where the magic happens' and asked me to test out his mattress."

"Oh no." Terrence shook his head. "That is not smooth."

"Yeah, babe, you have more game than that,"

Ronnie said.

"And that is how babies are made," Terrence replied.

Terrence started the next episode before the credits from the previous could even begin rolling, and the hours were swallowed up by the shambling horde. Josiah collapsed on Ronnie's chest where she snored open-mouthed on the couch.

"Whoa, when did we lose Ronnie?" Emma said between zombie attacks.

"She's sharking it," Terrence answered.

"What did you just say?"

"Sharking it."

"That makes absolutely no sense."

"When a shark stops swimming, it dies. Since Josiah, if Ronnie stops moving, she sleeps. Especially if Josiah is sleeping on her. So I call it sharking it."

"Ah, I follow now."

"She's going to be pissed she missed all this zombie action."

"You know she's going to watch them over again while she's working with Josiah."

"Oh I know. Man, I'm going to have a dark and troubled little boy."

"You were going to have that either way."

"True."

"So are you tapping out, or do we press on?"

"Are you kidding? We press on! I have to know if they get out of that warehouse alive."

Terrence and Emma remained locked in front of the screen until they watched the entire season of episodes. The zombies moaned while Ronnie and

Josiah snored in concert. When the season finale cliffhanger graced the screen, Emma gave Terrence a hug and retreated home.

In her car, in the dark, she could not get the trick line to her face fast enough. TNBoy80 had the hook clearly embedded in his cheek, sending an array of messages he may have even composed exclusively for her.

She took the next step, providing him with her burner phone number, and went to bed. When she woke up in the morning, she had a text message waiting for her on Eva's phone.

Cory: Good morning, beautiful Eva! This is Cory. Thank you for giving me your number. When can I take you out?

Emma cuddled down in her bed and curled the phone in close to her, debating how to respond. She wanted to say, *Tonight. I am going to murder you tonight.* She needed to pace herself, to ration Cory's demise, to pull his strings to tame the beast inside her.

Eva: Good morning, Cory. I would love to go out. What do you like to do?

Cory: Whatever you like. We could always go to dinner or meet for coffee.

Emma gagged. She could not even think about sitting down for another excruciating meal, another first date trapped at a table.

Eva: How do you feel about hiking?

Emma texted Cory conversationally in the days leading up to their hike. Seeing the text notification on Eva's phone caused her heart to flutter the same way it once did at a romantic prospect. Each message brought her one step closer, drew him in a fraction more.

Cory: How was work today?

Eva: Good. Nice and easy day.

Cory: What are you up to tonight?

Eva: I might go have dinner with my friends. I might pass out on my couch. Life choices.

Cory: LOL

Eva: What about you? How was your day?

Cory: It was good. I worked hard. Now I'm enjoying a nice beer and a steak.

Eva: Simple things.

Cory: I'm easy to please.

Eva: Don't tease ;)

Cory: I won't. I'll show you after our date. Assuming I don't cough up a lung on this hike.

***

Cory eased himself into the car beside Eva in the early morning light. Eva immediately found him simply plain. He embodied what she would imagine for a generic white guy. He had close cut blond hair over flat blue eyes. His features were passable, wholly unremarkable. He had tight cowboy jeans shoved down into cowboy boots with a tattered t-shirt.

Eva took him in from under her sunglasses.

"Good morning, girl. You are far prettier than your profile," he said as he settled in beside her.

"Thank you. Nice to meet you, Cory, after all our messaging. Thanks for coming hiking with me."

"Of course. This is actually my first hiking date. Are you a big hiker?"

"I've gotten into it recently."

"Let's see if I can get into it too."

"Have you hiked much before?"

"A little bit since moving to Colorado but nothing major."

"Where are you from originally?"

"Tennessee."

"Wow, how did you end up here?"

"My dad was military."

Eva pulled her car into the trailhead parking lot. She fetched her walking stick and hiking pack from the trunk and led Cory toward the mountain.

Walking up the trail, Cory's steps crunched behind her. Eva kept the pace slow and steady, swinging her stick forward and allowing it to bump against the gravel then swooping it in line with her stride and repeating. The sun crept up into the sky, casting sharp rays over the mountainside. The light broke among the trees and glared from the horizon. The air still maintained the hint of extra moisture, the fading cool edge of the night.

Eva evaporated momentarily in the mountain, dissolving in the thin air, until Cory spoke behind her.

"How far are we going?" he asked.

"We'll hike up about a mile. There's kind of a cool place off the trail I thought we could go to."

"That sounds good."

With each step upwards in altitude, Eva felt her anticipation building. The excitement swelled against her ribcage. The mile dragged on so long with Cory trailing behind her. She could hear him talking, but the words did not register in her brain. She was relatively certain she was even responding, but her mind sprinted ahead to the destination.

By the time Eva put her boots in the rough off the trail, her heartbeat was tingling in her entire body. She led Cory over the stringy clumps of green grass, around the protruding orange rocks, through the towering pine trees.

"Wow, you're really taking me out here," Cory panted. "This is like legit hiking. Just walking up the side of a mountain off the trail."

"Nearly there," Eva replied.

Eva fought the urge to sprint the final jaunt around a concealing clump of trees and reached back to ensnare Cory's fingers when they reached the spot. Sweat was beginning to break her scalp under her brunette wig. Cory wrapped his fingers around hers and pulled her closer to him, encircling her waist and bumping his hand into her pack. He pressed his body into hers and shoved his mouth against her lips.

"So what did you bring me all the way out here for? You a bit of a voyeur, girl?" he said with lazy eyelids and long syllables.

"Maybe," she teased. "Do you want a snack or some water first?"

"Yeah, definitely the water. I'll need to be hydrated for you."

"Awesome," Eva giggled coyly. "Check out that view."

Cory dropped his arms from around her and turned his back to her to glimpse the sprawling city spread out below them. He put his hands on his hips and leaned his pelvis forward, ogling the scenery. Eva slipped the pack from her shoulders and set it on the dirt in front of her. She reached into the main pocket and pulled out the spade to the shovel. Quietly, she reattached it to her walking stick handle.

Cory grew tired of waiting for her and looked toward her. As his eyes eased around in her direction, she heaved the shovel over her shoulder like a baseball bat. His unimpressive blue eyes met hers for the briefest instant. Then she swung the blade of the shovel around and slammed it into his head.

The impact sent Cory's body toppling to the dirt. His limbs landed haphazardly around his collapsed torso, his head nearly obscured by his shoulders. He lay frozen and crumpled for a second. Eva heard that familiar struggling breath pushing against the injury. Cory floundered in the dirt like a beached fish.

Eva walked slowly over to his jerking body. She pressed her foot into his shoulder until she flipped him flat on his back. She stepped over his body, placing a foot on either side of his torso. She raised the shovel directly above his head and swung it down into his skull until it cracked. His body fell still, his breath disappearing into the mountain air.

With Cory's corpse beneath her feet, Eva looked down at the unsuspecting city below. She stepped back and walked a few feet toward a large and wilting pine. She reached down and pulled a large, dead branch aside to reveal a hole, a perfectly dug grave she had hiked up and carved out days before.

No garage, no Sawz-All. She took Cory's body by the floppy ankles and dragged him over the dirt and rocks, dumping him into the hole. Cory's body folded on itself facedown, the dust settling on top of him.

Eva hopped down into the hole to tug his phone out of his pocket and remove the battery, dropping the pieces in the dirt beside him. Then she climbed back out to look down at him.

She changed her shirt into a spare from her bag, using the dirty one to swipe the blood from the shovel spade before tossing the shirt in after him. She popped the battery from the latest trick line phone and chucked it all into the pit with Cory. Then she fetched the shovel and heaped the earth back over him, swirling the dirt and rearranging the pine needles to obscure the struggle. As she hiked away, she looked back to evaluate her work. The swatch of mountain looked indistinguishable from the surrounding patches.

Emma returned to the trail but did not head down toward the car. Instead, she continued to ascend the mountain, winding back and forth across the face along the gravel path. Without Cory echoing her steps, she could concentrate on the Zen of her hike, the rhythm in her climb. The sun rose higher in the sky, and the warmth poured down the mountainside.

Emma melted into the hike. Her body hummed with the kill. In her mind, the shovel demolished Cory's face again and again, and the memory tranquilized her. She was not Eva anymore. Or Jennifer. Or Deidra. She was not even Emma. She was only the steps that dragged her up the side of this mountain, the one she felt like she owned with her kill hidden beneath its skin.

A large rock emerged on the hillside above her, dangling over her path. Its summit beckoned to her, jutting out of the mountain. Emma heeded and placed her hands on the rough surface to guide her legs on top of it. The pointed surface of the rock jabbed into the backs of her thighs. She still found it to be a most comfortable perch.

She pulled her pack up beside her and fished out a water bottle and granola bar. Breathing deeply and bathed in the crisp sunlight, she took leisurely sips of the water, chewing bites of her granola bar slowly and deliberately. She did not think; she did not analyze. She simply sat in the sun and ate.

Peace was what Emma felt. If she did not think about it, if she did not question it, if she only permitted herself to wallow in the echo of her murder, she experienced peace.

Maybe there never was an Emma. Maybe I was always Deidra, Jennifer, Eva. Maybe Emma was the persona and the lie all along.

This is who I am, she thought again, plain and simple. The thought flowed over her in waves as she lingered on the rock while the sun traced its arc in the sky.

CHAPTER 21

The months passed, and the men of the internet continued to fall. Brad, another man obsessed with photographing his own genitalia; Joe, the security guard who was unnervingly possessive before he even touched her; Alex, the twice divorced and obviously looking to use and abuse number three; and her favorite, Roland, the overpaid engineer who talked to her like she was a stupid child and seemed to think she should thank him for it.

Emma was surprised at how many men were willing to brave a hike for the hinted possibility of sex. Digging a hole in advance was infinitely simpler than dissecting a body and bleaching the bloody evidence out of her garage and trunk each time. Killing out in the open amplified the murder with a jagged thrill.

The seasons were turning against her though. The flirtation of fall tickled the trailing edges of the summer days. The night was starting to crawl both down into the dawn and up into the evening. Her hikes would soon not be an option, and that thought alone made Emma feel like she was suffocating, made her feel that crushing weight that compacted her into her couch all those months after Justin.

Pushed toward something drastic, she leapt into "Penny."

***

"Penny, I have to say, no bullshit, this is the wildest date I have ever been on," Carl said as he unloaded the tent from Emma's trunk.

"We just got here," Penny smiled coyly. "Nothing wild has even happened."

"Still. I would never have thought a girl would go camping on a first date."

Penny chuckled and tossed her hair over her shoulder. "I like camping. The guy I end up with has to love it too. So why not?"

"It's pretty trusting to take a stranger up in the woods and sleep in a tent together."

"Excuse me, we have separate tents. And you're not a stranger; we've been talking for a while now."

"True. But we only met in person today."

"Are you trying to talk me out of this?"

"No, not at all. I'm just saying you never know. I could be a serial killer or something."

"What makes you think *you're* not the one who should be scared?"

Penny stopped unpacking and grinned slyly. Carl laughed, shaking his head, and continued unloading the trunk. When his back was to her, Emma rolled her eyes.

The sharp sun roasted down between the trees,

warming the gravel and dirt of the campsite, making fall seem more distant than the calendar argued. The fake seasons of Colorado. The warmth of the daylight bred complacency that would be unnerved by winter waiting at the end of the sunset.

Carl dropped the tent bags onto the dirt and separated the zipper for his bag. He extracted the reams of rolled canvas, the piles tumbling around his hands awkwardly. Penny knelt down beside him and unfolded her own.

She stood and meandered around the bag, searching out a flat pad with a few rocks. She meticulously placed the tent base so that tall trees would obscure the rising sun and her feet would angle down the tiny decline. Carl tossed his haphazardly beside hers.

"There's a pretty big rock under there," Penny said. "And you're going to get baked in the morning."

You would, if you were going to be alive in the morning.

Carl looked down at his tent. "I know girl," he feigned confidently. "I'm laying it out here for a minute while I get the stakes and stuff out."

Penny concealed the laugh welling in her throat and planted the stakes at the four corners of her tent. From the corner of her eye, she watched Carl stand and drag his tent to one location, rub his chin briefly, then move to another.

"So you love camping?" Carl said, settling on another unwise location choice.

"I do," Penny replied. "It's quiet up here. None of the normal bullshit, you know?"

"Yeah, I hear you. Did you camp a lot as a kid? What got you started?" Carl stood to press a spike down with the sole of his shoe and stumbled when the stake bent beneath his foot.

"Yeah, I did camp a lot with my dad and my sisters."

Or my stepdad and my brother, she thought. *Half lie, half truth.*

"That's cool. I camped a lot too. Boy Scouts when I was young. Then, you know, just kegs of beers and four-wheelers. Lots of camping."

Oh yeah, and it shows.

Penny erected her tent and attached the final ties around the tent poles. The crackle of packaging rustled in the quiet mountain air, and she looked over at Carl. He stood lazily beside the crumpled pile of his tent, tearing open a wrapper.

"Snack break?" she laughed, restraining the eye roll behind her sunglasses.

"Yeah, girl, I'm working hard over here."

"I see that. What is that?"

"Peanut butter protein bar."

Penny felt a rumble in her own stomach at the distance between Carl's established tent and a kindled fire on which to cook.

"Do you have another?"

"Oh no. This is my only one," Carl said with pieces of protein bar rocking between his teeth. Then he took another hearty bite.

Don't kill him yet. Not yet.

The sun began retreating from the sky, hiding rays behind the tall trees. Penny's tent stood beside Carl's among the trunks. He had dragged out and set up the two camping chairs. Penny sent him into the surrounding hills to gather firewood while she dug through the cooler to assemble dinner. She only hoped he would not prematurely stumble across the concealed hole Emma had dug days before.

She heard his footsteps long before he tromped back into camp, dumping a load of wayward chunks of damp pine that would be hard to light, smoke like hell, then burn too fast.

"Looks good," Penny said. "Can you snag some kindling too?"

"I got this, girl. I'm your fire expert right here."

"My dad actually showed me how to start fire with sticks when I was a kid," Penny said, referring to Emma's stepfather. "I mean, I thought he was totally full of shit, but he actually did it. It started smoking at first until the kindling caught. My sisters and I spent the rest of the trip trying to do it ourselves but never managed to."

"I can do that. Used to do it all the time in Scouts. I can start one with rocks too."

"You'll have to show me."

"Oh," Carl hesitated, "I'm probably too rusty at it. It's been years."

***

The fire crackled loudly beside them, heat eating through the moisture in the wood, smoke billowing up into the night. It had only taken an hour, two trips for additional kindling, and a butane torch to accomplish, but Carl surely could have started it with a couple of rocks. By the time they had cooked their hot dogs through over the open flame, Penny's stomach lining contracted and burned with hunger. She kept thinking of that protein bar dripping from Carl's jowls, remembering she had to not kill him.

Yet.

Penny stood from her camping chair and moved around the fire to the cooler, bending down to fish another can out of the melting ice. Carl's steps scraped the dirt after her. By the time she stood back up, he appeared directly beside her.

Penny concealed the flinch at his proximity and gave him a wink. "Did you need another?" she asked innocently.

Carl did not speak; he was looking at her mouth. Penny knew what was coming. He gripped the base of her hair and pulled her mouth to his, kissing her more aggressively than Emma preferred. Penny responded in kind, leading and reducing his advances until she pulled back.

"Come on, girl," Carl said into her hair. "You didn't bring me all the way up here just to camp."

He wrapped himself around her, pressing his body against hers with his lips panting humidly against her neck. Penny's skin crawled, retreating away from the sensation. He reached with one hand and took a firm handful of her jeans, so hard it rocked her body against him harder.

Now.

Penny placed her hands on his chest and gently pushed him back until he released his clutch.

"You're right, Carl," she breathed, an octave lower into seduction. "I brought you here for a lot more."

342

The smirk infected Carl's face in the twisted shadows of the campfire, spreading far into grotesque features. Penny returned the expression, both faces reflecting the hunter poised to pounce, both convinced the other was the prey.

"Can't believe you let me set up my own tent for no reason."

"Give me a minute. I need to go get something."

Carl released Penny, and she retreated out of the ring of light from the campfire into the shadows of the night. In the dark, the cold edge of the air reminded her this would be her last kill for a long winter. Carl stared after her for an instant, snagging another beer and dropping himself back in the camping chair, his movements inflated by an irritating confidence.

Penny chuckled and took a second to appreciate the blissful anticipation at the precipice of her kill. She embraced the exhilaration humming on her nerves and accumulating under her skin, savoring the excitement that would be all too fleeting. She breathed in deeply to drink in the moment, the perfection of his ignorance, the thrill of her control.

She moved around the car and fetched the hefty rock she had planted against the tree trunk. She had selected it after pre-digging the burial hole. It fit in her hand comfortably, wielding a decent weight, and had a sharp enough edge to do the damage she needed. When she first saw it, she thought it looked like a bludgeoning rock.

Her palm cradling the rock, she moved up behind Carl, who was staring into the fire. She let her hand crawl up his shoulder and slide along his cheek. He dropped his head back and looked up at her with lazy lust in his eyes. She brought the rock crashing down into his forehead.

Carl's body jolted at the impact, arms and legs shooting out for an instant then flopping back down. His shoes scrabbled against the gravel, his hands groping at the arms of the camping chair. He let out the same wet grunt as all the men before him. Penny could hear the familiar confusion and anger in the primal noise. She stepped back to watch his body flounder in the pain.

Carl tumbled forward into the dirt. He landed flat on his stomach, droplets of blood spilling from his forehead. He struggled to prop himself up on his kneels then collapsed to the ground again. Penny ambled slowly around the camping chairs toward him. When she stood over him, she pressed her foot into his shoulder and forced him to his back. She wanted to look down at his face when she finished bashing it in.

A burst of breath exploded from Carl's mouth as she rolled him over. His eyes roved unfocused behind her. his face already partially obscured by the blood pouring out from his wound. Penny placed a foot on either side of his waist and stood straddling him, firming her grip on the now bloody rock. Once more, she inhaled the crisp mountain night air to savor every step of her process. She even allowed her eyelids to drop for a fraction of a heartbeat.

Carl popped up from the dirt and wrapped his hands hard around her thigh. Penny's eyes snapped back open as he pitched her over off of him.

Penny felt the heat of the fire as she careened toward the dirt. Her back landed against the stones lining the fire pit, and she scrambled desperately to get out of the reach of the burning heat. It took her a moment to reconcile the sensations of her fall. She clawed at the dirt until her fingertips found her rock. Then she sprang up and whirled around for Carl. There was only his small puddle of blood. Carl was gone.

Emma's heart stopped in her chest. The pretense of Penny abandoned her in the panic that raced over her skin.

Shitshitshitshitshit! Where is he?

Emma attempted to calm the fever flushing over her and listen for him. She only heard the wretched banging of her pulse in her ears and her ragged breathing. Her nerves felt like they were going to burst. She was done. She was caught. She was going to go to prison and be executed.

Before she could even think, Emma was running. She took large leaps over the dark ground. Even if it was the wrong direction, she had to do something; she had to find him. He could not have gotten too far with a squirting head injury. Her pulse slamming through her veins, Emma tried to strangle her breath. The panicked heaving deafened her.

Calm down. Just calm down. You can find him.

Emma spilled out between the trees, moonlight pouring down on the dirt and wayward blades of the sparse plants. She froze in the silver light and closed her eyes. Then, on the edge of her hearing between her gulps of night air, Emma heard the rustle. She sprinted toward the sound before she saw him, all her wayward emotions channeling into a singular focus.

I can still kill him. I have to still kill him.

Emma's pupils expanded away from the harsh flames of the fire. Her eyes dilated the moonlight and spread it thin over the landscape in front of her. She spotted Carl moving up the hill, attempting to circle back around the cars and get back to the road that brought them there. Back when he thought some girl from the internet brought him to the mountains to roll around in her tent.

Once she spotted him, the rest of the world fell away. She leaned back into her heels and launched forward on runner's legs. She felt every stride, every run, every race she had ever done culminating in this moment. The trees whipped past her, her footfalls crunching on the fallen pine needles.

Carl did not see her coming. He was lost in his own injury and the throbbing fear in his escape. He ran sloppily and slow, cradling his swelling wound with one hand. Emma sprinted toward him without thought, pumping her arms desperately across her body. She reached him as he rounded the crest of the hill and turned against the drop on the other side.

Emma dropped her rock at her feet and grabbed both his shoulders with her hands. Carl managed to wield his head around and give her another look of unadulterated shock as she shoved him hard away from his balance. He followed his shoulders to the ground, toppling hard into the scrubby grass. His arms and legs spiraled out against his fall as he rolled down the hill. His body came down on top of his neck, and a heavy, wet crack echoed through the night.

The sound of Carl's wayward limbs and full weight collapsing into the dirt punctuated the heavy silence that followed. Emma froze in the moment and released the pent up breath in her lungs, the faint outline of her air steaming against the stars. Her body throbbed with her raging adrenaline; it tingled and vibrated along the edge of her skin.

She dragged in several deep breaths of the crisp air, allowing her heartbeat to descend out of her ears and back into her chest. She discovered, as she crunched over the grass and needles toward Carl, that she was grinning again. Where did he think he was going? He could not escape her; she was in control here. Her panic dissolved into a manic sort of relief.

Carl lay in a heap on the ground, still breathing. His exhales struggled, restricted against the extreme angle of his neck. Emma stood over him for a moment, placing one hand against her chin and squinting down at his awkward shape in the dark.

Kill him. Just kill him now. He almost got you caught. Go find your rock and end this before anything else goes wrong.

Emma turned to start searching for the rock then hesitated.

But then it's over. Then he's dead. Then I have to go back to pretending to be that depressed basic bitch again. I'm not ready to let him go yet. I'm not ready to hibernate.

Emma looked back to Carl and crouched beside him. When she rolled him over, he was half-conscious, disoriented.

This is a horrible idea, a part of her said, as she moved forward anyway.

She took hold of his ankles and dragged him bumping and scraping back to the campfire.

"What in the hell is this?" Carl screamed as he regained coherency, his voice cracking as he lay immobile in the dirt.

Emma sat in the camping chair beside him. She crossed her legs in front of her, a beer can dangling from her fingertips. She had retrieved her bloody rock from the dark ground and placed it beside her, tapping her toe against it gently.

"Penny, what the fuck?" he yelled again. "What is this?"

Although Carl's booming voice was enraged, Emma detected the fear quivering at the edges of the words. The sounds were strangled by the tension in his throat. No matter how manically he glared at her by the firelight, Emma saw the tremble in his breathing and the sweat pouring down from his hairline despite how cold the night had become.

"Well," Emma uncrossed her legs and leaned forward, "I'm pretty sure you broke your neck up there."

Something about Carl's floundering emotions elicited a tranquility in Emma. He lay at her feet helpless while she bumped her toe against the rock she would use to murder him.

"I can't move. Penny. I can't move! You need to get me to a hospital."

"No, I don't think I'm going to do that."

"What? What do you mean you won't do that?

Take me to a hospital!"

"That's not going to happen, Carl."

"You broke my neck. You need to take me to a hospital. I need help, Penny."

"I broke your neck on purpose. I couldn't have you getting away."

"What? What the hell does that mean?" Carl yelled.

"I'm not done with you. I mean, the rock was supposed to finish you off. I've never had one run before. That was pretty exciting."

"What are you talking about? Penny, what the fuck is going on?"

Carl was struggling to move. The tension in his neck and the veins in his forehead tensed and bulged with each attempt before he puffed in frustration against the dirt. Emma could practically taste the sweet panic wafting up from him; she could tap in time with his heartbeat against her rock.

"I'm going to kill you tonight. That's why I brought you up here."

It felt good to say, to let the words spring off her tongue, the way she wanted to share them with Ronnie and Gladys so many times. Even if Carl would be dead and buried before daybreak, in this brief, irrational moment, Emma was not alone in what she was. She was not suppressed and censored and trapped down in the pit of her stomach.

"What? No! You can't kill me."

"Yes, I can."

A wave of power surged through Emma at the words.

Yes, I can. I can do whatever I want. I am in

control here.

She smiled.

"But why? You don't even know me. Why would you want to kill me? What did I ever do to you?"

Emma looked down at him calmly and sipped her beer.

"What the fuck?" Carl breathed. "What the fuck? What the *fuck*? This doesn't make any sense, Penny. I never touched you! You can't kill me. You have to get me to a hospital."

"No." Emma continued tapping the rock and took another sip of her beer.

She watched the thoughts move under his scalp, the swarm of panic on his face. His eyes flitted side to side as he groped at ideas.

"Help!" Carl bellowed, the sound shaking his limp body. "Somebody help me! HELP!"

"Huh, I guess they never teach guys that no one responds to a person calling help. It's fire, sweetheart. Even if you're getting raped in an ally, you have to yell fire."

You are just toying with him. Kill him already.

Despite the thought in her head, Emma continued to watch Carl squirm.

Carl looked at her bewildered for a moment then resumed shrieking. "Help! Help! HELP ME!"

His eyes had begun to water in all his screaming, and the droplets trembled in the corners of his eyes, ignited by the firelight. He breathed heavily, his eyes shifting around the sky above them. He dropped the disgust from his features, straining to look up at her. His eyes grew until Emma could see the flames from the fire dancing in them. For a brief second time suspended, and they were frozen, staring into each other.

"Please, Penny, I'll give you whatever you want. Anything." His tone changed under the heavy weight of begging. He was becoming boring.

When she did not respond, Carl's eyes flit frantically inside their sockets, drowning in the tears welling at the edges. He stopped looking at Emma, and his gaze fell distant.

"Oh my God. Oh my God. I can't die like this. I can't. I have parents. I have two sisters. You can't kill me like this. They're going to miss me. They're going to find you."

"Maybe. And perhaps I deserve it."

Emma dropped the can in the cup holder on the chair and slid down to her knees on the ground beside Carl, picked up her rock, and leaned in close over him. Below his immobile shoulders, she could feel his heart throbbing, hear his breath strain hard through his lips. Carl looked up at the real and honest version of Emma, completely unleashed.

"Fuck you, bitch," he snarled, a tear spilling out down the side of his cheek.

Emma heaved up the rock and brought it down onto Carl's face until it collapsed into a bloodied mess, spraying her face. Her clothes absorbed the spatter.

Later, while Emma twirled up Carl's tent and gathered his things to drop into the hole, she discovered another protein bar lurking in a pocket of his bag. Snickering, she ate it recklessly after the dirt settled on top of his remains.

CHAPTER 22

Winter descended with its fat Colorado snowflakes blanketing the mountains. Still full from her camping trip, Emma faced hibernation. Though she could carve up a body in her heated garage in any weather, she could not bury her evidence in the frozen earth. Anxiety infected the tranquility she had grasped on the sunny rock on the mountainside after burying Cory, and in the firelight after Carl stopped moving.

She realized she could not go dormant. The thoughts gnawed on the edge of her brain relentlessly. Her urge to kill seethed below her skin, filled her with poisonous restraint. She drew her thread of sanity with her online personas, resolving to play an extra-long game. She would select the perfect victim, cultivate the lie over the winter, and celebrate spring with his murder.

Emma escaped into her running shoes and her yak tracks on the snowy road to find her peace again.

The snow accumulated on her hat as she jogged

across town. The music throbbing in her headphones, the freshly fallen snow compacting under her steps. She allowed the thoughts to dump out of the back of her head with each stride, focusing on measuring her breaths against her pace, her warm exhales pluming in front of her face. For the first time since her camping trip, she captured some semblance of that quiet in her chest again.

A contradicting mixture of sweat and snow melting against her body heat wet Emma as she walked into the library. The rooms and bookshelves were relatively calm and quiet as most people sheltered from the storm at home. Emma embraced the solitude and sat down at a computer to create her winter persona.

"Kristy" flirted with reality; Emma could not resist. She could not commit months to a complete alternative fallacy. She needed to be able to immerse completely in Kristy daily, for an entire season.

Emma typed into the bio field, honesty leaking through her fingertips.

I am sick of the dating scene, I have been on too many first dates to count, and I am tired of searching through lies and playing games. I am looking for a real partner, someone who wants a relationship and a family. I am divorced. I am a professional who supports myself. I have great friends and a great life. I know

how to make myself happy. I don't
want to need you; I want to want
you. I am an avid runner and
hiker. I love to be outside.
Message me if you are serious and
would like to join me.

It was like she had been writing redundant versions of this profile for all these past years sacrificed to online dating, both authentic and as murderous fishing. Although her instincts balked at her putting any fraction of her truth into her future crime, it felt right to type it. She could kill the next guy who failed to answer the question she had been asking all this time.

Her grin remained plastered on her face even against the frigid air as she steadily jogged home.

By the time Emma acquired the next prepaid phone, Kristy's inbox had already begun to rack up suitors. Her alarmingly authentic and honest profile did not solicit the flood of messages the way the vague superficial postings of her previous personas did.

She skimmed through ScottyB0y who promised to show her how a man treated a woman properly. She skipped past MountainMan85 who said Kristy just had not met the right man (him) yet. She missed TNBoy80's canned, repeat message. He could not send it from his hole on the mountainside, and that made Emma grin.

Marco1819 caused Emma to hesitate.

I am not going to tell you that

you are beautiful. You surely already know that, and every other message in your inbox probably says that. I am not going to tell you that I am the one you need or the one you've been waiting for because how could I know that? We haven't even met yet. I only want to introduce myself. Your profile did not catch my eye (I hate that line), but it interested me enough to message you. I hope that this message interests you enough to message me back.

Emma read the message multiple times. Each time she rolled the words over her brain, something shifted in her chest. She responded to the message, feeling something besides the anticipant mixture of disdain and amusement.

"Oh, he's good," Emma whispered. "Now this is my guy. He'll be a nice, long challenge."

She did not even have to craft a reply, did not have to conjure Kristy's mind to find the words; they came out of her naturally.

I think that might have been the most honest message I have received on one of these sites. Consider me interested. My name is Kristy. Tell me more about yourself.

Was his an honest message? Emma hoped it was

for some reason, the same as she wanted to type "Emma" instead of "Kristy."

Marco1819 replied immediately.

Hi Kristy. You may not have guessed it already: I'm Marco. If we are continuing on this honest vein, I think I have been trying to figure myself out since my marriage ended three years ago. That might be too much information or make me sound too damaged, but it is part of who I am now. By day, I work a mundane IT job that pays the bills well. By night, I am an avid runner (yes, I used your same words though I never got into hiking). I have been training for a half marathon. Running keeps me sane. I read post-apocalyptic books and like comedy movies. And I run some more. Did I mention I like to run?

"Holy shit," Emma breathed. "He sounds like me. He better be full of shit."

The sensation in her chest was familiar. The light, airy flutter, like a small bird trapped inside her ribcage. She knew it well from the many times she thought the man on the other side of the message could be The One. It was hope flapping against the bars of her bones. Once she recognized the feeling, it dropped out of her chest and dripped into nausea in her stomach. Her brain wrapped around the darkness seeping out from her memory.

I could kill him for being full of shit.

***

Winter wrapped around the weeks, slowing the passage of time, weighing it down with fluffy snowflakes. With each passing day, Emma felt heavier. Each day, she longed to expose Marco's lies and introduce him to a blunt and forceful object. Each day unconsummated heaped upon her cells.

The same text appeared on her burner phone every morning, without fail.

Marco: Good morning, Kristy. I hope you have a great day.

The same text appeared on the trick line each night, without fail.

Marco: Goodnight, Kristy. Sleep well.

He is too good at this. He is too charming and too attentive for this to be authentic. If I slept with him once, all of this would disappear.

Emma felt expectant of the messages, needing even. Her morning completely began when Marco's text put a smile on her face, and she settled down to sleep effortlessly when that final chime in the evening sang.

He is making me dependent already. He is good at this game. Too good.

Still, none of her thoughts dissuaded the swoon

in her head when she read the words or the flash of exhilaration that climbed her spine whenever the trick line chimed. Beneath her flesh and her brains, her heart betrayed her and mounted acts of treason across her mind.

Marco's messages continued steadily each day. He did not falter or vanish. He dug beneath her skin with consistency. Nearly every time she picked up her phone, she could smile at a notification from him. He made her feel special, attended to. That was part of his game.

Marco: Tell me about your first half marathon. What am I in for?

Kristy: It was brutal.

Marco: How brutal? Should I back out now?

Kristy: Absolutely not. I am so glad I did it. It was so hard, and that made it such an accomplishment.

Marco: It does make you pretty amazing.

Kristy: You'll just have to catch up now.

It felt like he was stalking her, gathering intel to manipulate her. She caught each flare of infatuation and dosed it with a heavy swat of reality.

Play the game. Just play the game. Keep drawing him in closer.

Marco: Sometimes I feel completely behind my friends.

Kristy: How so?

Marco: They all have their families, and I'm back to dating like when we were in our 20s.

Kristy: I understand that!

Marco: My best friend just had a baby girl. I wasn't sure if I wanted to congratulate him or get stupid drunk and feel sorry for myself.

Kristy: I feel the same way about my nephews.

Marco: Maybe we should get stupid drunk together.

Kristy: We can. We don't have babies to take care of the next morning.

Marco: You might be brilliant.

The weeks passed with Emma growing more and more accustomed to the constant communication with Marco. She imagined his profile picture animating and coming to life. Her brain applied a calm and seductive voice to his messages. Her anticipation welled inside her. Winter suddenly seemed like such an exhaustively long season. How could she wait until spring to meet and murder him? If she waited much longer, he might have her completely duped and wrapped around his digital finger.

As she gauged her excitement increasing with each message, each perfectly worded correspondence, Emma resolved that she could not wait. She could no longer hibernate through the months of frozen ground. She was posing too great of a risk to herself, and she refused to regress into the Emma that got her here.

I have to kill him now before I totally buy his bullshit. I just won't bury the body. I can do this. I'm practically a goddamn professional now. Ditch the body. Leave no trace. I can do this.

Marco: Can I suggest an unconventional first date?

Kristy: Please do.

Marco: You said winter running is your favorite. In warmer weather, I usually do a run club downtown. They also do one at a northern location, which would be more convenient for you driving down from Denver.

My idea of a perfect date, Emma thought.

Kristy: That sounds great actually. When?

Marco: Thursday night.

Kristy: Send me the details.

On Thursday night, Kristy layered on fleece lined compression tights and shirts and laced up her favorite running shoes. She lingered near a vacant table near the run club setup, a Gatorade cooler perched on the end of the counter beside the sign in sheet and copies of the route maps. A strange nervous edge lined her normal pre-homicide trepidation. If she failed to recall her purpose, she could practically think she was on a normal date.

"Kristy?" The voice came from behind her.

Kristy turned around to greet Marco. A perfectly clean, straight, and white grin parted his face and scrunched his eyes up pleasantly. His wide eyes lined up below her nose. Somehow, she did not even notice that he was slightly shorter than her. At eye contact, at the sensation of his skin when they shook hands, a jolt seized somewhere in the coils of her spine. The impact struck low toward her center and undulated in vibrations down her bones and over her nerves. She scrambled to maintain her composure and find her voice.

"Marco," she returned. "I barely recognized you in your running gear."

"Same here, but you are the only girl in the place wearing winter running gear."

"Then we're both crazy. It's nice to finally meet you. I feel like we have been messaging and texting forever."

"I think we have. I have been looking forward to this all day. Do you want to hit the trail straight out?"

"No, let's get some water first."

Let me hear more of your bullshit to make killing

you all the sweeter.

They poured water into paper cups beside the run club sign in sheet, which Kristy had avoided both signing or touching.

"Are those Hokas?" Marco asked, spying her shoe peeking out from beneath the table.

"They are." She rolled her leg to angle her shoe up, as if to confirm for herself.

He chuckled. "You are hardcore about running then."

"I might have a problem. It's most of what I do when I'm not working. When I'm on the trail with my music, I run until I can't think anymore, and I just feel…I don't know…"

"Peace."

"Yeah, something like that."

"When did you start running?"

"Literally when I got divorced."

Marco laughed out loud. "How did you manage that?"

"The marriage was over. My husband had just left. I ran out the front door. In something ridiculous like bare feet, I'm pretty sure. I nearly got run over by a truck. I ran until I didn't exist anymore. Somehow, I felt better."

That was the truth, Emma! You are not Emma; you are Kristy. Stop talking like Emma.

"That is potentially the best running story I've ever heard." He smiled broadly. "I love it."

"We've been here all of five minutes, and I've already brought up my divorce," Kristy diverted. "I'm one of *those* girls."

"It's okay. We're divorced. It was bound to

come up eventually. You are not one of *those* girls. Not yet. Now, if you compare me to your husband at every point down to how I chew my food, you are most definitely the worst of *those* girls."

"Gross. Really?"

"Yes. And not even only one girl. Happened more than once. I have been on some awful dates. So many awful dates."

"I have too. I feel like I've been going on bad first dates for the last five years of my life."

"Exactly! I once went on a date with a woman and she brought her mother."

"Her mother?"

"Yes! And you want to know the worst part? I related to and connected with the mother more than the girl. It was the most surreal thing ever."

"That's pretty bad. I went on a date with a guy once who up and decided halfway through the date that his heart wasn't in it."

Why are you telling him that? He doesn't need to know that. He is exactly like him, and you will kill him just the same.

"Ouch. Better than a dine and dash. I have had those happen. I think I always knew they were coming. I could see it in the girl's eyes the second we met."

"Better than them sticking around long enough to get you invested. Then they split and give you the 'you're awesome but' speech on the way out."

"That is honestly the worst. If I'm so awesome, why are you leaving?"

"Right!"

"Aren't we just the saddest dating rejects?"

"At least we have plenty in common."

"So what is your escape plan if this date goes horribly?"

"Friend call with a fake emergency. We have a safe word I can text her."

"Classic. Wow, you didn't even pretend to not know what I was talking about."

Kristy giggled. "Well, you could be the Don Juan killer. You never know."

"I've heard about that guy. Picks up girls on online dating sites then kills them, right?"

"On the date, I'm pretty sure. My friend is a little obsessed with him or with me not becoming one of his victims. Did you know he kills with piano wire? Where do you even get piano wire?"

"Music store."

Kristy laughed again, deeper. "Fair enough."

"Or maybe those wire camping saws."

"Oh yeah, the ones with the handles. Wait, should I be worried that you know that? I run with a knife, just so you know."

And the pipe I plan to kill you with.

More laughter erupted out of Marco. "Should I be worried?"

The words between them dissipated, yet the space between felt inflated and comfortable. Marco maintained a wholesome grin on his face that appeared to be at home below his symmetrical cheeks. Kristy reflected that grin, drawn in, even in the silence.

Shit. I like him. I truly like this guy. I feel that spark. More than a spark. I feel a jolt in my marrow.

Get a hold of yourself, Emma. Do not be that naïve, stupid little girl who kept getting used. Do not be awesome but. He is the same as all the rest. They are all the same. You are going to kill him tonight, out in the open. If the Don Juan killer can do it, so can you. You can love Marco for being such a perfect victim. Before he rips your heart out.

"Wow, this is great dating conversation," Marco said. "I bet I sound like such a catch. Do you want to give me the 'you're awesome but' speech right now?"

Kristy laughed authentically. "Not yet. Let's go for a run first. Then I'll let you know."

"Kristy, can I confess something to you?"

"Already? Sure, why not?"

"My real name is not Marco. My name is actually Byron. After being burned so many times, it felt better to use an alias, like the dating profile screen names."

"Why are you telling me this now?"

"I'm not exactly sure. I just felt like I should."

"Can I confess something to you?"

"Please."

"Kristy is not my real name either."

What are you doing? she screamed inside her head. *Why are you telling him this?*

"What is it?"

"Emma."

What in the hell are you doing? It's okay. He can't tell anyone once you kill him.

"Hello, Emma."

"Hello, Byron."

"Now that we're honest, maybe it's time for us

to hit that trail."

The snowflakes fell slowly in the fading daylight. The sun disappeared behind the mountain edge and cast rose and amber hues over the fluffy flakes. They danced down to accumulate on the ground. Emma felt an exhilaration at the sight, at the razor chill in the temperature, at the pregnant silence encapsulating the world. For an instant embraced in her favorite weather, Emma forgot about Kristy and Marco, now Byron, and his murder. The surge of euphoria and the itch at the soles of her feet urged her to simply run and be free in her solitude.

"So this is your favorite running weather, huh?" Byron asked, tugging his hat down over his head and settling his headlamp on top of it.

The smile seemed carved into Emma's face as she nodded at him while slipping on neoprene gloves. Her winter gear compressed her tightly, feeling like a pleasant cuddle.

Kristy cracked unnamed; the façade fractured and shifted on top of Emma. The truth and Emma's voice kept escaping out of what should have been Kristy's lips. Emma reacted, responded, below the surface of the mask. She refused to hibernate while the persona liberated her. In every previous murder, the two had acted in concert, the fake identity enabling Emma to consummate her dark purpose, even when she left Carl alive to toy with him. Running in the snow, grinning at Byron, she found them instead at odds.

Kristy spoke from Emma's brain, reminding her why they were there, what they were planning to do. Still, the throbbing in her heartbeat infected the sensations along her nerves.

Don't be stupid. There is no such thing as a spark. There is no such thing as a good guy.

Byron approached the greenway and broke into a trot. Emma took stride after him, still wrestling between selves in her mind. Her hydration pack shifted heavier, sliding across her back with the weight of the pipe. She concentrated on the run.

Stride, stride, breath. Stride, stride, breath.

The physical act of running calmed her mind, quieted the collision of thoughts, sensations, and emotions. Everything steadily dissolved into the low acidic burn in her muscles and the sweet strain in her lungs. Byron jogged beside her, their paces synchronized, as the sunlight receded from the sky.

Darkness swelled around them. They activated their headlamps, and the two spotlights tangoed amongst the snowy debris before them. Emma became typically mesmerized by the descent of the snowflakes in her narrow cone of light. Byron startled her when he spoke between breaths, a large plume of steam rising in front of his face.

"Can I ask you something, Emma?"

"Clever play to ask me halfway through a run when we both know I'll confess anything."

Byron chuckled. "The thought may have crossed my mind."

"Go for it."

"How did your marriage end?"

"He cheated," Emma replied without even thinking. "Somewhere along the way, he decided he didn't want to be married to me or give me the family he promised me or be with me at all. Only he didn't tell me that. He let me go on compromising myself for him and sacrificing myself to make him happy, only to eventually tell me he was leaving."

"Jesus."

"Looking back, I should have known all along. I should have known he was never the kind of person to get married or have a family, that he never actually loved me. My friend knew from the beginning."

"You're right. You will confess anything while running. I'm sorry, Emma. I really am. He sounds awful."

"He is, but I think I'm more mad at myself for letting it happen. No matter how I tried, I still ended up repeating my mother's mistakes."

"I understand how that goes."

"Your turn. How did your marriage end?"

"Reciprocity. Okay. Well, cheating too. With my best friend, the best man at our wedding. I came home from some bullshit conference, walked in, and they were going at it in my recliner that he had bought me years before. I learned through all the awfulness that followed that they had had sex before she and I even got married then carried on behind my back most of the time we were married. They're married now."

"To each other?"

"Yeah."

"Oh no. How long did they wait?"

"Less than a year."

"Wow. I don't even know what to say to that."

The greenway rambled up a small hill then

intersected a street. Byron reached out and depressed the crosswalk button. Byron and Emma faced each other, bathing the falling flakes between in the weak headlamp light.

"I would say I'm sorry, but I know how patronizing that is to hear."

"Thank you."

"I will only say that I actually understand."

"I think you do."

The moment crystallized and froze like the ground beneath their running shoes for an instant. Emma sensed the penetration of Byron's constant eye contact, even below the glare of the headlamp, the gentle way he peered into her. Then the white figure illuminated, and they trotted through the headlights and continued up the trail.

The hill climbed steeper, and Emma's shoes slipped on the cold concrete hiding beneath the thin powder. Beneath her focus to not fall on her face, the moment was rising. Her entire body vibrated with anticipation, the way she felt holding the flashlight or the tire iron. Her cells were pointed, purposeful while another part of her, a deeper and softer part, wanted to only reach out and take Byron's hand, bury her face in his chest.

He has to die; you have to kill him.

She repeated it like a mantra with each stride.

Byron and Emma struggled up the crest of the hill and spilled out over the summit. Relief rushed over the muscles in Emma's legs when her feet found the decline. Byron released the same victory exhale that was bouncing out of her lungs at the same time.

"That hill was no joke. How about we sprint to that light post?" he said.

"Are you trying to race me?"

"Maybe."

"Okay. Go!"

Emma leaned forward and circled her legs beneath her torso with powerful steps. She launched off against her sliding shoes and drew her arms up to claw through the air. Byron darted out in front of her, clipping the snow in short and rapid strides. The light post seemed to move away the harder Emma sprinted; Byron leaped ahead of her by degrees.

The two winter runners galloped past the pole then dropped the run and settled beneath the light. Byron leaned forward, propping himself up on his knees, his breath billowing out in clouds that spiraled above his head.

This is it. This is the moment.

Emma pulled her hydration pack around her shoulder and slid her hand down along the water bladder. She wrapped her fingertips around the cold steel of the thin metal pipe nestled next to the swollen bag. She unsheathed it slowly, deliberately, her movement still dripping in doubt.

He has to die. You have to kill him.

Her footsteps crunched on the fallen snow as she moved toward Byron. Byron remained hunched over, hand fishing around in his jacket pocket. Emma raised the pipe high and arched her back for momentum. When she moved to strike forward, Byron turned around. Emma looked down and saw piano wire wound between his two anticipant fists.

The Don Juan killer and Emma faced each other. They locked eyes and froze, both fingering their murder weapons, perfectly matched, and the snowflakes continued to fall around them.

EPILOGUE

"Emma! Emma, are you ready yet?" Byron yelled, his voice echoing up the stairs to their house.

"Not yet!" Emma hollered back down. "I'm still getting Mila ready to go to your parents'."

Emma reached down into the crib and gathered her daughter into her arms. Mila's scent filled her nostrils, a sweet and intoxicating aroma that caused Emma's heart to swell. Mila collapsed into her shoulder, nuzzling against her skin and radiating her tiny heat against Emma's nerves.

She placed her hand in the center of Mila's miniature back and felt the wave of pure bliss crash over her head. Collecting the child's bag and blanket, she descended the stairs. Byron waited for her in the kitchen, chomping into an apple impatiently.

"Ronnie called while you were upstairs," he said.

"Yeah? What did she want?"

"Big family meal on Friday. She said she has news."

"Oooh, I bet she's pregnant again."

"Ha! I'm surprised she got pregnant the first time."

"You're telling me. Terrence can't stop gushing over Mila though. I know he wants a little girl."

Byron shifted his weight side to side and bit hard into the apple again. Emma stepped forward and ran her hand along his arm.

"Relax, babe," she said. "We will get there in time. We just have to drop Mila with your parents."

Byron smiled nervously and wrapped an arm around her lower back, drawing her and Mila closer to him. He pressed his cheek into Emma's face while leaning in to kiss their child. Then he drew back again.

"I know," he said, continuing to twitch from side to side. "I guess I'm nervous. This is the first time we've done this since Mila. I feel like we've been waiting forever."

"We *have* been waiting forever, but it was worth it." She kissed the baby's tiny cheek. "It will be just like riding a bike, I promise."

"The last time I took a break this long, I failed to go through with it."

"And look what that got you, a beautiful daughter and a passable wife."

"A beautiful wife."

"Did you confirm everything with the couple?"

"Yep, on the trick line, as you call it. We are set to meet them for coffee before retiring back to their place to 'play.'"

"Which site were these from?"

"SwingersOnly.com."

"You packed the bag with our toys and extra

clothes?"

"Of course."

"You've prepared the garage?"

"Yes, dear. Though I'm not looking forward to this daylong hike tomorrow."

"You'll learn to love it. I can't wait to see their faces when they see us play. Deep breath, honey. We're completely prepared. The rest will come."

Acknowledgements

This book is not the child of my brain alone. Rather, it is a collaboration from many minds and experiences amalgamated together. To protect the innocent, I will not name those brilliant women here, but you know who you are. Thank you for allowing me to crawl into your heads, examine your worst dating horror stories, and borrow your pain to create this one story. I hope all the murder I poured into the tale helped you to exorcist some of your dating frustrations.

Thank you to my partner, Mike, for meeting me at a keg party and sparing me from ever having to try online dating; to my children and family (blood and otherwise) for supporting and tolerating me in all my passions and obsessions; to "The Commune" for being such a part of this saga.

Thank you to Limitless Publishing for giving this book a home and amazing look. A special grateful nod to my editor, Felicia, for making the book read so much better. And love to my army of beta readers—Christina, Taylor, Kyle, Nev, Ben, Casey, Rebecca, Susie, Trisha, Eva, Demo—for helping me improve and evolve this story.

About the Author

Colorado-bred writer, Christina Bergling knew she wanted to be an author in fourth grade. In college, she pursued a professional writing degree and started publishing small scale. With the realities of paying bills, she started working as a technical writer and document manager, traveling to Iraq as a contractor and eventually becoming a trainer and software developer. She avidly hosted multiple blogs on Iraq, bipolar, pregnancy, running. In 2015, she published two novellas. She is also featured in the horror collections: *Collected Christmas Horror Shorts* and *Collected Easter Horror Shorts*. Bergling is a mother of two young children and lives with her family in Colorado Springs. She spends her non-writing time running, doing yoga and barre, belly dancing, taking pictures, traveling, and sucking all the marrow out of life.

Facebook:
http://facebook.com/chrstnabergling

Twitter:
@ChrstnaBergling

Website:
christinabergling.com

Goodreads:
https://www.goodreads.com/author/show/11032481
.Christina_Bergling

Word Press:
http://chrstnaberglingfierypen.wordpress.com/

Pinterest:
pinterest.com/chrstnabergling

Instagram:
instagram.com/fierypen/